WHAT MATTERS MOST

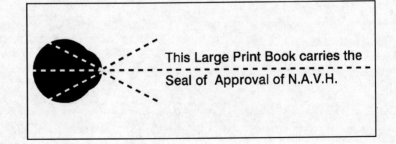

This Large Print Book carries the
Seal of Approval of N.A.V.H.

WHAT MATTERS MOST

KELLIE COATES GILBERT

THORNDIKE PRESS
A part of Gale, Cengage Learning

GALE
CENGAGE Learning·

Farmington Hills, Mich • San Francisco • New York • Waterville, Maine
Meriden, Conn • Mason, Ohio • Chicago

GALE
CENGAGE Learning®

LIBRARY OF CONGRESS CATALOGING-IN-PUBLICATION DATA

Names: Gilbert, Kellie Coates, author.
Title: What matters most : a Texas gold novel #4 / by Kellie Coates Gilbert.
Description: Large print edition. | Waterville, Maine : Thorndike Press, 2016. |
  Series: Thorndike Press large print Christian fiction
Identifiers: LCCN 2016029950| ISBN 9781410493897 (hardcover) | ISBN 141049389X
  (hardcover)
Subjects: LCSH: Large type books. | GSAFD: Christian fiction. | Romantic suspense
  fiction.
Classification: LCC PS3607.I42323 W47 2016b | DDC 813/.6—dc23
LC record available at https://lccn.loc.gov/2016029950

Published in 2016 by arrangement with Revell Books, a division of Baker Publishing Group

Printed in Mexico
1 2 3 4 5 6 7 20 19 18 17 16

To Leona Abbott Coates,
who bought me my first book
and fostered my love for story
with her bedtime tales.

1

"I'm sorry. We really need someone a bit more qualified. All of the positions we currently have available require a college degree — at a minimum."

Leta Breckenridge fixed her eyes on the woman standing behind the table lined with job application forms. "Oh — okay. Well, thank you for your time anyway." She placed the glossy brochure back in its spot on the table, taking special care to line up the edges with dozens just like it. Her fingers lingered for just a moment before she gave the lady in the suit a weak smile and moved on.

With a sigh, Leta pulled a pen and a notebook from her bag and marked off another company name from the list.

Taking time off work to attend the job fair this afternoon was turning out to be a waste of time. She couldn't even get her foot in the door at most of the companies she was interested in, even at an entry-level position. Not without having finished her degree.

Same story as always.

Determined not to let the situation get her down, Leta quickly glanced at her watch. She'd stay another half hour before getting ready to head back to the store. Maybe she could talk Mike into letting her make up the hours — and the lost earnings.

"Leta?"

She turned in the direction of a vaguely familiar voice just as Cassie Manning broke through the crowd, a wide smile planted on her face. "Leta, I thought that was you. Long time no see."

She quickly tucked the notebook back in her bag before letting herself get drawn into an embrace. "Hey, how are you?" Cassie smelled . . . expensive. Like the little samples Leta had collected from the Macy's counter last week while in the mall with Katie.

Her former classmate gave her a puzzled look. "What are you doing at the job fair?"

"I'm . . . uh . . . I'm here with a friend." She couldn't believe how easily the lie slipped from her tongue.

"Oh? What is your friend looking for? Maybe I can help." Cassie pulled a small gold case engraved with her initials from the pocket of her suit jacket. "I'm the human resources director for Greater Austin Enterprises. Have your friend stop by our booth. We're looking for candidates for our new division in Dallas, if she's willing to relocate."

Leta took the business card. "Uh, thanks. I'll let her know."

Her stylish former classmate, dressed in an impeccable plum-colored suit with matching heels, slipped the case back into her pocket. "What about you? Where did you land after graduating?"

Leta rubbed her sweaty palms against the fabric of her own skirt, one she'd been lucky to find in her generous roommate's closet. How was she supposed to explain she'd relinquished her dream of becoming a landscape architect and instead settled for working in the floral department at Central Market? Or that she'd taken on a second job at a dive bar just to make ends meet? *Yeah, let's tell her that.*

In a stroke of pure luck, her classmate's phone rang. "Sorry, I have to get this." Cassie turned and buried herself in a conversation, leaving Leta to ponder the best way to extricate herself before being put on the spot again.

In a quick move, Leta pulled her own

phone up and pointed to the screen as if she'd just received a text. She whispered, "Gotta go. Catch you later."

Cassie nodded. "Hold on," she said into her phone. She smiled in Leta's direction. "You've got my card. Call me for lunch sometime — okay?"

Leta nodded a little too enthusiastically. "Sure thing." She blew a kiss and scurried off down the aisle, past all the well-dressed job seekers pitching their hard-won credentials to waiting personnel directors like Cassie.

Outside, Leta slipped her sunglasses in place and hurried to the other end of the parking lot where her car was parked. Despite it being late November, the temperature lingered in the low eighties. She couldn't wait to get out of this skirt and back into crop pants and flip-flops.

An Austin winter didn't exactly replicate a Currier & Ives print, but despite the lack of snow, it had been known to turn cold and freeze on occasion. Sometimes without much warning. Given that, these temperatures were a treat.

She pushed the key into the ignition and started the engine with a relieved sigh. The used Chevy Blazer now showed close to 150,000 miles on the odometer. One never knew when the ole bucket of bolts would cough and take its final breath.

Leta headed north. Twenty minutes later, she pulled onto Burnett just south of 45th, then slowed in front of a small ranch-style house. Like many of the homes in the modest Brentwood neighborhood, the house she lived in had been built in the sixties. Her mother had rented it from Ben Kimey, a gray-haired widower who lived two doors away, when Leta was still in grade school.

Growing up, she used to know everyone up and down the street, even delivered her mother's infamous chocolate meringue pies to their neighbors on birthdays and holidays. Now, most of the residents were strangers and the houses had sadly fallen into various stages of disrepair.

Recently, Mr. Kimey agreed to pay for paint and Leta had done her best to spruce up the outside of the house, painting the front door a brick red, which offset the small covered porch nicely. She'd also splurged and lined the steps with ceramic pots filled with white azaleas. She longed to do more but simply couldn't afford the expense.

After parking in the narrow driveway alongside the house, she gathered her large file of leftover résumés and headed up the front steps. She went for her keys when suddenly the front door swung open.

"It's about time you got home." Her roommate grabbed her arm and pulled her inside. "Where have you been, anyway? Come in and sit. I met this new guy and —" Katie stopped midsentence. "Oh — the job fair." She slapped her forehead. "I nearly forgot. How'd it go?"

Leta tossed her bag on the sofa and slumped down beside it. "Just dandy."

Katie sank to the floor and sat cross-legged. "Uh-oh. That doesn't sound good. What happened?"

She let out a heavy sigh. "Nothing happened. That's the problem. Once these companies learn I don't have my degree, they won't even look at my résumé."

"Did you remind them you attended UT and finished three years before you had to leave? I mean, that should at least count for something."

Leta shook her head. "Not much. I mean, even the credits I earned don't exactly have broad application in the current job market."

There was sympathy in Katie's expression. "C'mon, it can't be that bad."

"It's like a merry-go-round. I can't afford to quit working so I can return to school, and I can't get a better job until I finish

12

school. At this juncture, I'm just going in circles and getting nowhere. I feel like everybody around me has been invited to the ball, and I had to stay home because I didn't have the right clothes to wear."

Her friend leaned forward and patted her knee. "Leta, I know you. You're smart and innovative. There's little doubt you'll figure all this out. I promise you have a bright future ahead. You'll attend that ball someday."

"Maybe — if I can get a lucky break somewhere along the line." She knotted her long blonde hair at the back of her neck. "Enough about all that. Now tell me about the new guy. Let me live vicariously through you."

"At twenty-six, you might want to make time to start dating. You can't stay single forever. I mean, I know your schedule is tight, but there are plenty of online options to meet people."

Leta held up her palms. "I know, I know. Enough about my sad life. Now spill."

Katie's eyes brightened, the way they always did when a new guy came onto the scene. Leta tried not to feel jealous. Her roommate was blonde and cute and had a personality that just drew everyone to her, especially men.

As her roommate had so eloquently stated, her own busy schedule had pretty much squelched any kind of social life.

Katie drew a big breath. "Well, his name is Bart. That's his nickname. His real name is Rubart Nelson. I mean, who names their kid Rubart?" She popped up and darted for the kitchen. "Want some sweet tea?"

Leta shook her head.

Her roommate withdrew a glass from the cupboard and moved for the refrigerator. "He said his grandmother used to call him Ruby." Katie visibly shuddered as she loaded her glass with ice. "How lame is that? Anyway, I met him at Halcyon over in the Warehouse District. He was behind me in line to get coffee and we just started talking." She reached for the pitcher. "He was so easy to talk to. We ended up sharing a table and sat there for nearly three hours."

"What does he do? For a living, I mean?" Katie had a tendency to date men in dead-end situations who often lacked the monogamy needle in their moral compass.

Her friend stopped mid-pour. "That's the best part. He's in commercial real estate. Leases retail space in shopping centers." She grinned. "And — get this part — he drives a BMW and wears khakis, polo shirts, and leather loafers."

Leta raised her eyebrows. "Well, that is an improvement." The last one, a drummer in a band that played on weekdays out at the Broken Spoke on South Lamar, had a wardrobe of holey jeans and Hooters T-shirts. The loser had broken her best friend's heart and nearly drained her bank account.

Katie returned to the living room, glass in hand. Leta stood and hugged her, nearly spilling the iced tea. "I'm glad. Really, I am." She slipped the glass from her friend's hand and took a deep swig.

"Hey, I asked if you wanted some."

Leta handed the glass back half empty. "Sorry," she said, grinning. "And I'm going to have to cut this discussion about your fabulous love life short because I've got to get going. I have to be at the store in less than an hour, and I want to shower first." She headed down the hall.

"Someday *your* great guy will show up. You just wait and see," her roommate shouted after her.

Leta laughed and hollered back over her shoulder, "Ha — I guess my mom isn't the only one who lives in a fairy tale."

2

Leta picked up the box cutter and slid the blade along the taped seam, then lifted the cardboard flap to reveal dozens of stemmed white hydrangeas and creamy lilies flown in from Oregon. When added to a blend of simple white tea roses, narcissus, and lisianthus . . . the simple holiday bouquets would be gorgeous. Especially if she popped all that white with a couple of red ilex berry branches.

She lifted a single stem from the box and pulled the delicate lily to her nose. Even while in bud, the spicy-scented bloom lit up her senses. How could anyone deny there was a creator when holding one of these intricate works of art in their hands?

The packing list went into the file in the rack by the sink, then she lifted the blooms one by one, clipped the stems, and nestled them in galvanized steel containers filled with room-temperature water. Later she'd

16

store what was left over from the bouquets in the back refrigerators and maybe sell the remaining blooms individually, capturing a tidy profit that would make her store manager happy.

As if on cue, Mike moved in her direction from the checkout stations. Behind him trailed a tall middle-aged woman with overdone makeup and a nest of blonde hair clipped high on her head. Loose tendrils hung carelessly around her face — that messy look that seemed so popular. The woman's height gave her an easy view of Mike's balding head, camouflaged by a severe comb-over.

"Leta — I'd like you to meet Ms. Wilder. Today is her first day."

She lowered the floral clippers onto the counter, wiped her hands on her apron, and glanced at the woman's store badge for a first name. "Nice to meet you, Denise."

"No, it's D-e-n-e-s-e. Two soft *e*'s like in *egg* — last *e* silent. Denese," she countered in a thick accent.

"Oh, excuse me." Leta peeked closer at the name tag pinned on the women's ample chest. "Denese," she repeated.

Mike grinned. "Ms. Wilder is from Hungary. Moved here as a young girl fresh out of school." He gave his new employee a wide smile.

Mike had a thing for pretty women with . . . *assets*.

Leta held out her hand. "Welcome, Denese. What department are you going to be working in?"

"Yours," Mike announced. "I want you to show her the ropes. Once trained, she can pick up enough hours to reduce the need for overtime."

Her heart sank. There went the extra money in her paycheck she'd come to count on. That would mean more hours down at the Hole in the Wall serving inebriated college students instead of making bouquets of gorgeous flowers, which was the closest work she could get to landscape architecture, at least for now.

Mike must've sensed her concern, because he was quick to add, "We're going to have Ms. Wilder back up the bakery manager as well."

She tried not to let the fact she'd be sharing her valuable hours with the new hire get her down. Instead she dredged up all the enthusiasm she possibly could. "Well, welcome aboard. Here, you can help me move these new arrangements into the floral case."

"Okay, well, I'll leave you two at it then."

Mike smiled and turned for the checkout counters. "I'll be right over there if you need anything."

Denese wiggled her fingers after him. "Bye, Mikey. Me thank you a lot."

Leta groaned. As with some of the woman's other parts, she wondered if the thick accent was even real.

"Well, better get started, I guess." She showed Denese the cramped storeroom — a closet, really — and the binder where she kept the work plan and standards she'd developed to maximize sales and gross profit. Next she explained how the receiving and rotation schedules were set up.

Finally, it was time for her dinner break. "You okay here for a few minutes?"

"Oh yes, you go ahead." The new hire shooed her away with her hands. "I be very fine right here until you return."

Leta gave her a reluctant nod and headed for the employees' lounge, where she quickly gobbled her tuna sandwich and washed it down with a soda. Then she turned her attention to a newspaper someone had left strewn on the Formica-topped table and flipped to the classified section where, like always, her eyes scanned the columns for employment opportunities.

Tonight, in the middle of the column on

the second page, she spotted a new listing that looked interesting.

Are you someone with an inquisitive nature and a keen ability for research? If so, then this high-profile public relations firm is looking for you!

Leta's heart beat a bit faster. She scoured the remainder of the ad. Nothing mentioned a college degree was required. As far as she could tell, she met what they were looking for. She was dependable, discreet, and hardworking and had the ability to work without a lot of supervision. Even better, the hours were flexible, allowing her to work around her shifts at Central Market.

Elated, she carefully tore out the ad and tucked it into her pocket before she had to get back out on the floor. It wasn't a good idea to leave Denese with a soft *e* on her own for long. Not on her first day.

She packed up what was left of her lunch and crammed the brown sack in the trash can before pushing her way through the metal double doors leading to the floor. Still thinking about the job listing, she made her way down an aisle lined with organic cleaning materials and headed back toward the floral department.

As she passed the toilet paper display at the end of the aisle, her heart suddenly lurched. She stopped. "What are you doing?" she hollered with a level of volume that turned more than a few heads.

Denese looked up from behind the counter. In one hand she held a white hydrangea stem, and in the other, a bright yellow chrysanthemum. "Oh, you be back already?" She glanced at the wall clock, then at Leta. "I hope you don't mind, but the bouquets in that case were rather bland. I took liberty of adding *much*-needed color."

Leta swirled around. Horrified, she saw that her beautiful bouquets in the case had all been wrecked with brightly colored blooms and hideous bows. Every one of them looked like a cheap mess you'd find . . . well, anywhere but Central Market. Anywhere but in *her* floral case.

"Well, look at that."

Leta heard her boss's voice and turned, hoping to pull him aside to complain about the situation. Before she could say a word, Denese trumped her with a self-congratulation campaign.

"Oh, Mikey, I so tickled to be working for you. Really, I am. You were very right. The floral department eez perfect place to showcase my design talents. I can't wait to decorate some cakes too."

The bald-headed store manager stood there all gaga-eyed. Like he was in junior high and the cute girl had just paid attention to him.

Denese swept her arm across the counter, showing off the destroyed bouquets as if they were vowels in a game show. "So you like?"

Mike beamed. "Very much. You really have an eye for these things, Denese." He turned to her. "Don't you agree, Leta?"

Frustrated, she clenched her fists and shoved them into her pockets. "Oh, you bet."

Beyond the end of the beverage aisle, a man caught Leta's eye. He had dark hair and was dressed in a suit and tie. He stood watching, his hands loaded with cheese wedges and crusty sourdough bread.

He looked at her and smiled, taking in the scene.

Leta did her best not to appear nonplussed by the situation.

Obviously, he must think this was funny. Right now she couldn't claim to share his sense of humor.

She let her eyes linger in his direction. His gaze was steady, and just when Leta thought she could stand it no more, he nodded and moved on down the aisle, still grinning.

Normally, Leta stayed past her scheduled shift to clean up, sometimes even off the clock. But not tonight. She now had a headache forming, and just needed to go home before she said something that wouldn't be in her best interests.

Granted, she'd handle this matter, but any resolution would have to be done with some careful thought and execution.

"Hey, I hate to do this," she said, rubbing at her now pounding temples. "But I feel a terrible migraine coming on. I think I'd really better nip this headache by getting in a quiet place and trying to sleep it off."

"Oh, absolutely — you go right on ahead!" Denese assured both Leta and Mike she was capable of finishing off the shift by herself. "I got everything here very under control."

"Excellent," Mike said, still grinning. "I knew you'd be a perfect fit." He turned to Leta. "Don't you think she's a perfect fit?"

She nearly growled in response as she grabbed her bag from behind the counter and headed for the front of the store without saying another word. Not even when one of the checkout clerks bid her good night.

With her cranky attitude in tow, she stormed out of the open glass doors and into the parking lot.

How dare that woman show up and mess with everything!

Yes, she was likely overreacting. But in the short time Leta had left that Denese woman, she'd ruined the focal point, layering, and balance in the bouquets she'd so carefully assembled.

From Mike's reaction, she could only imagine there would be more to come. Much more.

She marched across the asphalt to where she'd parked near a lamppost. Her hands shook as she unlocked the door and slid into the front seat.

Who did that woman think she was, coming into her department like that and remaking all her bouquets? Clearly she did not grasp even a basic understanding of the elements and principles of design, let alone the techniques of floral placement.

Maybe Leta hadn't officially obtained a degree, but she had enough training to know what worked from a visual standpoint — and what did not.

Bows! Denese even used cheap drugstore bows.

Leta gripped the steering wheel. She knew she was overthinking all this, but she couldn't help it. While working in the floral department at Central Market was not her dream job, the functions she performed were as close as she'd been able to muster at this point in her life.

She felt pride in her work, relished the fact that customers would sometimes drive from as far as neighborhoods near Lake Austin when they needed flowers just because of her. While she may never design a landscape master plan anytime soon, this job gave her an opportunity to showcase her talent on a much smaller scale. Now even that was being threatened.

Leta started the engine and shoved her car in reverse.

Despite the fact this Denese woman obviously had Mike's favor, Leta would just have to find a way to set some very firm boundaries with this new employee, let her know it was *not* okay to —

A sudden jolt followed by the sound of crunching metal forced Leta's attention back to her driving. She gasped, her eyes flying to the rearview mirror.

Oh no! Where did that car come from?

She clapped her hand over her mouth. Her heart pounded.

Don Castillo from produce rushed across the parking lot and swung her door open. "Leta, are you all right?"

"Yes, yes — I'm fine. I think." Leta's

entire body shook as she climbed out. She took a big breath and moved to the rear of her car to survey what she'd done. She hadn't been going that fast. Maybe the damage would be minor.

How could she have been so reckless? Her mind instantly went to the stack of late notices she'd tucked in the kitchen drawer at home, and she prayed the pile didn't include her car insurance premium.

A tall, lean man in a suit and tie got out of the driver's side of the car she'd smashed into.

Heat spread across her face and her eyes filled. Why couldn't she seem to catch a break? "I am *so* sorry. I really didn't see —"

The man tipped up his face in her direction, revealing warm brown eyes. "Boy, you're really having a bad night."

It was then Leta realized he was the man with the dark hair from inside the store.

She could barely breathe, now feeling even more humiliated. This was the second time he'd seen her at her worst tonight. "Like I said, I'm really sorry." Leta gestured back at her vehicle. "My insurance is in the car. I mean, my insurance card is in my purse —" She swallowed. "Uh — in the car."

The look on the man's face softened.

"The damage appears minor. Nothing that can't be fixed." He pulled his wallet from his pocket and slid a card from its slot and held it out to her. "Here's my insurance information."

Leta hesitated. "There's a —" She searched for the right words while keeping her eyes averted from his broken grille and the big dent she'd put in his front bumper. "There's a slight possibility I don't have insurance." She held her breath, dreading his reaction.

He briefly surveyed her old Blazer, then moved his gaze back in her direction, looking her up and down. Leta caught her breath, surprised at the tiny thrill she felt even while in this uncomfortable predicament.

"Well then" — he broke into a grin — "I guess it's a good thing I do."

Before she could take his card or say anything more, he slipped the card in his front shirt pocket, smiled, and got back into his car, leaving her pondering what had just happened.

No one was that nice.

As he pulled away, he waved back at her through the window.

Don stepped forward and inspected the back of her car. "Whoo-ee! You got lucky on that one. But I think you're going to lose that bumper. Stay put, I'll be right back."

She watched her co-worker return to his truck and scrounge in his glove box. Finally, he lifted a piece of wire with a big grin. "This should do the trick," he hollered.

He began wiring her bumper up to the body of her car and shook his head. "Ain't every day a gal plows into a senator."

She blinked. "A what?"

Don looked up. "That dude you hit. He's a senator. Don't you watch the news?"

"Not usually," she answered, cringing inside.

"Well, he's been on the tube a lot lately. All the pundits are talking up Nathan Emerson as a candidate who could draw votes from both sides of the aisle and eventually take the presidency."

Her eyebrows lifted. "Of the United States?"

"Yup." Don gave her a weak smile before burying his head and continuing his task. "Detractors claim an independent could never take the White House."

Normally, this conversation would bore her to tears. She wasn't all that interested in politics, frankly. Despite being told in school that all those politicians represented the interests of people like her, they didn't. Not really. "We the people" seemed a nice catchphrase, but she doubted her vote would ever alter the course of anything that really mattered.

Besides, she had more important things to consider. Like how she was going to pay to fix her car in the event she was no longer insured. Looking at how this entire night had been going, she wouldn't be surprised to find her luck had run out in that regard as well.

Still, this new information added yet another layer of angst to her evening. She hadn't smashed into just anybody — she'd backed into a senator.

Don stood and brushed off his hands. "There, that should at least get you home."

Leta placed her hand on his shoulder. "Thank you, Don. I owe you big-time."

"Eh — *de nada, chica.*" Don walked her to the driver's side of her car and opened the door. "Didn't look like the senator's car got hurt all that much either. Don't worry about it, Leta."

She climbed in and waited for him to close the door behind her. "Thanks for all your help, Don. I really appreciate it."

"Aw, now, like I said, it's nothing." He winked. "I'll run over to the salvage yard out on Congress and pick you up a replacement bumper. Won't cost a dime — old Rodney owes me," he assured her. "Bring this car to my place next week, and I'll put it on for you while Carlena shares some of the pork tamales she cooked up last week. The best you ever ate. And I'm not just saying that because I'm her husband." He winked again and stepped back from her door. "You drive careful now."

She thanked him again and started the engine for the second time that evening. After carefully looking in all her mirrors, she maneuvered through the parking lot and out onto Lamar Boulevard.

Life sure had a way of dishing out hard stuff. She could handle the big things. It was these series of small setbacks that could catch her off guard and make her vulnerable to her emotions.

Leta bit her lip as she thought about it all. Only then did she remember the employment ad. Even if only for a minute, she let the notion of a better job lift her spirits.

3

Until today, Leta had never seen a man's bare backside. But there in front of the reception desk at Heritage House, a white-haired man stooped with age shuffled across the lobby, dressed in a shirt, socks, and shoes, but no pants.

"Lester, did you forget something?" Lucy, a buxom, middle-aged nurse with a blazing red mass of curls, scurried after the man. She stepped in front of him, hands planted on her hips. "C'mon, Lester, let's get you back to your room so you can put your britches on."

"I don't remember where I put 'em." The elderly fellow glanced in Leta's direction, a smile teasing the corners of his mouth.

Lucy snatched the walkie-talkie belted at her side and pressed her thumb against the button. "Mona, I need some help in the lobby. It's Lester again."

A younger woman in nursing scrubs immediately appeared, and together they herded their white-haired friend through the lobby and toward the hall.

Lucy looked back over her shoulder and smiled apologetically in Leta's direction. "Sorry about the show, sweetie." The red-headed nurse turned and followed Mona and Lester down the hall.

Leta pulled the clipboard from the counter and signed in.

"Your mom had a good morning," the receptionist reported, taking the clipboard from Leta's hand. "They made pottery in craft class, and she seemed to enjoy participating." Their eyes met briefly, sharing an unspoken understanding that *participating* could be widely defined in a place like Heritage House. Regardless, every resident would be included at whatever level suited his or her ability.

That's what she loved about this place. Unlike so many care facilities she'd researched, the worst being those with dank hallways that smelled of stale cafeteria food mingled with the faint sweet stench of urine, Heritage House was bright and cheery, and their staff was filled with caring individuals who treated the residents with dignity and respect — even those who walked around without their pants.

32

Lester was somebody's husband, somebody's father, likely somebody's grandfather. More than that, he was a child of God, and the staff here honored him as such.

She rode the elevator up to her mother's room and pushed the door open. "Mom?"

Her heart saddened at the sight near the window, the familiar profile sitting in an easy chair, gazing outside with a blank look on her face.

No matter that she'd walked in to find the scene dozens of times. Seeing her mom in that condition could still be likened to discovering a stranger in her mother's body.

Leta dropped to the floor at the base of the chair and nestled her head in her mom's lap, taking in the familiar feel and breathing in her mother's scent, letting her mind drift back to a time when she would've felt her mother's fingers smoothing her hair.

"Sorry I didn't make it yesterday, Mom." She lifted her head and joined her mother in staring out the window. "I've had a lot going on lately."

Outside, a lone dried-up leaf fell from the otherwise green live oak. Leta's eyes followed the way it gently listed this way and that, riding on an unpredictable breeze until lightly landing on the hard ground at the base of the tree.

"Did you bring my slippers?"

"What? Oh, no, Momma. I didn't." She stood and rubbed her mother's shoulders lightly.

"But I need my slippers. How can I dance without my glass slippers?"

"I know. I'll bring them next time. I promise." She kissed the top of her mother's head. "The gal at the front desk tells me you made pottery today in craft class."

Her mother probably wouldn't remember.

"Hey, Thanksgiving is next week. You like pumpkin pie and sage dressing. Ah . . . you always made the best dressing."

The words were out of her mouth no longer than a second before her heart grew heavy with a flood of memories. Hard memories.

During any given holiday, her mother was famous for putting on a feast for what she called "scragglers like us." People who had no family to gather with for holiday celebrations.

On that one particular year, guests were already arriving — their landlord, Ben Kimey, from two doors down, Mrs. Childers and her sister, who also lived on their street, a woman who worked at the post office, and Tom and Rosa Garcia, a young Hispanic

34

couple who attended a Bible study with her mom. So many that not one more chair could be placed around the tables wedged between furniture in their tiny house when her mother's hairdresser unexpectedly brought her new boyfriend. "Leta, honey — put some more place settings up to the counter," her mother told her.

Sylvia Breckenridge made sure no one was alone for Thanksgiving.

Her mother was already a bit flustered because she'd forgotten to turn the oven on. By the time she realized what she'd neglected, dinner had to be pushed back at least an hour.

But that was only the beginning. The real kicker happened later, during dinner.

Everyone had taken his or her place. Mrs. Childers and her sister and the Garcias on either side of her mother's beautifully set table, with Ben at the opposite end from her mother. Leta, the hairdresser, and her boyfriend were seated at the counter.

Her mother picked up her linen napkin and placed it carefully in her lap, just so. Then she looked to the other end of the table. "Wilson, would you bless our food, please?"

Looking puzzled, Ben brought his hand to his chest. "You mean me?"

Leta's mom smiled. "Well, of course, darling. You always say the blessing."

Nervous glances were exchanged.

"Mom, that's Ben. Our landlord." Seeing the frightened look cross her mom's face, Leta quickly slid from the bar stool and went to her side. "Mom, are you okay?"

"I — I'm fine," she assured her, but not before Leta noticed a flash of something she'd never seen before — a ghost of an expression in her mother's eyes, a flutter of fear. "And of course, I'm sorry. Ben, would you do us the favor of blessing our food before we dig in?"

Later in the meal, her mom made the same mistake when she served Ben his piece of pumpkin pie. "Here you go, sweetheart." Then, to everyone else, "Pumpkin is Wilson's favorite." She swiped their landlord's cheek tenderly with her fingers.

Leta pushed her bar stool back abruptly. "Mom — Mom, that's not Daddy. That's Ben."

This time her mother's eyes teared up as she realized what she'd done. She glanced around wildly, looking confused. "I . . . I know that." She quickly excused herself, claiming she had a headache. "Leta, please finish serving the pie, would you, honey?"

Once she'd left the room, Mrs. Childers

piped up. "Leta, has this happened before?"

Everyone's eyes followed her as she moved to serve the dessert. "Um, well, not that I've noticed. Not really. Mom's been under a lot of pressure lately. She, uh, she really wanted all this to be lovely for everyone, and I think it might have been a little too much. I'd wanted to help her more, but school is . . ."

She could hear herself chattering, told herself to stop. But she couldn't seem to help it. How could she admit she'd been seeing things for a while now — things that left her concerned? Scared, really.

Her mother just wasn't herself lately.

There'd been that time she found her mother's shoes in the refrigerator, and all the occasions where she'd misplaced her house key, one time even locking herself out of the house.

Leta grew even more concerned one day when her mother came out of her bedroom dressed for church.

"Mom? What are you doing?"

"Leta, dear, you need to get dressed. We're going to be late."

Confused, she slid her book aside. "Late? For what?"

Her mother's hands went to her hips. "For goodness' sake, sweetheart. For church. Now go get ready."

When Leta explained it was Friday, her mother quickly recovered. "Oh, well . . . I've been off by a couple of days ever since the news preempted my favorite show. How silly of me!" She waved her hand and acted like the error was simply a foolish miscalculation.

Leta had thought so as well at the time. But after the Thanksgiving episode with Ben, she could no longer deny what was happening. She knew.

Leta stood and brushed a stray strand of hair from her mother's face and tucked it back in place, then pulled her momma's hand into her own and sat with her, silently looking out the window.

Back then she hadn't entirely understood what was happening to her mother. To them. And the unknown scared her.

It still did.

"Momma, I've got to leave now. But I'll be back tomorrow." She kissed the top of her mother's head, the same way her mother had kissed hers many times over the years. "Bye, Mom. I love you." She gathered her things and moved for the door.

"Leta?" her mother suddenly called out, surprising her.

Hope surged.

"Yes, Momma?" She rushed back to her

mother's side. Moments of lucidity were rare, and she desperately wanted to capture and savor each one.

Her mother grasped her arm. "Don't forget to bring my glass slippers. I need my glass slippers." She turned and looked out the window, her head bobbing slightly. "I can't dance without my glass slippers."

Leta's heart felt like a stone in her chest.

Sometimes she was so lonely for some connection to her precious mother — the one trapped somewhere deep inside that addled mind — she could barely stand the ache.

Ignoring the knot in her throat, she forced a laugh. "Don't worry, Mom. I'll help you dance in whatever shoes you wear. I promise." She gave her mother a tight hug and again headed for the hall.

Before she made it through the lobby and to the front doors, someone called her name. Edith Styles, the director at Heritage House, stood at the front desk, waving her over. "Could I have a moment before you go?"

Leta quickly glanced at her watch. She needed to be at work in less than an hour, and traffic could get really snarled between here and Central Market this time of the day. "Yes, Ms. Styles? What can I do for you?"

"This will only take a few minutes, I promise," the woman said while showing her into her office. "Have a seat."

Ms. Styles certainly wasn't one for small talk. She was direct and to the point — always. Still, Leta had found the director of Heritage House to be extremely caring and protective of the people under her care. Despite her brisk nature, Ms. Styles impressed Leta with her intolerance for any amount of slack when it came to attending to the residents of Heritage House.

Leta would forego the warm fuzzies, knowing her mother was being well cared for. As long as she had breath in her lungs, she would make certain that was the case — no matter how many jobs she had to work to keep her financial head above water.

Across from her, Ms. Styles folded her hands on the desk. "I'm afraid we have a problem."

Leta cleared her throat. "Look, I know I'm a tiny bit late on the payment, but I had some issues with my car." She paused and tried to make eye contact in an attempt to gain sympathy. "I accidentally backed into someone and —"

"Look, I understand you are doing all this

on your own. I know it may be a lot for you to handle." Ms. Styles's lips pulled into a grim line. "I'm not without consideration for your personal situation. But your account has grown considerably more delinquent."

"But when we spoke months back, you agreed to let me assign my father's pension money over. Combined with Mom's social security benefits, the deficit can't be much, and I promise I'll do everything I can to bring things current as quickly as possible. I'm looking for employment now that will bring in a bit more. You have my word I'm doing all I can."

Ms. Styles's eyes softened. "I know you are, Ms. Breckenridge. Believe me, Heritage House wants to work with you. Your mother is precious, and it is our goal to support her, and you, in every way possible. But about the assigned money — we just received an insolvency notice from your father's pension. I'm sure you were mailed notice as well."

Leta's mind raced to the pile of unopened mail at home. Yes, she'd seen envelopes from the fund, but she'd thought they were her regular monthly statements — certainly nothing that needed her immediate attention. Since she'd assigned the funds over

41

and the money no longer came to her, she'd simply thrown the mail on top of the pile, intending to open it when she had more time.

How could she have been so stupid?

Inside, she groaned. This was the second time that mail pile had come back to bite her. First the insurance bill, now this.

"I — I will look." She hated the way her voice sounded, lacking the confidence she needed to convey to Ms. Styles that she could be trusted to bring the account current — eventually.

Anything could be fixed with a bit of grit and some hard work. Her mother had taught her that.

Ms. Styles shook her head. "I'm sorry, Leta. This is by far one of the hardest parts of my job, but . . ."

She searched the woman's eyes for some soft place to land, some chord that would resonate and alter the direction of this discussion. For her mother's sake, Leta couldn't afford to mess this up. "What are you saying?"

Ms. Styles stood and circled the desk. She sat in the chair next to Leta and placed her hand on her arm. Not especially a good sign.

"I'm saying we've got a problem. I've looked at this situation and evaluated your financial status. Ms. Breckenridge, as much as we love having your mother here at Heritage House, I would be remiss if I led you to believe there is any possible way for you to afford to keep her here." She patted Leta's arm. "While I feel extraordinary compassion for your predicament, I have to consider the big picture here. My responsibility is to all the residents here at Heritage House. I'm afraid it's time to insist you bring your mother's account current, or . . ." She let her words trail off.

Leta bit her lip and watched Ms. Styles pick up a file from her desk. Her heart pounded. She nervously rubbed her palms together and considered the ramifications of what was transpiring.

If this was the end of the road — if her mother couldn't stay at Heritage House — then where would she live? Bringing her home, even with round-the-clock nursing, was not an option. First, the expense was even more than Heritage House, even if she could find an individual she could trust with that level of responsibility. In addition, all the experts had advised that her mother would deteriorate more quickly in a secluded environment. She needed a residency program where she would be safe but also have access to the best experts who were trained to work with dementia patients.

The last time Leta had hunted for the perfect facility, it'd taken weeks — time she'd carefully maneuvered around her jobs. Few facilities in a lower price range offered what she'd found here at Heritage House.

As if reading her mind, Ms. Styles opened her file. "I've taken the liberty of doing a little research for you." She offered a piece of paper to Leta. "Here is a list of facilities that I think might be better suited to your budget. Some are very nice."

She scanned the list. Most were state-funded facilities — in her mind, the bottom of the barrel in terms of what she'd ever consider for her mom. She looked up and knew Ms. Styles shared the same assessment, despite the encouraging statement.

She couldn't help it. Tears burned in her eyes.

For years, her widowed mother had sacrificed to make sure Leta had all the love and material things any little girl down the street with a father might enjoy. Certainly, they weren't rich, but her mother gave up her dream to make sure Leta was cared for in the best way possible.

Now it was her turn. The responsibility to provide the very best for her mother fell flat in her lap. Hers alone.

She looked down, surprised at how her hand trembled while holding the paper. Fighting despair, she did her best to thank Ms. Styles for the list.

"I — I'm sorry. No matter what, I'll still bring the account current. As soon as I'm able, that is. And I promise that won't take long. I'll figure out something quickly." Her voice snagged as she pushed out the words. "It was — uh, incredibly nice of you to look for some alternatives."

Given the course she knew this disease would take, she couldn't stop her mother from simply fading away one small step at a time. But giving her a secure living environment while that was happening was paramount.

Her mother needed her. If she didn't find a way around this financial mess, she'd end up letting her down.

She swiped at her wet cheek.

From the looks of things, no matter how hard she'd tried to live up to her obligations as a daughter, she'd miserably failed.

4

Leta weighed her options on the drive home, which were admittedly limited given her current financial state of affairs.

Early after her mother's diagnosis, there'd been a revolving door of caretakers, mostly premed students without specialized training. Some didn't always show up — especially during finals week — forcing Leta to finally turn to a higher level of care. But qualified nursing was very expensive. In what seemed like no time, she'd quickly gone through what little savings her mother had accumulated.

About that same time, her mother's medical team suggested it was time Leta moved her mom to a long-term care facility.

She'd wanted to resist and keep her mother home, but the advice had been spot-on. When placed in an environment with programs designed for people suffering in a similar manner, her mother had thrived —

at least initially. But over time, the fingers of this ugly disease had choked out even that benefit. Now her mother was trapped inside her broken brain and more isolated than ever.

Leta pulled into the driveway.

Without the pension funds, she would have no choice but to move her mother from a patient-funded program. Still, not just any facility was acceptable.

Just last week, a local news station featured a report about an elderly man suffering from Alzheimer's disease who lived in a state-funded facility in north Austin. His family grew concerned when he became fearful around relatives and had unexplained bruises. The man's two daughters placed a hidden camera in the room and were shocked by what it captured — a video showing workers pinching the elderly man and being forceful with him, even calling him names.

The report broke Leta's heart.

While she knew these types of incidents could happen at any facility, the chances were significantly increased when the caretakers were not highly skilled and paid accordingly. Of course, skilled care drove up the cost for residents, bringing her back full circle.

Where was she going to find a safe place of high quality that she could afford?

She got out of the car and moved to the front door, jabbed the key in the lock, and opened it.

"Oh — oh, I'm sorry!" Leta turned her head to avoid the scene playing out on the sofa.

Katie laughed. "Hey, you only interrupted a kiss. Don't freak out." Her roommate climbed off the sofa. "Bart, this is my roommate, Leta. And this is Rubart Nelson, my — uh, my new *friend.*"

He stood and brushed his fingers through his sandy-colored hair. An embarrassed smile graced his lips. "So pleased to meet you," he said, extending his hand. "Uh, we were planning on heading to dinner. Would you care to join us?"

A nice-looking guy, and polite too. Could Katie have broken the chain of losers after all?

She returned the smile and shook his hand. "Thanks, but I'm going to have to pass. I have some calls to make, and then I need to get to work."

Katie gave her boyfriend's hand a squeeze. "See? I told you Leta never makes time to play." She brushed his cheek with a kiss. "Y'all get acquainted while I change," she said before heading down the hall toward her bedroom.

Leta and Bart looked at each other with sidelong glances, an awkward scrutiny born of knowing things about each other not learned firsthand but through their mutual friend.

"So, Katie tells me you are a real estate developer?" She tossed her bag on the counter.

"Yes, I primarily do site acquisition for big boxes."

"Big boxes?"

"Retail chains," he clarified. "Walgreens and OfficeMax, primarily. Sometimes we do projects for a few restaurants."

"That must be interesting. Want some iced tea?" she offered.

"No, we're going —"

"— to dinner. That's right." She went for the fridge.

Over the next few minutes, they made small talk. Leta learned he'd moved here from Dallas. His father owned a chain of barbeque restaurants. "Really? Your family is the Nelsons of Nelsons' Famous BBQ? I love their brisket."

He grinned. "I'm a Big Mac kind of guy myself."

"Are you kidding?"

He shook his head and chuckled. "Nope. Hamburgers all the way."

Katie bounded back down the hall and into the living room dressed in a cute red dress with matching shoes and a white cardigan tied over her shoulders. She'd recently ordered the polka-dot number off the internet, not caring that she'd be eating bologna sandwiches for a few weeks to compensate for the expenditure. "You sure you don't want to change your mind?" she asked.

"Can't. But you guys have a nice time." Despite the angst churning in Leta's gut over the conversation with Ms. Styles and the recent development with her mother's care, she forced a lighthearted smile. "Take a bit of advice. This guy might be a great catch, a nice date and all, but you might want to be the one to pick where you go for dinner."

Her roommate looked between the two of them, puzzled.

"Nice meeting you," Bart said as he opened the door for Katie.

"Yeah, you too."

They headed out, leaving Leta to dwell on the mountain of problems piling up. Her job, her car repairs, and now her mother.

No matter how she sized up the situation,

the current state of affairs was overwhelming.

First things first.

She grabbed her bag from the counter and retrieved the ad torn from the newspaper — the one from the public relations company. Certainly, applying was worth a shot. A job that paid more money could solve a lot of problems.

She took a deep breath and dialed the number.

The Ladd Agency was located in a nondescript commercial office building off the corner of Colorado and 15th, just blocks from the state capitol building. Leta rode the elevator to the fourth floor, rehearsing in her head what she would say.

Hi! My name is Leta Breckenridge. I'm so glad to —

No, too perky.

Hello, I'm Leta Breckenridge, the girl who called last —

Stop already. They knew she was the girl who called. She took a deep breath and tried again.

I'm Leta Breckenridge. Thank you for inviting me in to talk about the position you advertised.

Yes, that was it. Perfect.

51

The elevator doors dinged and slid open to a large and well-appointed lobby. She glanced again at the tiny gold doorplates mounted next to the floor numbers in the elevator.

Yup, this was the right place.

Fluorescent lights buzzed overhead, a bright and cruel backdrop exposing the way her nerves caused her hairline to break into a sweat.

She focused on the shiny floor tile and told herself to get a grip.

Then, as if by magic, she heard her mother's voice in her mind. *Sweet girl, why are you so nervous? If this job is to be yours, God will make sure it's so. Quit worrying.*

Buoyed by the sentiment, she firmly gripped her bag. Before her newfound confidence could slip away, she stepped up to a reception counter stationed prominently at the rear of the lobby. The woman at the desk was on the phone. She held up a finger while she wrapped up her call, leaving Leta to look around a bit more.

The wall behind the reception desk displayed a bright, shiny metal logo with backlighting.

THE LADD AGENCY.

Classy, she thought while taking in the sleek décor. Chairs in cream and beige fabric, chrome tables, and a massive rug in that shaggy look that was so popular formed a seating area to the left.

"I'm sorry." The receptionist stood. "You must be Leta Breckenridge."

"Yes." She nodded enthusiastically — maybe showing a bit too much enthusiasm, actually. She swallowed. "I have an appointment with Jane Ladd."

The impeccably dressed woman smiled. "Certainly. She's expecting you. Let me alert her you've arrived."

Minutes later, a tall, slender woman appeared, dressed in a zebra print jacket and black slacks. Large gold hoops hung from her ears, accentuating her stylish chunky blonde haircut. Very trendy — especially for someone who looked to be in her forties, maybe even early fifties.

Leta was never very good at guessing a woman's age. Of course, this woman had likely had some work done.

"So, you must be Leta." The woman extended her hand with a wide smile.

Taken aback by the warm greeting, Leta nodded and shook hands. "Thank you for inviting me in to visit with you about your opening."

"We're delighted you came in." She guided her down a short hallway to her private office and motioned to a chair. "Have a seat," she said while moving to the other side of her desk. "Frankly, the Ladd Agency is a bit different than most. In a lot of ways, really, but most of all we treasure talent."

Leta cringed. *Oh, here it comes.*

"We've found that a hardworking individual with a certain drive and intellect, someone with that innate ability to ferret out information — well, you just can't teach that." She smiled at Leta. "Not that education isn't important, mind you. It's just not the primary way we measure a candidate's ability to effectively assimilate into the Ladd Agency team."

Leta had to pinch herself. The words coming from this woman's mouth were an answer to prayer. Literally.

The woman moved into the chair behind her large glass and chrome desk. "I'm getting ahead of myself a bit. First, introductions. I'm Jane Ladd. I personally started this firm nearly twenty years ago." She leaned back and steepled her fingers. "The entire public relations network in this town was quite the boys' club back then." Her eyes twinkled. "But those old boys underestimated Jane Ladd."

Leta swallowed against the dryness in her throat. She'd done a little research, and Jane

Ladd's accomplishments were impressive. She got up her nerve and said so. "The internet claims the Ladd Agency is the most respected PR agency in Austin — well, in most of Texas. And that you have strong national media connections and a satellite office in Washington, D.C."

Ms. Ladd slapped her hands together. "That's what I'm talking about."

The reaction startled Leta, but she tried not to let it show.

Ms. Ladd pointed a manicured red nail in her direction. "Right there — you can't train someone to incorporate that kind of initiative. It's inherent. So tell me. What else did you find?"

Hoping Ms. Ladd couldn't hear her pounding heart, Leta took a deep breath and responded, "Well, I — I discovered you served as a senior-level assistant to a former White House communications director before starting your firm. You love Austin. Never married. And your favorite food is homemade tamales. Hand rolled. Shredded pork, never beef."

Ms. Ladd grinned. She leaned toward her phone and pressed a button. "Elaine, could you bring me in a new hire packet? I think I've just found my candidate."

5

Nathan Emerson stood on the massive front stoop of a Tuscany-styled home nestled on a cliff overlooking the chiseled landscape west of Austin, with its vista of speckled yucca, prickly pear cactus, cedar scrub, and an occasional live oak. Before he could ring the doorbell, the heavy wooden doors swung open.

"There you are! You're late."

He kissed her cheek. "Hello, Mother."

She swept him inside and closed the door. "Good thing I had Porter hold off putting on the steaks." Her heavily jeweled hand pushed at the back of her coiffed silver hair, a familiar gesture his mother used whenever she felt put off by his actions.

"Mmm. What kind of steaks? I'm starving," he said in an attempt to neutralize the moment. Despite the fact that both her husband and son were physicians, she'd never embraced the volatile hours of those in the medical profession. Now that he had the added responsibilities of serving in the senate, which was quickly becoming nearly a full-time endeavor, his schedule had only gotten worse, especially when he was in session.

He followed her to the kitchen. "Hey, Porter. How's it going?"

The gray-haired man turned, holding a large platter filled with steaks in one hand and a large set of tongs in the other. "Hi, Nate. So glad y'all could join us for dinner. Hope you're hungry, because I have here some of the best T-bones in the state of Texas — three inches thick and hand cut from King Ranch beef aged to perfection."

Nate gave his stepfather an appreciative smile. "That sounds great. I'm starving."

His mother swept imaginary lint from the sleeve of her fine-gauged cashmere sweater. "We employ a full-time chef, and Porter still thinks he has to buy groceries and do the grilling."

Her husband winked at Nate before leading them out to the back balcony overlooking a pool. Generous uplighting showcased Mexican palms and pots of flaming red hibiscus, like a scene one might see in a travel brochure for an ocean-side resort in Cabo.

"I urged Porter to stay busy — men who doddle in retirement grow old much faster — but I didn't mean for him to take up house chores. I was thinking more in line with joining an astronomy club or the like. Use that expensive telescope he ordered last year but lets sit in the library collecting dust."

His mother wasn't pushy exactly, but she held no compunction about sharing her opinions generously. She urged quite frequently, and Porter wasn't the only target of her persuasive tactics.

As bulldog as she appeared, Nate knew his mother had encountered struggle in her life . . . and deep pain.

Her first husband, Nate's father, had been found dead one evening at the bottom of a pool. Senator Emerson was a favorite in their voting district, loved by liberals and conservatives alike for his no-nonsense approach to politics. A rarity in Texas politics at that time.

While his death was ruled an accidental drowning, it was heavily rumored his demise may have been purposeful. Media accounts subtly mentioned marital problems caused by an overbearing wife who had her sights on the gubernatorial mansion and perhaps beyond.

His mother had quickly quashed the suicide rumor by carefully putting out an innuendo of her own — that his father had simply overindulged in Don Julio, his favorite brand of tequila. He'd gone for a swim to relax before bed and fell asleep while floating on his back and looking up at the stars. Something he often did to dissect his thoughts about what was on the political horizon.

Nate was thirteen at the time. Soon after the tragedy, his mother moved him to an exclusive residential school outside of Wimberley, where he'd met kids with last names that read like a directory of billionaire dads.

She married Porter less than two years later. His stepfather quickly became an ally, arguing to bring Nate home to live with them. He advocated that public schools would provide an excellent education, especially if augmented with personal mentoring.

And he did — mentor, that is. Helped Nate get through med school and, at his mother's urging, opened more than one research door for him to walk through. His mother certainly had incredible influence on his life, wanted or not. But he credited Porter Wyatt with the man he'd finally become, and he was grateful.

Once he'd been bold enough to ask Porter how he put up with his mother's constant pushing. His stepfather just smiled and said her need to control everything was in order to feel safe, and that was his job — to make her feel safe.

"Is there anything I can help with?" Nate offered as Porter carried the steaks over to the hot grill.

Porter chuckled. "Nah, stand back and watch the master work."

"Son, can I get you something to drink? A bourbon, perhaps?"

Despite having told his mother on numerous occasions he didn't drink alcohol, Nate simply smiled and declined her offer. "I would take some sweet tea, though, if you have some."

"Of course, dear." She retreated inside, leaving him and Porter alone underneath the night sky. The house was located far enough outside the metropolitan area that the lack of city lights allowed for a brilliant showing of stars.

"Your mother might have an agenda," Porter warned.

"Yes, I figured. Especially when her invitation didn't include Tiffany."

"She means well."

Nate slowly nodded. "Ah yes . . ."

"Here you are, Nathan." His mother re-appeared and handed him a glass.

He raised his eyebrows. "Lemonade?"

His mother's brows knit together in confusion. "Isn't that what you asked for?"

He and Porter shared a look. "It's fine, Mom. I love lemonade."

"So, do you think the Cowboys are going to do anything this year? Or just more of the same?" Porter moved the steaks from the searing station onto the hot grill and lowered the lid. "ESPN is reporting that Tony Romo's injuries are continuing to hinder his performance. Another injury and he might be finished."

"Yup, that's what I'm hearing." Nate didn't really care for football, but he found following the game made for good politics and lively conversations over dinner. "Word has it Kellen Moore is being groomed as a potential replacement. He posted an impressive 50–3 record while at Boise State."

His mother leaned against the balcony wall, watching them. He knew it was coming any minute.

He was surprised when she waited until they were seated around the dining table.

"Nate, I need to talk to you about something that is concerning me."

He placed his knife and fork on his nearly

empty plate and swiped at the corners of his mouth with a napkin engraved with the letter *W*. "Oh? What's that, Mother?"

"You've been dating Tiffany Shea for some time now, haven't you?"

He nodded, indulging her. "Yes, that's true."

She looked at him like he was a petulant child. When he didn't add anything more, she brushed at the back of her hair with her hand and continued. "If you are serious about running for governor, I urge you to carefully consider giving her a ring for Christmas and follow that up with a June wedding. News cycles matter, and you should maximize how this can be played and keep you in front of voters."

Nate laughed. "You want me to get married so I can get some camera time?"

She lifted her chin. "I wasn't trying to be clever here. You can bet Wyndall Holiday is taking his run very seriously. If you are going to unseat that savvy campaign machine he's got going, you're going to have to take every advantage coming to you. Including marrying Tiffany in a perfectly timed manner."

Nate drew a deep breath. "First, yes, I may propose to Tiffany at some point, but that has not been set in stone. So let's not get ahead of ourselves. Especially when I haven't even decided to run for the governor's seat. My research at the institute would have to be put on hold, and if I do that, I stand to potentially lose out on a lot of funding. My team is the best there is, but no leader is still no leader. We're on the brink of opening some doors in the field of human cognition and associated brain function. I don't want anything to detract from swinging those doors wide open." He carefully laid the napkin on the table next to his plate. "I can barely juggle my political duties now. I'm not sure it makes sense to add to that load with a run for governor." He tried to smile. "I'm sorry, Mother. I don't mean to disappoint you, but it could well be that the timing is just off this go-round."

The petite woman, who had won the 1965 Miss America pageant by performing a delicate ballet, looked across the table at him, her features now transformed into something resembling a bulldog. She flung her napkin to the table. "Nathan, you always do this."

"Do what?"

"You lose focus. As a child, you'd save and save to buy a racing bike. Then at the store, a trail bike would catch your eye and you'd change your mind. And then —"

"Mother, my political career can't be equated with purchasing a bicycle. Or whatever other incident you are about to invoke. This is my choice alone. As of this moment, I choose to use my talents and limited resources serving my constituents in the senate, where I can make a difference in steering the medical funding matters I care about — and I plan to remain available to my research. My life's work."

Her eyes narrowed to a slit. "Oh? And who do you think is funding that little project of yours?"

"Vera — no." Porter set his fork down.

Nate frowned. "What are you talking about?"

His mother leaned back in her chair. "All that money that keeps pouring into your pet project comes from donations — charitable giving that is often orchestrated by people with influence."

Nate locked eyes with her. "I'm well aware of your personal donations and the fact you've garnered much support in the way of financial funding for the Institute of Brain Sciences. But —"

"And that support will continue, won't it, Vera." Porter smiled at his wife, doing a little urging of his own.

"Of course it will. Who do you take me

for?" She turned to her son. "Don't misunderstand. I am not making threats. I'm simply trying to convey a very important matter you seem to have overlooked."

"And that is?"

"Many of your largest donors also contribute to a political action committee that was formed about this time last year. These donors would like to see you elected to a higher office."

Her words finally hit him, and he reacted to the blow as if it were physical. "You registered a PAC on my behalf? Without my knowledge?"

"Not on your behalf exactly. True, Concerned Citizens for Texas cares about what you care about politically. We live in a hotbed of volatile issues right now — immigration, oil drilling and the environment, gun rights, the definition of family, and safety from threats coming from outside America. We live in a highly dangerous time." Her face softened. "Look, Son. I'm not trying to make you leave your important research behind. I'm simply asking you to take a look at how moving into the governor's mansion could further those interests. Surely there is an individual who could take the helm temporarily until you could return to your very important work at the institute, which I'm quite proud of, actually."

Porter stood. "He'll think about it, Vera. But for now, it's time for dessert." He cleared the table with as much intent as he had on clearing the tension in the room. "I'm making Bananas Foster."

At the end of the evening, both his mother and Porter walked Nathan out to the circular drive where his car was parked.

His mother frowned. "Did you get a new car?"

"What?" He slid his keys from his pants pocket. "Oh, no. Mine's in the shop."

Porter patted him on the shoulder and grinned. "I told you to quit driving those foreign jobs."

"I agree," his mother added. "How does it look that you don't drive an American-made vehicle?"

Her husband placed his arm around her waist. Teasing, he pulled her close. "I was talking avoiding repairs, not politics."

She gave them both a shrewd grin. "So was I."

Nate pulled the rental car door open, remembering the girl who had backed into him. The panicked look on her face when she realized what she'd done, and the relief when he told her not to worry.

"Someone didn't see my car and backed into me in a parking lot. Not a lot of damage, but I had to leave my car in the shop for a couple of days." He leaned over and kissed his mother's cheek.

"Well, I hope they were well insured," she said.

Nate couldn't help but grin. He shook his stepfather's hand. "Thanks for a great steak."

"Don't be a stranger, Son." He patted the top of the car. "There's more where those came from."

Later, as he drove away, he turned up the radio and let his thoughts return to the girl at Central Market.

He'd spotted her when he'd first walked in the store, was drawn to how intensely she worked at placing the flowers just so. Perhaps it was a bit curious that he would spy on a floral clerk. But there was something about her obvious pride in her work that he appreciated.

She'd been crushed to find that same work disassembled at the hands of another. He certainly knew how that felt.

Six months ago, he'd pushed a very important funding bill through committee, one that would secure reading programs in some of the most illiterate counties in Texas.

Hours of lobbying his peers in both the senate and congress were necessary to bring the bill to the floor for a vote.

The prospects of success looked good down to the final hours, when Governor Holiday's cronies stepped in and convinced key members of the house to vote the sponsored bill down in order to divert the funds to one of his pet projects — a new sports stadium in north Dallas that would be used by multiple high schools in the affluent area.

Yes, he knew that look in her eyes.

He appreciated the way she'd squared her shoulders. How she'd no doubt used calculated discretion in tempering her response. Like him, she knew timing was everything. And that sometimes winning meant appearing to lose initially.

Clearly, she'd already had a horrible night when she failed to look in her mirror and backed into him, sending her pretty eyes wild with dismay.

Nate pondered the warm feeling it had given him to exhaust her cause for concern. The look of appreciation in her eyes was well worth the expense of letting her off the hook. Just a couple of words of reassurance and her world settled back into its right place.

Suddenly he understood what his stepdad meant about making a woman feel safe. Because by taking away that girl's angst, he'd felt like a hero.

6

"They hired you? Leta, that's wonderful!"

"I know, right?" She handed Katie a soda from the fridge and followed her roommate to the sofa. "I mean, I thought I'd have to go through at least several rounds of interviews."

Katie plopped onto the cushions and tucked a comforter around her yoga pants. "Sit and tell me every detail. I want it all."

Leta slid in next to her. "Well, she said —"

"No, from the very beginning. Where is this place located?"

"Not far from the capitol. On an upper floor of a really nice building."

Katie took a swig from her soda can. "Oh my goodness, were you nervous?"

"Yes! My hands were shaking as I opened that office door. I mean, we both know what was riding on this and how much I needed to land that job. The ad didn't say a college degree was required, but I really expected to hear the same old song and dance. I have to admit, I was really surprised to discover otherwise."

"What was she like? The lady who interviewed you?"

"Oh, Jane Ladd is really smart and she looks amazing. Like someone who stepped out of the pages of a magazine or something. Anyway, the salary is really sweet given this is a part-time gig and temporary in nature. And perfect for working around my other commitments."

"So, what will you be doing exactly? More importantly, are there any cute guys?"

Leta rolled her eyes. "Apparently, she was impressed with my innate curiosity and the way I research information on the internet. The time I spent checking her out really paid off."

"Yeah?"

"She seemed to like that I knew stuff about her." Leta took a sip of her soda. "From the sound of things, I'm going to be doing a lot of that. Research, I mean."

Katie knotted her hair. "What kind of research?"

"I'm not entirely certain. But guess what? I finally get my very own cubicle — do you know how long I've waited to say that?" She looked at her friend, barely able to contain her excitement. "I know I'm being silly, but this is the real thing. In a real office working with educated people. It's not landscape architecture, but this job is sure right up there. And did I mention the salary?"

Katie grinned. "A couple of times."

"I report to work on Monday. The way I figure, I'll be able to put in my hours there, then go to the store in the evenings. Shouldn't be a problem now that Mike's got that new gal on board." She tried not to let her mind wander to Denese Wilder's poor taste when it came to floral arranging and the havoc she'd wreak if left on her own for long. "I still plan to work every extra hour I can manage at the Hole in the Wall — at least for now." According to her calculations, she could bring her mother's account at Heritage House current in just a few months. That is, if Edith Styles would work with her a bit.

Leta smiled to herself. She'd done it — despite her lack of degree, she'd landed a real job with potential for the future. A job with the kind of money that could eventually remove the financial pressure she'd been under, or at least lighten everything up a bit. She'd be able to take care of her mom, and who knows, maybe at some point she'd even find a way to return to school and get that degree.

"What about you, Katie? You never spilled about your date last night."

"Bart is wonderful. He's attentive and charming, smart, and has a great job." Her roommate beamed. "He even picked up the entire tab. And opened the car door for me."

Leta sat there for a moment, relishing this new direction in both of their lives. Each had weathered more than a storm or two lately. Katie seemed starved for a relationship with a man she could count on, especially after that long string of disrespectful losers. Perhaps this guy, Bart, was finally the one who would fit the bill and be what Katie deserved.

As for her? Well, she too now seemed to be standing in a ray of sunshine. For too long her horizon had been shadowed with problems. Maybe now her luck was finally turning.

"Ms. Ladd, the governor and the first lady are here."

Jane looked up from her desk. "Thank you, Elaine. Show them in."

Minutes later, in walked the bigger-than-life and charming Wyndall Holiday and his stunning wife, Amanda Joy, a woman who clearly revealed how the new forties in-cluded looking like you were in your thir-ties. Well, except for the tiny dark spots sprouting on the backs of her hands. Why did some women break the bank on cos-metic improvements but leave the small, telltale signs undone?

Jane stood and swept from around her desk to greet them.

"Jane, you are looking gorgeous as ever." The governor brushed her cheek with a kiss.

She'd elect to take his remark as a compli-ment, especially given he had a well-known propensity for the young and pretty ones. At least when he was out of the camera's eye. "Wyndall, so good to see you again." She moved to his wife and pulled Amanda Joy into a quick embrace. "Darling, you look stunning. And rested. My, that trip to Bali really must have been the ticket." She grinned at them both. "I need to book some travel for myself — when I can carve out some time."

Wyndall chuckled. "Who are you kidding, Jane? You aren't the kind of woman who vacations, not unless you're trailing an oil tycoon on a yacht in the Mediterranean."

"Yes, you might be correct on that one." She grinned and padded across the thick, plush carpet, returning to her place behind her desk. She motioned them to take a seat. "Now, let's get down to business. We have a lot to talk about."

The governor took his wife's hand, and they sat.

Jane opened a file on her desk. "I'm not going to pull any punches here," she said, looking intently at both of them. "The telephone poll we conducted shows that Nathan Emerson is connecting with the public. His numbers came back high. Voters trust him and believe he has integrity and cares about the issues on their minds."

Wyndall waved off her remarks. "Integrity — bah! Every candidate has integrity until it gets down to the nitty-gritty. Politics are easy when it's all about shaking hands and telling the ladies' circle members you've never in your life tasted better chess pie. Let's see how that boy ranks when some serious issues bite that little fella in the behind. After he's taken some punches and gotten the wind knocked out of his ideals a bit. Then he'll be just like the rest of us. You mark my words on that."

Amanda Joy laid a graceful hand on the sleeve of her husband's tailored suit jacket. "Wyndall, dear, I think what Jane is trying to convey is that we've got some work to do here to bring those very astute assessments of yours in front of the people." She parted her pink lips and gave Jane a brilliant smile. "What, in your opinion, is the best way to do that, Jane?"

The governor wove his fingers through his wife's. He grinned and nodded. "Yes, yes, by all means. Let's put a game plan in action to neutralize the situation and tackle some of that pretty-boy ambition before he gets a first down."

Jane leaned back in her chair. "Everybody has dirt. We'll find Emerson's and splay it out for the world to see. And at just the right time. The Ladd Agency won't let you down."

Amanda Joy gave her dark, glossy hair a slight toss. "And this will be . . . uh, discreet?"

Jane nodded. "Absolutely discreet. We've just hired someone who will be perfect."

The governor's eyes took on a gleam. "Someone?"

"Yes. She's young, naïve, and hungry."

"But is she up for a job like this?"

Jane closed her file and slid it to the side of her desk. "Absolutely. I checked this girl out carefully. She's bright. Really bright."

Amanda Joy glanced at her husband, then back at Jane. "What do you mean, 'hungry'?"

"She's underwater financially. Working multiple jobs to keep her mother, who has dementia, in a care facility."

The governor scowled. "Janie, is that wise? That's pretty close for comfort."

"I considered all sides of the situation. Believe me, she's the perfect candidate for what we need," Jane answered. "Won't be a problem."

The governor stood and helped his wife to her feet. "Sounds like you've got everything handled." He straightened his suit jacket.

"Like I promised, there's none better in this business, Wyndall. We'll deliver." She extended her hand.

They shook. "Good to hear, Janie."

Amanda Joy added, "Yes, I don't have to mention how important this is to — to the people of Texas. To the nation, really. I'm glad we can rely on you."

Jane showed her guests out and walked them through the lobby. As the elevator doors opened, Wyndall placed his manicured hand against his wife's back. "It goes without saying, I suppose, but if you take down this Emerson kid before he makes a touchdown and send me home with the trophy, there will be a very nice postgame bonus in it for you."

Jane smiled at her clients with confidence. "Don't worry. We'll have Senator Emerson sidelined before the halftime show," she assured them. "Y'all can count on it."

7

Luckily for Leta, her roommate had a love for fashion and spent nearly all her excess income, which wasn't a bunch, on clothes.

"Here, what about this?" Katie pulled a cute green full-skirted number from her closet. "This would get you noticed."

Leta shook her head from where she sat cross-legged on Katie's bed. "No, I need something more professional looking. Something a little more . . . uh, unnoticeable."

Her roommate laughed. "Well, you're looking in the wrong closet. This gal don't wear anything plain. Wait, maybe . . ." She paused, her hands scrambling at the back of her closet. "This!"

Leta smiled. "Yes, that's more what I had in mind." She reached for the simple navy sheath dress with cap sleeves and ornamental gold buttons down the bodice.

"It figures you'd like my church dress."

"Church dress?"

Her roommate plopped down on the bed. "Yeah, my mom bought that one. Apparently, she didn't care for my regular wardrobe either."

Unlike the relationship Leta had enjoyed with her own mother prior to the illness, Katie's mom seemed to always rub her the wrong way. "She cares far more about her silly rules than about me," Katie claimed. "And I hate playing her game."

Perhaps that was true. But Katie still attended church every Sunday with her family, just as her mother wanted.

Leta stepped to the mirror on the door and held the dress up against her. "Well, that may be so, but this is absolutely perfect." She glanced around. "Do you have any shoes to go with? Maybe some simple black pumps?"

Katie pointed back at her closet. "In the shoe box at the back." She shook her head. "So you're going to go all corporate on this one?"

She stared back at her roommate, puzzled. "Well, yes. I want to make a good impression on my first day." Maybe she could open a credit account at one of the department stores and purchase a few other things as well.

Katie plopped back onto the bed. "Well,

you deserve this, girl. You better get a move on, though, or you'll be late. And don't worry, you'll make a great first impression."

That thought played foremost in her mind later that morning as she rode the elevator up to the Ladd Agency office. With this job, she'd been given a golden opportunity, and she wanted to make the most of it. Everything rode on performing well, proving that she was worth investing in even without the education certificate to back up her abilities. Here was her chance to build a career. Up to now, her only chance.

She took a deep breath, trying to muster all the confidence she could. The pressure to succeed seemed to increase in her mind with every floor number that lit up on the overhead panel.

Finally, the elevator stopped climbing. A ding sounded.

Her hand tightened on her handbag as the doors opened. She drew a deep breath and stepped out with confidence.

And fell.

The heel of a shoe she was not accustomed to wearing caught on the edge of the elevator floor as she stepped out, and she went down — hard. So hard her knees banged against the shiny lobby tile and pain instantly shot into her consciousness. Her eyes welled with unbidden tears.

She scrambled to get up, her gaze darting to see if anyone noticed her horrible arrival on the career scene.

"Oh my goodness! Are you all right?" The woman who had greeted her the other day hurried to her side from behind the reception desk.

Leta clutched the receptionist's arm to steady herself as she lifted from the floor. "Uh — I think so." Her face reddened with embarrassment. "I — well, that was quite an arrival."

"Do you need to sit down?"

She shook her head. "No, really. I'm fine." She brushed her hair back in place and straightened her dress. It was then she realized the heel that had caught was now broken, leaving her feet at perilously unequal heights. "Oh no!" she said, surveying the disaster.

The receptionist glanced down at her dilemma. "Don't worry. I have an extra pair of shoes in my desk. Looks like we're about the same size, I think. You want to try them on and see if they work for you?"

Leta thanked her and followed the woman back to the reception desk. "I'm Leta Breckenridge. I start today. Working, I mean. I start working here today."

The lady smiled. "I'm Elaine. And yes, I remember you coming in for the interview. Jane alerted me you'd be starting this morning and asked me to have you report directly to her upon arrival. Here," she said, handing over a pair of athletic shoes that looked to be her size. "Sorry, it's all I've got."

Leta nodded her appreciation and quickly slipped them on, knowing she now looked absolutely ridiculous, but there was nothing she could do about it. "Thanks. And it's nice to meet you."

"Go on back." Elaine pointed to the hallway. "Second door on the left."

With her confidence now shaken, Leta scuffled across the lobby floor and made her way to the door leading to Jane Ladd's office. She lightly knocked, her knuckles keeping beat with her pounding heart.

The door swept open.

"Leta. Come in. We're so glad to have you with us here at the Ladd Agency." She glanced down at Leta's feet. A puzzled look crossed her face.

"Uh, long story. But it involves a broken heel."

Jane nodded. "Of course, it's happened to me before too." She pointed to her guest chair. "We've got a busy first day planned for you. But first, why don't you try these?"

Her new boss opened a desk drawer and handed her a pair of really cute Mary Janes. "Sorry they don't have heels," she said. "But that's what I wear when I can't tolerate these stilettos one more minute." She smiled then, putting Leta at ease. "Look, the job is simple in terms of responsibilities. You'll be reporting directly to me, working on a project-by-project basis with clear goals and expectations."

Leta nodded. "Sounds great. I can do that."

Over the next half hour, she learned a bit more of what would be expected, then Jane stood. "That's about all I have for your orientation. Now let's introduce you to the staff. The Ladd Agency is made up of a small team of individuals who are extremely bright, visionaries able to think outside the box and who work with very little direction. I think you'll fit right in." She placed her hand on Leta's back and guided her through the office, making introductions.

The receptionist, Elaine McNamara, had been with Jane from the very beginning. So had a guy everyone called Markle, who she learned was brilliant despite his brooding nature. He ran IT for the agency.

A woman probably in her midthirties, dressed in a white button-down tunic over leggings and knee-high boots, was named Erin. She wore chunky bracelets and lots of turquoise jewelry.

"Erin grew up in Nacogdoches," Jane said. "She's one of the best researchers on the team. Feel free to go to her with any questions that might come up when I'm not available."

There were two more guys, also researchers. Dan and Mike Williams. Jane had known their mother for years. The two women had gone to college together.

The only person not stationed at a cubicle was Bernard Geisler. Like Jane, he had his own office. The guy wore a black suit, white shirt, and black tie. His hair was thinning on top, but he wore it longer — past his ears to where the ends curled up. His eyes were small, dark, and piercing, tucked behind thin wire-rimmed glasses.

Frankly, he unnerved her a bit.

"Welcome aboard, Ms. Breckenridge." His voice was low, and the way he said her name was creepy. She felt more than relieved when they moved on to the break room, the supply closet, and the all-important restrooms.

Finally, she was led back to a guy who was introduced as the human resources manager. Jane smiled. "I'll leave you here in

Dawson's capable hands to get the necessary paperwork completed."

Leta filled out a myriad of forms and provided a urine sample to prove she wasn't under the influence of any illegal substances. There were tax forms, insurance papers, and acknowledgment forms confirming she'd received the employee handbook.

Dawson handed her another form. "You'll need to sign this confidentiality agreement," he said. "And we'll need an emergency contact name."

She paused.

Who did she put now that her mother was no longer the person to call if she suffered an accident or got sick and couldn't communicate her wishes? She had no one, really. It'd always been just her and her mom. Now her mom was not . . . well, not exactly present.

Sure, she could put Katie's name on the form, but her roommate tended to be a bit scatterbrained and lost more phones than most people owned in a lifetime. Six months from now, she'd likely have an entirely different phone number.

"Is there a problem?" he asked.

"Oh — no. Not really," she quickly assured him. She pasted on a smile and pulled out her phone. "I just couldn't remember the phone number off the top of my head." Her thumb scrolled until she found her neighbor's name and number. He was old and didn't often drive. But Ben Kimey would have to do.

"Okay, I think I'm all finished." She handed back the stack of paperwork.

Dawson nodded. "Good. Welcome aboard. I'll let Jane know we're done here."

Minutes later, her new boss showed back up, looking especially chic in her tangerine sweater and cream-colored slacks. Everything about Jane Ladd was so put together, so polished.

Leta could only hope to be like that someday.

"So, are you ready to get started?" Jane asked, waving for her to follow.

"You bet!" She followed her stylish boss down the hallway and to the cubicle she would now call her work home. Next to the computer monitor sat a stunning floral arrangement, one of the very bouquets she herself had put together at Central Market the night before.

She looked up, confused.

"You shouldn't be surprised." Jane winked. "You're not the only one who does her homework."

Leta nodded. "Of course. They're beautiful. And that was really thoughtful."

Jane smiled generously. "I'm glad you like them. I was hoping you would appreciate the gesture." She opened the file lying on the desk. "The instructions for your first project are all explained here. Mainly, you'll be taking a look at the voting records of three senators covering the past two years and charting your findings on an electronic software program. Very user friendly. If you have any questions, buzz my assistant. Or ask Erin."

"Thank you, Ms. Ladd. I will."

"Oh, please. It's Jane."

Leta nodded. "Jane."

Now alone, she opened a drawer and slid her purse inside, then moved into her chair and swiveled around. With a tiny smile, she drew a deep breath and ran her hands along the top of her work space, fully embracing her good fortune.

You're right, Momma. God is indeed good.

She squared her shoulders and opened the file, excited to begin.

There on the very first page was a photo and name she now recognized — Senator Nathan Emerson.

The guy she'd run into in the parking lot.

8

Leta rushed into the side door of the Hole in the Wall and grabbed her apron from the hook to the right of the backroom sink. Nearly out of breath, she tied it on and pushed through the swinging door.

"You're late!" Max barked from behind the bar. He turned to the shelves lined with bottles and pulled a fifth of tequila down.

"I know, I'm really sorry. Traffic on Guadalupe was backed up because of an accident," she explained. "It won't happen again."

Max's bloated sausage-like fingers gripped the bottle as he poured a generous amount into a shot glass and tucked a wedge of lime onto the rim. "Here, this goes to the table over by the billiards." He pointed to a group of guys in cowboy hats. "And watch yourself. They've been here awhile."

She nodded, grabbed her tray, and loaded it with the shot of tequila and the longnecks he handed her. "Thanks. Got it."

Frankly, this job pretty much sucked. And the pay was abysmal. But the tips she made in the few hours she worked each week made the difference between real groceries or eating ramen noodles three meals a day.

She ignored the leers and catcall whistles as she approached the table of guys.

"Hey, babe. Where ya been all my life?" one of them bantered as she served their drinks.

With her free hand she caught the guy's wrist before his open palm smacked her backside. "Not allowed," she firmly chastised. "Try that again and you're out of here. Understand?" She might need this job, but no one was going to cross that line.

She collected the empties from the table and returned to the bar for another round.

A fellow server wiped the counter with a rag. "All the rowdy ones are here tonight." Nancy nodded in the direction of the stage. "Saddles and Spurs are playing later tonight, and they're all getting primed and juiced up for the show."

"Yeah, well, it's time to cut that last table off."

Nancy nodded. "I'll let Max know."

With any luck, her new part-time job at the Ladd Agency would lead to something more and let her leave this job behind. Anything was possible, especially if she worked really hard and proved herself.

She'd had a great first day. The people were nice. Well, except for the man in the corner office. He was just weird.

In one of her braver moments, she'd asked Erin about him when they were alone in the break room. "Bernard Geisler is special ops," her co-worker said, emphasizing the term with air quotes. She shrugged and stirred creamer into her coffee.

"Special ops? What's that?" Leta asked.

"None of us knows, really. He doesn't really work with the rest of the team, though, so don't worry about it." Erin grabbed her magazine and coffee and headed for the door. "I know what you're thinking. We all think he's odd, but a word to the wise. Don't go there." She lowered her voice and looked around, even though they were alone. "He and Jane are tight, and you don't want to get on her bad side."

Erin must've seen the look of confusion on her face, because she quickly clarified. "In this outfit, you're either one hundred percent on the team, or . . ." She let her words trail off and stared at Leta.

Leta frowned. "Or what?"

"Or you're outta here," Erin answered,

91

her voice barely above a whisper.

Erin's warning had been a lesson to her. She couldn't afford to allow her snoopy nature to get the best of her.

Leta walked behind the bar to the beer taps and filled four glasses. She waited for the foam to settle before placing them back on her tray.

She needed that job, so she didn't need to be asking a lot of questions about Bernard Geisler.

Even if he was now sitting alone at a table by the wall staring at her.

9

"So, how do I look?"

Nate pulled his attention from the view out of the rear town car window and turned to the woman beside him. "What? Uh, you look fine."

Tiffany Shea, the stunning brunette he'd been seeing for a couple of years, slapped her compact closed. "Well, that was astounding affirmation."

"Sorry, I —"

"Yes, because what you should have said is, 'Tiffany, honey, you look amazing. That little black sequined number, those four-inch stilettos, the crystal chandeliers dangling from your ears — babe, you're definitely hot.' " She gave him a coy smile and slid her hand in his. "What's the matter, Nate? You've been distracted ever since you picked me up. Don't you want to go tonight?"

"No, it's nothing like that."

"Well, good. Because this little gala brought more clients into my firm than any hard-core marketing I did last year. And if you work this event right, you might find your campaign coffers filling up." Her deep brown eyes twinkled. "Some very deep pockets will be attending tonight."

He gave her a weak nod, knowing every politician had to be mindful of building financial support for whatever was next. It's just that he had a lot of soul-searching to do before he determined exactly what his political future looked like and what direction he might take. "Thankfully, there's still plenty of time before donor maintenance becomes an issue."

Tiffany flashed a brilliant smile, showing off a set of perfectly white veneers that rivaled any celebrity's on television. "Well, sure, if you stay in the senate. That's not my point. We both know a huge swell of support is building for the gubernatorial race. You have to consider your options, don't you think?"

He squeezed her hand. "I think I don't have to decide anything tonight."

"Okay, agreed," she said as their car pulled up to the entry of the Driskill. "But don't close the door on running. Not when there are people ready to throw their support your way. Important people."

By important people, Tiffany likely meant her father, Frank Shea, and his wealthy oil clients. The kind of people who had the money to shore up considerable influence — especially when it came to regulatory matters that could affect their bottom lines and their shareholders.

Tiff was extremely smart, and beautiful. Any man would be taken with her, and he was certainly one of them. Still, sometimes he thought she drank too much of her father's power-driven Kool-Aid.

Their driver opened the car door and Nate slid out. He helped Tiffany from the car, and together they made their way through the massive entry of the historic Driskill Hotel, with its magnificent columned lobby, marble floors, and stained-glass domed ceiling extending four floors high.

He didn't normally notice architectural elements, but his mother had recited the history of this place a number of times over the years, always reminding him that President Lyndon Johnson had first laid eyes on Lady Bird while standing in this very spot.

"Good evening, Senator Emerson. Miss Shea."

Nate nodded at the concierge, who had done his homework and no doubt memorized the guest list. "Good evening."

The man, with his precise haircut and impeccable suit, stepped forward and directed them to the Grand Ballroom. "I hope your evening at the Driskill Hotel is an enjoyable one."

"Thank you." Nate linked arms with Tiff, and together they moved for the grand staircase.

She leaned over and whispered, "You know that in 2001, beginning his first term, president-elect George W. Bush leased the Driskill Ballroom for two weeks to hold cabinet selection meetings and press conferences."

"Is that so?" He laced his fingers with hers as they entered the crowded room.

Tiffany almost smiled, then waved at one of her law partners across the room by way of dismissing his mocking tone.

This fund-raiser was no doubt going to be a dreary repeat of dozens he'd attended before, where powermongers from throughout Texas brought their agendas disguised as urgent needs essential to society.

He didn't mean to sound cynical. It was an honor to serve in the senate, to represent constituents relying on him to make a difference. With that role came a level of influence and prestige many would consider a

golden coin. But that shiny penny sometimes had a tarnished underside.

Sadly, in politics there were people who
used the system for personal gain. Events
like these seemed to pull them out of the
woodwork, the ones who worked the angles,
pressed their agendas — individuals who
stopped at nothing to attain their goals, even
if they had to convince themselves the ends
justified the means.

He placed his hand on Tiffany's back and
guided her through the crowded room
toward a lobbyist group he'd had lunch with
earlier in the week — three individuals who
worked for the state's hospitality association
and wanted him to vote against an upcoming bill that would impose additional regulations on swimming pool access for the
physically disabled.

"Senator Emerson," one of them said,
extending his hand. "So glad to see you
again. Have you made any decision about
what we discussed earlier?"

The sole woman of the group wedged
herself into the conversation. "Bill, Bill —
let the man get a drink first." She flashed a
brilliant smile at Tiffany. "And you are?"

His confident companion stepped forward. "Hello. I'm Tiffany Shea of Shea,
Bailey, and Gutteridge."

He smiled to himself, noting how she always introduced herself in the same manner, adding the firm name as if it were an extension of her surname. He'd teased her about it once.

"Oh, I do not," she'd argued.

"Yes you do." He rarely contradicted her, especially over something so inconsequential. To soften his antithetical assertion, he'd brushed her long brown hair aside and kissed the back of her neck, a trick he'd picked up from Porter. His stepfather was a master at defusing the impact of anything his mother didn't find agreeable.

"So nice to meet you. I'm Joanne Franzenberg." The woman waved over a tuxedoed server and slid two glasses of champagne from the tray he carried.

Nate held up an open palm. "None for me, thanks."

Bill, looking impatient, took the extra glass from Joanne's hand. "So, tell me, Senator. I'm not one to dog-whistle my politics. The figures we supplied clearly show how small hotels across Texas would have to close rather than face the liability of missing the compliance date. Do you think you could swing your support our way?"

Nate patted him on the shoulder. "I haven't made a final decision. But I did manage to get the speaker to place an extender on the agenda until I've had enough time to thoroughly review the issue. There's not likely going to be a final vote until after the first of the year."

Satisfaction bloomed across Bill's face. "Well, that's good news."

The others nodded enthusiastically. "Yes," Joanne said. "We appreciate that, Senator. That at least gives us time to mount a proper campaign to stop this attack on small business."

Tiffany lifted her hand and waved at someone he couldn't quite see in his line of vision.

Nate nodded at the group before him. "Could you excuse us?" He shook their hands and then he and Tiff moved on, walking in the direction of the person Tiffany greeted from across the room. "Who are you waving at?" he asked her.

"Your mother."

Inside he groaned. His mother was the queen of agendas, and no doubt she'd be working the room on his behalf.

He quickly chastised himself for instantly leaning toward the negative and forced a smile as she made her way in their direction. She was his mother, after all, and he knew she only had his best at heart.

"Nathan, dear." She planted a kiss on his cheek, then turned and embraced Tiffany. "Sweetheart, don't you look darling tonight."

"Thank you, Vera."

Porter patted his shoulder. "We're going to have to get the two of you back over and let me practice my grilling skills again."

Tiffany smiled. "We'd love that. Wouldn't we, Nate?"

"Yes, yes, of course. I'm up for one of those fine steaks any day."

"Well, look who's here!" The booming voice belonged to Governor Holiday. He sidled up, drink in hand, with his beautiful wife close behind. Amanda Joy Holiday, as Tiffany had once pointed out, entered every situation smiling and camera ready.

Nate extended his hand. "Good evening, Governor. Mrs. Holiday." He reached to embrace the governor's wife, but not before he noticed a brief sour look slip across his mother's face, one she quickly replaced with a broad smile.

"Well, hello, Governor." His mother brushed the first lady's cheek with a kiss. "So good to see both of you this evening."

Out of the corner of his eye, he saw a camera crew break through the crowd, the glaring bright lights from the camera nearly blinding him.

"Excuse me, Governor, Senator Emerson. Could we get a few minutes?" Without waiting for a response, a man Nate recognized from a local television station pointed a microphone their way. "Political pundits everywhere project that while several candidates are jumping in the race to unseat you, Governor Holiday, they assert that in the end it will be the two of you in the final runoff."

While no question had yet been posed, Nate knew what was coming.

"Either of you care to comment?"

Governor Holiday smiled into the camera. "Well, let me just go on record right now and tell your viewers that I would be delighted to face off with this admirable gentleman in the upcoming election. While our positions rarely match on many of the issues voters care so much about, Nathan Emerson is a fine young man. Fine *young* man. I think he's done rather well in his freshman year." A slight grin played across his face. "But we might all be getting the cart before the horse a bit. First, Nate here has to declare his candidacy." He turned to face Nate. "Isn't that right, Senator Emerson?"

All eyes turned to him as the camera

pointed his direction. The sound level in the room lowered considerably as they waited for his response.

"Thank you, Governor. While I believe the polls reveal Texas voters appreciate a *fresh* approach to these issues, at this juncture I've not made any decision to leave my senate seat and run for governor."

The reporter interrupted. "But isn't it true a political action committee has been formed to fund your campaign?"

Out of the corner of his eye he saw his mother lift her chin and smile.

"Like I stated, I've not made any decision. That said, as those polls show, my efforts are clearly hitting the mark with voters, and I can promise this." He paused for effect. "I am committed to serving the needs of the people of the great state of Texas, in whatever form that might take. Prior to being elected, I dedicated my efforts to making a difference in medical research, searching for the kinds of scientific breakthroughs that would have great impact on people's lives. Especially those suffering from brain injuries and mental illness, and seniors experiencing cognitive impairment. More recently, I've been profoundly grateful to have the opportunity to also serve in the government sector, working to advance not only these issues but also the kinds of things that matter a great deal to all of us." He smiled into the camera for good measure. "But no — I've not made any decision about running for governor."

"Thank you, Senator." The camera pulled back.

Governor Holiday stepped forward. "Uh, just one question, if I might."

The cameraman redirected his shot.

"You have something you want to add, Governor?" the reporter asked.

The skin around Governor Holiday's eyes tightened. "Where do our citizens suffering with physical disabilities fit into this plan of yours?"

Nate scowled. "Excuse me?"

"You recently worked to table some very important legislation that would significantly improve access for the disabled." The governor tossed the accusation into the conversation, likely hoping to blow up Nate's credibility and create collateral damage.

That was what he hated about politics.

"If you are referring to the bill meant to promote better access into hotel swimming pools, then you would be accurate. I asked for the bill to be held until such time as we can assess the financial implications to our small business owners. Once that is deter-mined, I'll be the first to foster a vote among my peers that will carefully weigh the concerns of everyone, create some middle ground, and form a plan that will not implode our tourism economy, while ensur-ing complete access to all necessary public areas for our treasured physically disabled citizens."

Satisfied he'd staved off Holiday's guerilla potshots, he smiled and added, "Now, you'll have to excuse us."

The following morning, media across the state ran headlines quoting what he'd said. Op-eds accused the governor of being out of touch. One popular online blog included a cartoon drawing of a large swimming pool lined by wheelchairs with this quote under-neath: "I'm feeling like a swim today. How about you, Joe?"

Calls came pouring into his office with statements of support. According to his mother, donations to the PAC skyrocketed in the aftermath.

It seemed everyone wanted him to run. His mother, certainly. And Tiffany. His loyal constituents and voters from across the state all encouraged him to jump into the race. It wasn't hard to imagine all of Texas was behind him if he chose to run.

All but one.

He doubted Governor Holiday was terribly happy with any of this.

10

Leta loved to study, to delve in and learn everything she could about a particular subject. Her mother had often taught that knowledge was power, and she believed her.

In the fifth grade, she'd been assigned to give an oral presentation on the Alamo and its history. Motivated to do her very best, she'd spent hours browsing through encyclopedias and clicking on websites back when surfing the net was still fairly new.

When she'd stumbled on the news that the Daughters of the Republic of Texas had collected and stored artifacts from the Battle of the Alamo in a museum in San Antonio, she wouldn't rest until her mother relented and packed a small overnight bag for the two of them, and they made the drive south on I-35. Together they headed for the museum and spent hours talking with the curator.

Using her mom's Kodak pocket camera,

she took photos of key objects belonging to the Alamo defenders, which she later mounted on a foam core board to share with her classmates. On another board, she created a timeline depicting the chronology of events leading up to the 1836 battle, the famed thirteen days of glory, and the sad aftermath. For good measure, she included a side note about the Battle of San Jacinto, which paved the way for the Republic of Texas to become an independent country.

The project garnered her a top grade, and the disdain of some of her classmates, who accused her of trying to be the teacher's pet. Their taunts didn't matter compared to the thrill she felt knowing she'd outshined the others and had presented the best report in the class.

For this current project, most researchers would simply look at the legislative history archives available online to determine voting records. For Leta, that approach was not nearly enough.

She went much further and accessed hours of live streaming video of actual committee meetings, taking copious notes of opinions and concerns expressed while the senators were responding to testimony. She hoped the effort would provide important context that might not be apparent when viewing a simple voting account.

It was during this process that Leta discovered some very interesting information. Senator Nathan Emerson, the guy she'd backed her car into, was on three legislative committees: Finance, Health and Human Services, and a special appointed panel on aging.

Prior to his election, he was incredibly active in issues related to brain health. As a senior-level research doctor at the Institute of Brain Sciences, he directed a consortium of scientists studying cognitive impairment and the velocity of decline in functionality in patients suffering dementia.

That last one especially piqued her interest.

While some of the detailed testimony was difficult to understand, according to his record in the senate, he'd voted to enhance funding of a study that included biomarker analysis and synuclein causes of Parkinson's and Alzheimer's.

The way he brushed off her lack of insurance the night she slammed into his car had sparked an affinity. This new information made her downright admire the guy.

She hated to admit it, but politics had never held her interest. To her, elections were just about a bunch of people with overinflated egos promising anything to garner votes. Once elected, it seemed like all politicians forgot their constituents and did whatever would keep them in office. The lines between right and wrong often blurred, and only the interests of people with power and wealth were ever really served in the whole process.

Just watch the news and you'd learn the truth of that.

Besides, what good would her one little vote do? She doubted any politician would ever make her own life easier.

But despite her disregard for the political process, something deep inside told her this Emerson guy was different.

She told Katie so as they folded laundry.

"It's amazing, really. Every vote cast by Senator Emerson has benefited people. Did you know he alone argued to stop funding a study to find out the mating habits of armadillos? I mean, how does that help anyone?" She pulled a shirt from the dryer and handed it to Katie. "Instead he rallied support for an increase in incentives to build new nursing facilities for people like my mom. Even though the effort was spear-headed by Governor Holiday, a guy from across the aisle politically, that Emerson guy put personal ambition aside and did what was best for the residents of Texas."

Katie tucked a corner of the shirt under her chin and matched up the sleeves. "What's up with you and this new interest in politics?"

She remembered the nondisclosure paper she'd signed. "Oh, nothing, really. I just think Senator Emerson's approach to all this is refreshing. Don't you agree?"

Her roommate added the folded shirt to a stack on top of the dryer and reached inside the drum for another. "I think he's cute. That's what I think."

Leta rolled her eyes. "C'mon. Get serious."

"I am serious. The guy is seriously good-looking." She smoothed wrinkles from the fabric of her favorite polo. "And don't tell me you didn't notice."

"You are completely missing the point." A tiny smile nipped at the corners of her mouth. "Okay, yes. Maybe I noticed. But that's not apropos to the conversation we're having."

"Oh really? If you think political appropriations are more important than a hot guy, that might answer why you have no dating life."

"I don't date because I work three jobs and spend my spare time traveling back and forth to Heritage House to be with my mother."

Katie scooped the stack of folded laundry into her arms. "Yes, I know all that is true. But if you hermit away much longer, you're going to grow old all by yourself."

"Hey, I haven't even turned thirty yet."

Her roommate let out an exaggerated sigh. "My point exactly. Your social life is that of a fifty-year-old." Katie pulled Leta's favorite UT Longhorns sweatshirt from the dryer. She held up the garment with the frayed hem and little hole at the neckline and grinned. "Of course, your wardrobe might not be helping much either."

Leta brushed off her roommate's teasing. While what Katie claimed might be true, there was little she could do about it at this juncture.

She would not let her lack of social life diminish the good mood she experienced over her findings.

Jane Ladd seemed equally impressed with the results of her efforts.

"Excellent work, Leta." From behind her desk, her new boss leaned back in her leather armchair and flipped a page in the report. "Truly superb work. And thorough," she said, not even bothering to look up.

Leta beamed inside as her boss praised the data she'd so carefully collected and then meticulously catalogued. "Thank you. I hope you don't mind that I went a bit beyond what you assigned."

"Mind? I wish all my researchers were this self-motivated." She placed the report on her desk, appearing duly impressed. "This is truly an excellent show of ability, Leta."

Jane's accolades sent her spirits soaring, carrying her off on waves of possibility.

The decline in her mother's health had nearly taken her under. The past few years had sucked the air from her dreams and left her wondering if she'd ever land on solid ground again.

Now the dismal outlook had turned. She'd landed a great job, and her employer was pleased with her effort. For the first time in a long time, she felt hopeful.

Who knew? Maybe if she kept working hard, the effort would pay off and this job would turn permanent. If she let herself really dream big, a promotion might be in her future, with an accompanying raise.

She'd be able to catch up her bill at Heritage House in next to no time, and the financial pressure she'd been living with would evaporate. If things went really well, she might be able to quit her job at the Hole in the Wall and cut back her hours at Central Market — maybe even eventually terminate her position there as well.

How would Mike respond when his new pet employee drove down profits with her atrocious design ability and Leta was no longer there to turn things around?

Not that she'd have to care. Not if she'd secured a full-time job with a future and insurance and vacation pay.

She was probably getting ahead of herself. And it wasn't really like her to give in to resentment. Her mother would certainly chastise that kind of attitude.

For now, she needed to focus on the next assignment. Jane wanted her to trace the source of funding for several political action committees, including one recently formed called Concerned Citizens for Texas.

"If you want to know who the whales are in this town, follow the PAC money," Jane told her.

Leta didn't bother to hide her confusion. "Whales?"

Jane leaned forward over her glass-topped desk and steepled her fingers. "Like the highest of high rollers at casinos, these are the biggest of the wealthy donors. Their numbers are few — less than a hundred on the liberal and conservative sides combined."

She nodded. "Okay, I see."

"We have a client with political considerations," Jane explained. "He's paying us a lot of money to tell him who's supporting his issues in the upcoming elections."

Leta tried to take in everything Jane said. She didn't realize public relations included all this work related to legislative matters and elections. But maybe she shouldn't be surprised. Especially given that Austin was the seat of Texas politics.

Jane stood. "Is something the matter?"

She quickly shook her head. "No, of course not — no problem. I'll get right on it."

"That's what I like to hear." Jane handed her the file. "Our client is very anxious for this information. If you can turn this project around quickly, you'll be rewarded."

"Thank you, Jane. I'll do my very best," she promised.

"And Leta?"

She tucked the file under her arm. "Yes?"

"Everything we do here at the Ladd Agency is highly confidential. This project is no different. You are not to mention any of the work you perform or the results outside my office. Not even to co-workers."

The woman she admired smiled as if to rub the sharp edge off her warning and put her at ease.

Leta nodded. "Yes — yes, of course. I understand."

Back in her cubicle, Leta eagerly started to work. Here was another chance to show Jane Ladd what she was capable of doing — another chance to shine.

Still, something inside went on high alert at the extreme secret nature of the project. Who was this client?

And again, what exactly was *special ops*? That Bernard Geisler guy gave her the creeps.

Even Katie had agreed it was a bit strange that he'd slipped out of the Hole in the Wall without even ordering a drink once she'd noticed him.

She'd looked him up, but there was next to no information online. He didn't even have a LinkedIn profile.

She shook her head. Didn't matter.

The important thing was to perform the job set before her, and carry out the assignment exceedingly well.

Mediocrity was not an option.

11

Nate Emerson gunned the gas pedal on his Audi A6 TDI, enjoying the amount of torque in the turbodiesel engine. Unlike many of his congressional peers, he seldom utilized the services of a town car, preferring this car as his chariot of choice. While not extremely expensive, the car mixed function and fun in equal parts.

Someday, when he was no longer in the spotlight and didn't have the media assessing his every purchase, he'd like to buy a sports car. Nothing really spendy. Maybe a Porsche Boxster, cherry-red.

Until then, he'd enjoy this sensible black number that had served him so well, a car he'd missed while she was in the shop.

He thought again of the girl who had run into him and wondered briefly if he'd see her in the store tonight. She'd been so terribly distraught over the damage she'd inflicted on his car, he couldn't possibly be angry. Even if she had put a nice-sized dent in his front bumper.

Though not exactly close to his home, Central Market was the only grocery outlet to carry his Ossau-Iraty, a creamy and slightly nutty-tasting cheese made of sheep's milk from the western Pyrenees of France.

He'd first tasted the delicacy when his mother and Porter took him on a graduation trip to Europe. His mother believed it was her job to make sure he was exposed to culture. "You're destined for big things, Son," she'd said. "I intend to show you there's more to this world than bluebonnets and longhorns."

Nate parked in a spot near the entrance to the store. As he tucked his key fob into his pants pocket, he couldn't help glancing around for her car.

When he didn't see her vehicle, he tucked away his slight disappointment and stepped through the sliding glass doors, making his way to the rear of the store where the cheese carousel was located, next to the wine aisle.

He selected several packages of Ossau-Iraty and placed the cellophane-wrapped wedges in his hand-carried grocery basket. He rounded the aisle and headed for the bakery.

That's when he saw her — the girl.

For some reason he couldn't explain, he hung back and again watched her work. Alone in the department, she pulled a long-stemmed pink rose from a bucket and expertly clipped the stem at an angle. Before placing it in the vase, she lifted the bud to her nose and took in its scent. Her eyes closed, the aroma seeming to bring her immense pleasure.

He smiled at the delight expressed on her face, appreciating that a simple rose made her that happy.

She opened her eyes, caught him watching her. Her expression turned to surprise, and then a slow smile dawned on her face. She waved.

He waved back before making his way over. "Hey there. Nice seeing you again."

Her hand went to her temple, and she rubbed the spot as if nervous. "Are you sure?" She grinned and stepped from behind the counter and extended her hand. "Thank you again for being so nice the other night. I mean, when I backed into your car and all."

"No problem. Accidents happen." He smiled back at her. He felt oddly nervous as he shook her hand. "Just got my car out of the shop yesterday, and she's as good as new."

"Oh, good. I — I'll try to stay out of the parking lot tonight until after you've had a chance to leave." Her laugh showcased her dimples.

Suddenly, he remembered his manners. "I'm Nathan Emerson."

"Yes," she said. "Senator Emerson. I know who you are."

Normally, he resisted connecting the label to himself when first meeting someone, reluctant to come off as pretentious. But he liked when she said she knew who he was. He could only hope their political views were aligned and the fact she knew he was a senator was an advantage.

"I like your voting record," she said, immediately putting him at ease. "And the things you care about."

"Oh?" He admired how little makeup she wore. While he'd never said it out loud to anyone, he thought women who covered up their natural beauty with a bunch of expensive products seemed a bit inauthentic. "It's always good to hear my efforts are aligned with that of my constituents."

She hesitated a second or two, glanced at the floor before looking back up at him. "My mother . . . well, she suffers dementia. She's in a residential care center."

His heart ached upon hearing that news.

"Oh, I'm so sorry." He was well aware of the burden created for the families of those suffering these types of diseases. And he heard the emotion in her voice.

"Uh, thanks. I mean, she's doing well. Considering."

Nate nodded. "I hate that debilitating disease and what it does to families. It must be very hard for you."

Their eyes met. He sensed deep sadness behind those blue eyes. A sadness he wished he had the ability to erase.

Nate shifted the basket and reached in his pocket for his wallet. "This is my personal contact information. If there's ever anything I can do to help you and your mother, please call me." He gave her an earnest look and offered his business card. "I mean it. Call me anytime."

She took the card. "Thank you."

He stood there several more seconds without moving. Feeling a bit awkward, he shifted his stance. "Well, I guess I'd better get going."

Her face broke into an easy smile. "Nice seeing you again."

"Yeah, same here. Take care."

Reluctantly, he turned and moved for the line of people in the checkout lane.

It wasn't until he was halfway home that

he realized he'd forgotten to go to the bakery department for his pastries.

Worse, he never asked for her name.

12

Leta sat on a thick quilt covering the bed, brushing her mother's hair. When she was little, her mom used to do the same for her each evening before she went to bed, while listening to her tell all about her day.

With each stroke of the brush, she tried to dwell on happy thoughts and ignore how their roles had reversed.

"Jane Ladd is so put together, Mom. And smart. For some reason, we really seem to connect. I mean, I think she admires how hard I work and that I'm thorough. And resourceful." She paused the strokes. "Just like you taught me to be, Momma."

Outside the window, tiny multicolored lights twinkled from the row of hedges that circled the courtyard — the only indication that Christmas was next week. She'd wanted to put a tree up in her mother's room, but as she'd learned last year, safety regulations prohibited the effort. Beyond potential accidents with electrical cords, any change in their living environment seemed to agitate dementia patients.

"This job could lead to everything we need, Mom. I'm already well on my way to bringing our account here at Heritage House current, thanks to a cash bonus I earned on this last research project."

She told her mother all about the assignment she'd just completed. How she'd worked for days, spending every possible moment poring over public information.

Her first stop had been the attorney general's office, where she inspected volumes of financial disclosure reports. She'd spent time in the secretary of state's office tracking filings for the various entities she identified that had contributed to the Concerned Citizens for Texas PAC. No doubt the process was complex, but her hard work paid off again when she hit the pot of gold, so to speak.

She finally had her hands on the name of the true founder, and was shocked to realize the influential woman who formed the PAC was well-known philanthropist Vera Emerson Wyatt. Senator Emerson's mother.

Leta shifted her legs to keep them from going to sleep. "I'm not sure what all this means, Mom. There's a lot of moving pieces, some of them very secret. The more I get involved — the more I learn — the more I become confused."

She didn't mention how quickly Jane had buzzed Bernard Geisler on the phone, how he'd scrambled into the room and snatched the report off the desk. He'd read her findings with much interest, his brows furrowed and sweat glistening at his sparse hairline.

She'd sat and watched in silence, finally having to glance away when he licked his lips and used the back of his hand to wipe the moisture away.

When he'd finished looking over her work, he handed the report back to Jane. "Good. That's good information," he said before turning and leaving the room without even acknowledging her.

She also didn't tell her mom how her gut had churned the whole time. How she'd forced herself to brush off the concern building inside. This was a good job, one she'd waited for, and a position she was really good at.

In the face of never finishing her education, which hindered her dream of becoming a landscape architect, this opportunity could furnish their financial needs and build her badly tarnished self-esteem.

She remembered how easily she'd looked

Senator Emerson in the face when he showed up at the store. How she'd used her newly discovered confidence and boldly interacted with him despite the fact he was a senator — and someone she'd backed into only days earlier.

This new assurance could only be attributed to her new position.

"Mom, a guy came into the store a while back. His name is Nathan Emerson, and he works hard to support people like you. Senator Emerson wields a lot of influence on certain legislative committees that form the laws and regulations that affect patients with brain disorders and dementia. He's also the founding director of the Institute of Brain Sciences. The guy really cares, Mom." Her heart tickled inside her chest. "I — I think he likes me. I could tell from his eyes. You know what I mean, Mom?"

Leta gave her mother's hair two more strokes before placing the brush on the bedside table. She clambered off the bed and nestled her head in her mother's lap. "You were right, Mom. God is good."

She wasn't sure how long she stayed like that in her favorite spot, with her head there in her mother's lap, before she felt her mom's fingers in her hair. Softly stroking. "Yes," she said. "He is."

Leta quickly popped her head up. "Mom?"

Her mother stared out the window with the same emptiness in her eyes, the same void as always.

A slow, disappointed breath leaked from between Leta's lips. Her eyes welled. She wiped away the moisture, then carefully wove her fingers through her mother's and squeezed. "I love you, Mom," she whispered. "If you are in there somewhere, please know how very much I love you."

From across the room, an image flashed across her mother's old Magnavox television. The familiar profile instantly caught her attention.

Leta pulled her fingers free and scrambled for the remote on the bed table. She quickly turned up the volume. "Mom, that's him. That's Senator Emerson."

The guy she'd just been talking about stood on the steps leading up to the capitol building. He wore a beautifully tailored navy suit and a red tie. The camera zoomed in to catch a close-up of his face as the announcer's voice-over began.

Key political strategists from across the state of Texas and beyond predict that Senator Nathan Emerson is poised to launch a challenge against incumbent

Governor Holiday. An unnamed source reports that Senator Emerson is quietly but aggressively courting key endorsers and is developing a behind-the-scenes strategy for entering this very important race.

Officials from both sides of the aisle warn that Senator Emerson could pose a real threat to the governor serving a third term, especially given Holiday's recent drop in poll numbers.

An image of Governor Holiday standing at a podium appeared on-screen.

The governor's camp claims they welcome Senator Emerson into the race. Holiday's political architecture has been in place for months, and his message remains clear — as a husband and father, he understands the importance of preserving traditional values like faith, family, and freedom for future generations. As the state's chief executive officer for the past eight years, Governor Holiday has made protecting children, families, and these values the focus of his administration.

Leta watched with acute interest. Looked like a lot of people were paying attention to Nathan Emerson these days, especially the governor.

Before she could ponder what that might mean in light of her work at the Ladd Agency, the television monitor again switched to a film clip of Senator Emerson. Her new acquaintance stood chatting with a group of men.

Her stomach fluttered.

Nathan Emerson was no doubt fierce and bright and attractive in a decidedly hand-some way — all angles and lines and broad shoulders. Even in their short exchanges, and especially given what she'd learned in all her research, she'd determined he had the mind of a scholar and was a force to be reckoned with. Those qualities, coupled with his sincere kindness, made him one of the most attractive men she'd encountered in some time.

Maybe ever.

She sat back, realizing the impact of the thoughts that had just run through her mind. While not ready to openly admit it, she was clearly attracted.

The announcer's voice blurred as she let her mind wander to what that could mean — to the way he'd looked at her that night in the store and how, impossible as it seemed, he might feel the same about her.

The idea sent a thrill through her entire

body. She felt the corners of her mouth lift as she let herself savor the idea.

She reached over and squeezed her mother's hand again. "Look, Mom. That's him. That's Senator Nathan Emerson. Isn't he amazing?"

Just then, something else on the television caught her eye. A woman — gorgeous in a black sequined dress, high heels, and big sparkly earrings peeking out from long, curly auburn hair — moved forward. Looking like some model who had just stepped off the pages of *Vogue* magazine or something, she flashed a brilliant white-toothed smile and placed her hand on the senator's arm.

In a gesture that suggested intimacy, he placed his hand on the small of her back.

Senator Emerson wrapped up what he was saying, but his words blurred together as Leta focused on his hand as it guided the woman away from the cameras.

He . . . he has a girlfriend.

The thought came quickly like a sharp needle, piercing her fantasy and draining her of the elation she'd felt only moments ago.

You fool. Of course he has someone. Look at him.

Leta swallowed against the dryness growing in her throat, her hand heavy as she pointed the remote toward the television and clicked it off.

"No-no-no-no-no!"

She startled at her mother's voice. "Sorry, Mom. I forgot," she said, turning the television back on.

Immediately, her mother calmed.

Leta lowered the volume, then stood and moved to the window. She stared out at the darkness, acutely aware of how utterly hopeful she'd been. How much she'd wanted to see if there could be more than just a spark between her and Nathan Emerson.

How could I have misunderstood that look?

Mentally, she stepped back and got a grip on reality, realizing she'd been acting like a silly schoolgirl, easily swept away by an infatuation that would never be reciprocated.

She took a deep breath and forced herself to refocus. Thankfully, she hadn't been stupid enough to tell anyone else what she'd been thinking about Senator Emerson — not even Katie.

She rubbed her forehead, determined to find the silver lining in all of this.

There were a lot of positives in her life right now.

The fact still remained she'd landed a

great job. With any luck her employment would go full-time and the financial burden she'd been under would lift permanently.

No doubt, she had much to be thankful for.

Leta shifted from the window to find her mother had lifted from her chair. With a dreamy smile, the petite woman swept back and forth across the industrial beige carpet, waltzing to some unheard minuet.

Leta couldn't help but smile. She held out open palms. "Hey, Cinderella, may I have this dance?"

With confidence, her mother gripped her hands. And for a magical few moments, Leta became a child again as she and her mother whirled around the tiny room in imaginary glass slippers.

13

The following Monday dawned bright and crisp. While people in other parts of the country were shoveling snow and loading up their fireplaces with wood to keep warm, here in Austin Leta drove with her car windows partially down.

She passed Auditorium Shores on the way to the office. The trail was lined with running enthusiasts enjoying a bit of sunshine, albeit jogging in sweatshirts and long pants this time of the year.

The Ladd Agency offices would be closed through the holidays, starting tomorrow. Without the extra paycheck coming in during those weeks, she'd have to schedule more hours at Central Market and a couple of extra shifts at the Hole in the Wall to make up for the lost income.

In the last weeks, she'd easily adjusted to having extra money in her budget. That was not a good thing, given the temporary nature of the job at the Ladd Agency. Still, the extra income had allowed her to get back on top financially, and for that she was grateful.

She was waiting at the elevators when her phone alerted she had a message from Jane.

I'd like to see you in my office after the company meeting this morning.

Immediately, she feared the worst. Her work had been highly praised, but no new assignment had been forthcoming. She didn't want to think the worst. But it was entirely possible the need for her position was at the ending point and Jane wanted to tell her so.

No matter how she tried to ignore the prickly notion, the concern followed her right into the staff meeting like a cocklebur she couldn't shake off.

"Good morning, everyone," Jane said upon joining her employees in the small conference room. She set her steaming coffee mug down on the granite table and motioned for everyone to take a seat. "As you know, we close operations until after the first of the year, but before I send you all home to enjoy the holidays, I have something important to share."

The dozen or so people in the room exchanged curious glances. Jane took a sip of her coffee before continuing. "We've had a good year. Revenues are up as we've enjoyed a steady stream of work. Occasionally more work than we've been able to manage." She looked across the table. "We brought Leta on to help out, and she's done a fabulous job."

Leta smiled. "Thank you. I've loved being here."

Despite the praise, she felt her insides tighten, knowing that her temporary employment might be about to come to an abrupt end. She never wanted to sit across the desk from that Edith Styles woman again and be told she had to consider moving her mother to another facility. If she lost this job, she'd have to find another. And quick.

Jane leaned forward in her chair, adjusted the black and gold scarf at the neckline of her pretty cream-colored blouse. "I'd like to send you all off to enjoy the holidays with some good news." She paused and looked around the room with a huge grin. "We've taken on a new client. A very influential and highly visible political candidate. We'll be assisting Governor Wyndall Holiday in his bid for reelection. While it's not yet official, most believe the governor will have no serious opposition in the May primaries. His major contender heading into the general will be Nathan Emerson. Emerson currently holds a senate seat and has done very well pushing a health care–related agenda."

Leta's ears perked up. The announcement was not all that surprising, given the projects she'd been asked to work on, but she couldn't help wondering what all this would mean, especially for the man she admired.

"Ten months sounds like a long time, but in the world of election cycles those weeks will pass in a flash. There's a lot to do ahead." Jane nodded at her human resources director. Dawson handed her a stack of sealed envelopes. "So expect to return after this short holiday break ready to tackle some hard work. Until then, consider this year-end financial gift a token of my appreciation. Please know you are all valued here at the Ladd Agency." She circled the room, handing out the envelopes to everyone, including Leta. "I hope you all have a wonderful break."

Her co-workers dispersed from the table, no doubt anxious to begin their holidays. "Merry Christmas, everyone," Elaine called out before turning to Erin. "Honey, you going home to Nacogdoches to be with your folks?"

Erin nodded. "Yup, leaving this afternoon."

The older woman gathered the used coffee mugs onto a tray. "Well, drive safely. Lots of crazy drivers out there this time of year."

Dan Williams pushed his glasses up on his head. "Yeah, take care," he said. "See you after New Year's."

In the lobby, Erin waved goodbye. "Merry Christmas, everyone."

"Yeah, sure. You too." Leta clutched the envelope and made her way to Jane's office. She poked her head inside the open door. "You wanted to see me?"

"Yes, come on in." Jane waved her inside. "Sit down."

Leta took a deep breath. "Look, I just want to say how much I've enjoyed working here." She held up the envelope. "And you certainly didn't have to do this."

Jane smiled. "Like I said in the meeting, your work is stellar, and I wanted to reward you."

Leta felt her hands shake. Nothing noticeable, but her nerves began playing a mournful blues tune in every fiber of her being. Even after hearing the firm had a lot of work on the horizon, she couldn't help believing Jane was about to inform her this was the end of her good run.

Jane looked past her. "Isn't that right, Bernard?"

Only then did Leta notice Bernard Geisler sitting in a chair at the side of the room. Those tiny, dark eyes stared at her from behind wire-rimmed glasses. He said nothing, instead he simply nodded in agreement.

"Sit," Jane offered, pointing to her guest chair. She leaned back at the corner of her desk and grabbed a file, slid a sheet of paper from inside, and held it out. "We'd like to offer you a full-time position here at the Ladd Agency, beginning after the holidays."

"Full-time?"

Jane grinned.

Flushed with relief, Leta quickly glanced down at the offer written on the paper. Her breath caught. She looked back up at Jane with raised eyebrows. "You're kidding, right?"

Jane shook her head, still smiling. "I think that's a fair offer, and there will be opportunities for financial advancement as we help you grow your career."

"But — but this is six figures!"

Jane moved to the chair behind her desk. "We maintain a small staff. My employees are handpicked and highly rewarded for their dedication, drive, and *loyalty.*" She leaned back against the plush leather, the stacked gold bracelets at her wrist reflecting light from the window. "I believe you have all those qualities and more. And I'm an astute judge of character. So what do you say, Leta — you in?"

A flush of adrenaline rushed through her body, lifting her onto a cloud of possibility. Nothing in her wildest dreams had stretched this far.

Her car was barely holding together, and her mother's care and rent gobbled up what little income she could cobble together with multiple jobs, leaving little left over for much else. Her clothes closet held none of the kinds of wardrobe items she saw in store windows or online. She never dared to go out and have fun like other girls her age — like Katie so often enjoyed.

Her mother's health situation had usurped her ability to afford anything extra. Now here in her hands rested the keys to changing all of that. All she had to do was unlock the door and step through.

In her excitement, she could barely respond without her voice shaking. "Yes! Of course I'm in." Her hand involuntarily moved to cover her mouth as her mind still tried to take in what was happening.

Her heart fluttered in excitement. *A six-figure salary!*

Jane glanced over at Bernard. She slapped her hands together and stood. "Excellent! Welcome aboard."

Leta grinned and even ventured a glance in Bernard's direction. "Thank you. This is a tremendous opportunity. I'm extremely grateful."

Jane guided her to the door. "You go home. Enjoy the holiday break. Then come back ready to work. All right?"

Leta nodded. "Yes — all right. Sure." Before turning down the hall to leave, she paused and looked back. "Merry Christmas!"

Moments later, she passed through the now empty lobby, past the professionally decorated tree filled with bright white lights and glittery ornaments. She made her way to the elevator doors, clutching the bonus check and the offer letter to her chest, thinking of her pitiful tree at home with its string of barely working lights and chipped ornaments.

"Yes," she whispered to herself as the elevator doors opened.

This year, it was indeed going to be a very merry Christmas.

14

Two days before Christmas, Nate leaned against the glass-topped display counter and pointed. "Let me take a look at those, please."

The man nodded, his head perched on a crisply starched collar. "Yes, sir. Fine choice." He pulled out a velvet-lined tray and set it before Nate. "These brilliant-cut diamond bracelets have clarity and color qualities of the highest nature, sir."

Nate reached for one and admired how the large stones sparkled as the halogen lighting above the counter caught the facets. "Yes, these are really nice."

Inside, he could almost hear his mother's voice. *A bracelet? What's the matter with you, Son? It's time for a ring.*

In many ways, she would be right. Tiffany was every man's dream. She was beautiful, accomplished, and incredibly intelligent.

The first time they'd met he'd been sitting in a conference room. He'd gone for legal counsel regarding a grant program he wanted to establish for the institute. She walked in with the senior partner, confident and well-spoken.

During the entire meeting, she'd sat silent, taking in the discussion before articulating her thoughts. "That strategy is viable. But there's a better approach. One that will make you less obligated and will free you to call the shots." She went on to remind everyone in the room how often researchers ended up beholden to their financial bene-factors — how restrictive and politically motivated that environment could be. "I suggest an alternative. Private funding by benefactors who are not profit-oriented will provide far more flexibility in terms of direc-tion and will allow for adjustments in focus as you weigh research findings and what that means to your project."

Tiffany Shea made a compelling argument that day — one the institute ultimately fol-lowed with great success.

The time they'd spent first in strategy meetings and later in group social environ-ments had led to more intimate settings — dinners at nice restaurants, time at the gym, Sunday afternoons sipping French-pressed coffee and eating croissants at a little shop downtown.

It seemed they had much in common, and an easy friendship formed.

While it was not intentional, he woke up one day and realized the friendship had extended past casual, and by everyone else's standards they were dating.

He was the first to voice the revelation. Tiffany just smiled. "It was inevitable, don't you think? We're perfectly matched. That, and I think you're extremely attracted to me."

He laughed. "Oh, you think so?"

She ran her manicured finger up his sleeve, traced his jawline. "Yes, I know so."

And he had been. Only a blind man would not be attracted to Tiffany Shea. She was the whole package, and as his mother so often reminded him, a perfect wife for a rising political star.

"So? What do you think about the bracelet?" The clerk's voice brought his mind back to the present. "Would you like me to box it up?"

He handed the bracelet back. "This is a stunning piece, but before I decide, maybe I should look at some rings."

No expression registered on the man's face. "Certainly, sir. Right over here."

The diamond solitaires in the case caught

the light and sparkled. But that was not what caught Nate's attention.

Outside the store window, he glimpsed a familiar figure.

"Uh, I'll be right back." He apologized to the man behind the counter and hurried out to the sidewalk. Several yards ahead, the girl from the grocery store walked with multiple packages tucked under her arms. The girl with the mother who had dementia.

Despite a couple of trips to Central Market, their paths had failed to cross. He'd wondered about her often over the course of the past weeks.

"Hey," he hollered. Why hadn't he been smart enough to get her name? "Excuse me." He waved his arm, feeling a bit foolish but determined to catch her attention.

She turned.

He picked up his pace and jogged in her direction. Breathless, he smiled when he finally reached her. "Hey, I saw you and I . . . well, I just wanted to say hello."

Great, he was a Texas state senator who had just come off sounding like a kid at a junior high lunch table.

Nate grinned. "Let me start over. I saw you walk by and just wanted to say hello."

Thankfully, she smiled. "Hello back."

"Looks like you've been shopping."

She lifted the packages. "These? Well, yeah. Kind of last minute, but I'm playing Santa this morning."

"Every year I vow to get my shopping obligations done early. Every year I'm in the stores frantically hoping to find gifts at the last minute. So I get where you're coming from." He held out his hands. "You look like you could use some help."

The corners of her mouth lifted into a shy smile, and she shifted the bulkiest of the packages into his waiting hands. "Hey, thanks. I appreciate it."

"Listen, I could sure use something hot to drink. You up for a cappuccino?" He nodded toward a storefront ahead of them.

She hesitated slightly, then gave a hearty nod. "Sure, why not?"

As they started walking, he told himself the elation he felt could simply be explained as . . . well, as what? No label would be entirely accurate. All he knew was that he was glad to run into her again and that she agreed to go have coffee.

He held the door open to the bright red entrance to LavAzza, a trendy little Italian coffee shop blocks from the capitol.

She stepped inside. "Mmm. Why do these places always smell so enticing?"

He followed, nodding in agreement. "I

know. I love that aroma." They chose a table over by a wall painted bright yellow. "Wait here and I'll go get our drinks. What do you like?"

"Anything hot and with frothy milk." She grinned up at him. "Surprise me."

"You got it."

As he moved to get in line, an overweight woman in yoga gear cut in front of him. Her frizzy hair smelled heavily of patchouli and was pulled back by some clip-like thing, revealing a tattoo on her neck: *Bite Me!*

He stepped back, allowing her ample room.

She turned. "Hey, aren't you that guy I see on television sometimes? You're in government or something."

He patiently folded his hands in front of him and nodded.

"Well, listen — I've got a problem I need help with. My neighbor's got one of them yappy dogs. A Chihuahua or something like that." She shrugged. "Anyway, the stupid thing barks all the time. Keeps me and my husband up at night. You know?"

Inside, he couldn't help but groan. "I'm sorry to hear that."

"Well, maybe you can do something about that?" She looked at him hopefully.

He took a deep breath and smiled back at

her, then slipped his iPhone from his pocket and thumbed the face until the information he was looking for appeared. He grabbed a napkin from a nearby table and wrote down a number and handed it to her. "Here, this is the name of the city manager — the person who issues and upholds the ordinances in your area. Call him and make a report. That should take care of the issue." He forced another smile. "I hope that helps."

She raised her eyebrows. "Well, thanks. I'll do that." She turned back around and stepped up to the counter to place her order.

Nate glanced back over at the table, realizing he had yet to get Market Girl's name. She smiled at him and raised her eyebrows, seeming to also appreciate the unique nature of the woman in front of him.

Minutes later, he returned carrying steaming cups of cappuccino. "Somehow I think this is going to be the better part of my entire day." He nodded back in the direction of the tattooed lady, who was busy shoving a pastry in her mouth as she walked out the door.

She laughed and slid the cup and saucer closer. "One of your constituents?"

He sat and leaned back in his chair, enjoying the way her cheeks dimpled when she smiled. "Ha — one who probably voted against me in the last election. But give me time and I might be able to win her over." He handed her a long-handled spoon, enjoying their easy banter. "Look, I'm embarrassed to admit this, but I don't even know your name."

Something inside him revved as she looked over at him.

"I'm Leta Breckenridge," she said after positioning the spoon on the side of her saucer.

"Well, it's nice to formally meet you, Leta Breckenridge." Nice name. It fit her. "You were hauling around quite a load." He glanced at the floor near her feet where she'd tucked her packages. "So, I'm assuming you enjoy this Christmas shopping thing?"

"Gifts for my mom. She loves chocolates and pastries and music boxes."

"Ah yes." He nodded. "Appreciation for food and music are often the last senses to diminish in the dementia patient." The minute the words were out of his mouth, he wanted to take them back. It was a stupid thing to say, something a researcher would utter. Not a friend. "I'm sorry. I didn't mean to —"

"Oh, please — it's fine. I find it strangely

comforting that you get it." She sipped her steaming drink, leaving a hint of white foam at the corners of her mouth. He wished he knew her better. He'd reach and wipe it away.

She must've noticed him looking. "What?"

He grinned and pointed.

"Oh." Her cheeks blushed slightly as she wiped the foam off with her napkin. She shook her head and laughed. "I've never figured out how to drink these without —"

"Every time I'm around you, I like you more," he blurted, surprised he'd so freely admitted his . . . his what? Attraction?

How could he possibly be so easily attracted to this girl when he was securely in a relationship with a woman who everyone knew was remarkable and, frankly, perfectly suited to him?

"So, you appreciate me because I'm a slob?" She laughed again. "Or is it because I backed into your really nice car? I mean, people like me . . . we're hard to find."

They laughed and drank their cappuccinos, talking through a refill. He learned she loved the Christmas season. Poinsettias and decorated pine trees, even though trees in Texas were nearly always fake. The way entire houses and neighborhoods were blanketed with lights.

He told her that thickly frosted sugar cookies topped with tiny silver beads were his favorite. "When I was a kid, my mom used to help me roll out the dough and cut out shapes. The minute she'd look the other way, I'd swipe frosting out of the bowl with my finger and tuck it in my mouth."

"Me too! Only I'd get caught when Mom noticed some at the corners of my mouth, and it'd give me away. Some things never change." As if to punctuate her anecdote, she dipped the tip of her finger into the frothy white foam in her cup and brought it to her mouth, letting some carelessly collect at the corner of her mouth, causing them both to chuckle.

He really liked that about her. She didn't take herself too seriously.

Their discussion turned more poignant then, as she described how hard her mother had worked to establish family traditions during the holidays, despite the fact it was only the two of them — and how heartbreaking it had been when her mother turned ill and everything changed.

The sadness in her eyes as she described the first Christmas Eve she'd had to leave her mother at the nursing center and return home to an empty house created a surge of sympathy deep inside him.

"In the early stages of her decline, I begged God to heal her. Pleaded and screamed. I didn't understand. I knew he could — heal her, I mean. And maybe he still will." She shrugged. "I don't know."

"Maybe that healing manifests most in our courage and strength to go on — and still trust things will work out," he said softly. While true, the statement sounded a bit hollow. He wished he had the power to erase that pain and make Leta's situation better.

Her features shadowed, and she looked down at her cup. "You know, I've never really confided how lost I feel sometimes without her."

Nate took a deep breath. "Yeah, I get that. My dad died when I was thirteen. He drowned in our pool." The confession seemed to spring out of a mouth not his own. He could barely remember a time he'd discussed that sensitive topic with anyone — let alone a girl he'd barely met. Living with his tight-lipped mother and then entering a life of politics had trained him to never put personal information out there that could become fodder for the gossip mill.

Her hand seemed to instinctively reach across the table, and he felt her fingers on his own. "Oh, Nate. I didn't know. I'm so very sorry."

Her touch somehow punctured his soul, and he began to spill out everywhere. As did the details.

"Rumors flew, of course. He was a senator as well, and media outlets hinted at suicide."

She looked at him, their eye contact potent, palpable. "How hurtful. I can't even imagine what that must've been like," she muttered.

"I was promised it wasn't true," he quickly assured her. "But then, rumors never have to be true to do damage." He slowly slid his hand from hers. "Once the notion was planted inside my head, I could never fully camp on my mother's assurances. Know what I mean?"

She nodded.

"I asked myself if there was something maybe I had done — or not done. At night, images of my dad knowingly downing a bunch of alcohol and then walking down the pool steps with purpose haunted me for years." He couldn't help the tears that pooled. He knuckled them away, embarrassed. "Still does."

Faint strains of "Have Yourself a Merry Little Christmas" drifted from the ceiling speakers. Nate and Leta both sat in silence with their cups on the table, strangers oddly connected over the dim outline of shared pain.

Later, when they'd finished their drinks and realized it was time to go, Nate risked a brief hug before they headed toward the door. "Thank you for agreeing to have coffee," he said. "I really enjoyed getting to know you more. And I hope you have a merry Christmas, Leta."

Her face told him she was as reluctant as he to part ways. "You too, Nate."

It wasn't until Nate was on his way home that the full impact of those hours spent talking over coffee, the gift of opening up and sharing his soul with another human being who understood, fully registered. How easily they'd formed a community of two, knit by shared loss and the scars that remained.

The freedom with which he'd shared such private matters with Leta Breckenridge startled him.

Why, he wasn't certain, but he'd never expressed those feelings before. Not to his mother, or Porter, or any of his frat brothers at school. Not with friends or his pastor. He hadn't even confided in Tiffany, the girl he'd recently contemplated making his wife.

At that moment, another realization startled him even more.

He'd never returned to the jewelry store.

15

If, as John Steinbeck wrote, Texas is a state of mind, then Austin, an eclectic and high-spirited city filled with artists, musicians, and freethinkers, was the perfect capital city.

Leta Breckenridge never knew where she fit in, exactly. Unlike many of her fellow classmates at UT, she didn't run in the circles of earthy students who ate organic fare and spent their evenings in dark, smoke-filled rooms listening to moody musicians.

Neither was she one who wore Tony Lamas or tight jeans, who followed the rodeo circuit, or who pulled on running shoes every Saturday morning to participate in the sponsored run du jour.

Frankly, her social life was just as Katie claimed — dismally nonexistent.

So when Erin Robertson peeked her head around the cubicle wall and invited Leta to join her and some friends for dinner, she didn't hesitate to say yes.

"I thought we'd just catch an early bite somewhere downtown."

"Yeah, sure. That'd be great." Leta closed the Excel spreadsheet she was working on and grabbed her purse. "What did you have in mind?"

"The Roaring Fork. They have great fish tacos and this green chili mac and cheese to die for."

Twenty minutes later, they joined a small group already seated at a table beneath a large chandelier made of deer horns.

"Hey, everybody." Erin hung her purse on the back of a chair. "This is my co-worker Leta Breckenridge. These bozos are Troy and Ben."

The one with the longer hair grinned. "Hey, nice to meet you."

Erin pointed to a girl with short platinum hair worn spiky. "And Tatum."

Leta slid into her seat. "Hi. Thanks for letting me hang out."

"No problem." Troy reached across and shook hands. "How long have you guys worked together?"

Erin took the menu Ben offered. "Leta started at the Ladd Agency not long ago." She quickly scanned the menu. "I don't know why I'm looking at this. I already know I'm getting the mac and cheese." She handed the plastic-covered menu off to Leta.

There was a time she'd never have been able to accept this invitation, never afford menu items priced at twenty dollars or more. Thanks to her recent good fortune, she could now live a little.

She had to admit, acting like other women her age felt good. In fact, life in general was pretty good.

With the bonus money, she'd been able to write a fairly good-sized check to Heritage House, which included an amount over her monthly obligation. "The overage is a small charitable donation for anyone who can't quite afford things this month." The gesture surprised Edith Styles. "I'll do more when I'm able," Leta promised.

She'd also splurged a little and used some money to upgrade her sad wardrobe. She bought several pairs of new shoes and a purse, a few dress clothes. She'd even had a professional haircut, the first in over a year.

While it wasn't hard to quit her job at the Hole in the Wall, leaving Central Market was a bit harder.

"You can't quit now," Mike begged. "I don't have anyone trained to take your place."

"What about Denese?"

Mike shook his head. "Had to move her into produce last Tuesday."

"You did?"

"Yeah, too many customer complaints."

So, her nemesis had been yanked out of her beloved floral department like a bunch of bad weeds. "Well, sure. I'll stay on until you find someone good."

Besides, with any luck, she might run into Nate — oh, not literally, but she couldn't help but hope she might look up to see him standing at the end of the aisle, smiling at her.

While she hadn't seen him since the afternoon they'd spent talking in the coffee shop, the hours she'd spent with Nathan Emerson that day had been a special gift that carried her clear through the holidays.

He was so easy to talk to. Rarely did she ever open up and share at such an intimate level, revealing feelings often reserved for only the closest of friends, like Katie.

Likewise, she doubted Nate had confided in anyone else about his father. And she'd seen that thing in his eyes again, that look that made her heart beat faster.

She smiled thinking of him as she looked over the menu.

Erin leaned over to Leta. "Do you like

fish? You can't go wrong with the salmon."

"So, hey, I got tickets to South by South-west. Anyone else going?" The guy with the longer light brown hair, the one named Ben, looked across the table at her. "What about you, Leta?"

She shook her head. "I hate to admit this, but I've never been."

"You've never been to South by?"

Tatum rolled her eyes. "Don't be a schmuck. I've lived here two years and I've never been either."

Troy turned to her. "You've got to be kidding me!"

Ben grabbed his beer. "Man, you guys are missing out. You gotta go. Let me see if I can get my hands on some more tickets."

Erin pulled a tortilla chip from the basket on the table and dredged it through a tiny cup of salsa. "Tickets are on sale already? March is still a long way off."

Troy leaned forward and grabbed a chip. "Be here sooner than you think, and the tickets to all the hot venues sell out quick. Last year I snagged entry to a live taping of the Jimmy Kimmel show."

Tatum banged her shoulder against his. "You're such a celebrity habitué."

He bumped her back. "And you use words that are too grandiloquent."

"Hey," Erin said, interrupting their banter. She lowered her voice and nodded in the direction of the door. "Speaking of celebrities. Isn't that Senator Emerson?"

They all turned and looked. Especially Leta.

Ben let out a low whistle. "Who's the classy babe?"

Erin frowned at him. "That's his girlfriend. I saw on the news Emerson plans to announce his bid for governor soon."

Troy rubbed his stubbled chin. "Should be an interesting race against that Holiday guy."

Leta heard the entire conversation but couldn't pull her attention from Nate and the beautiful woman by his side. Tiffany Shea. She'd looked her up.

The waitress appeared at the table and took their order. Reluctantly, Leta returned her attention to the table. "I'll have the salmon. And a salad."

"Dressing?"

"What? Oh, uh, ranch is fine."

Leta snuck another look and watched as Nate and his lady friend were seated at a table by the window. Despite feeling like some sort of spy, she continued to sneak glances every few seconds while pretending to stay engaged in the conversation at her own table.

Erin rummaged in her purse and pulled out a photo of her family and passed it around for her friends to see. "That's the whole bunch of us at Christmas."

Ben pointed. "Your guy?"

Erin shook her head. "No — that's my brother." She passed the photograph to Leta. "He's single, by the way. Interested?"

She grinned and played along. "Depends. What does he drive?"

Her comment elicited a laugh around the table, so she added, "I'm not picky. A Maserati will do."

She tried to sneak another glance, but a small group had gathered at Nate's table, blocking her view.

"What about you?" Troy asked. "You got family nearby?"

The waitress showed up. She waited to answer until their salads had been served. "Just my mother." She didn't offer anything more, instead she simply picked up her fork. "These marinated artichokes look delicious."

Tatum scooped a bite and nodded in Nate's direction. "So, do you think he has a chance?"

Troy lifted his empty glass to the waitress. "If he makes it through the primaries, he'll likely give ole Holiday a run. I mean, look at him. He's what, twenty years younger? That's reason enough to vote for the guy. Governor Holiday is a fossil." He chuckled. "I bet he doesn't even know how to tweet."

Erin looked at her from across the table. "Oh, he doesn't have to know social media. He has people. Huh, Leta?"

She shrugged, not entirely crazy about the direction this conversation was taking, given the sensitive nature of the work at the Ladd Agency. "Yeah, he probably does."

Worse, she didn't feel comfortable mulling over the odds of Holiday beating her new friend in a run for higher office.

She placed her fork on her plate and scooted her chair back. "Hey, y'all excuse me? I'll be right back." Leta wiped her mouth with the corner of the linen napkin, stood, and headed toward the bathroom.

In the privacy of her stall, she leaned back against the door and tried to catch her breath. She needed to get a grip after seeing Nathan Emerson again. This time with his girlfriend in tow.

Had she misread his interest?

Sure, they'd spent time together one afternoon over coffee, even connected at a deeper emotional level than is normal for casual friends, but that obviously hadn't altered his relationship status. He already had a girlfriend. One who looked like she regularly shopped Neiman Marcus.

Of course Senator Nathan Emerson couldn't possibly be attracted to someone like Leta. She'd completely misunderstood. He was just being uber-nice, that's all.

But even as she told herself this, she could see him running down the sidewalk calling out after her, all frantic as if he —

Leta, get a grip!

She shook her head and erased all those silly notions. No one in their right mind would consider he had even a moment of romantic inclination toward her. That was just crazy.

They were friends. That was the extent of it.

With her head now clear, she opened the stall door and walked to the sink. She squirted some liquid soap into the palm of her hand and turned on the faucet.

The bathroom door opened.

In walked . . . *her.*

Nate's girlfriend smiled and walked up to the vanity mirror. She leaned forward and checked her face. Noticing Leta staring in the mirror, she smiled. "Hi."

Embarrassed, Leta dipped her hands under the running water. "Hey," she offered back. "Nice evening."

The comment sounded lame, even to her own ears. But she couldn't come up with anything else. Not when her gut twisted and her mind suddenly turned into pudding left out in the sun too long.

Tiffany reached in her bag and pulled out a tube of lip gloss. She removed the top. "This is a great restaurant. Eat here often?"

Leta watched her slide the applicator across her red lips, wishing she too could pull off that look. "No — my first time."

Tiffany reattached the lid and slid the tube back into her purse. "Well, if you haven't ordered yet, try the salmon. It's to die for."

Yes, she'd heard that.

"Well, have a nice evening." Tiffany gave her a wide smile before heading for the door.

"Yeah, you too."

Alone again, Leta reached for a paper hand towel from the basket on the counter. She wiped her hands and tried to quiet her pounding heart. Tried to quit thinking about Nate kissing those perfect red lips.

She chastised herself again.

Don't be stupid. Both of them are completely out of your league.

Leta rejoined the table just as the waitress showed up with their entrées. She sighed and took her seat, determined not to look over at the happy couple.

Erin pointed her fork at Leta's plate. "Man, that salmon looks delicious."

Leta nodded. "Yeah, it looks really good. So does your mac and cheese."

Despite promising she wouldn't, she snuck another peek at the table near the window.

Nate noticed her then. Their eyes locked, and he smiled and waved.

Her tablemates noticed as well.

"What, you know Senator Emerson?" Erin asked, frowning. "Why didn't you say something?"

Tatum spoke up. "Tell you what, I'd sure vote for him. He's gorgeous."

Troy rolled his eyes. "And that is exactly what is wrong with America. You don't vote for somebody because he's a pretty boy. You cast your ballot for the guy who's going to make a difference."

"You didn't make that remark when we were talking about his age," Erin interjected. "Besides, you're being sexist."

"What?"

"A smart woman can make a difference too, you know." Erin scooped a steaming bite of mac and cheese.

"Yeah," Tatum agreed. "Just look at Hillary."

"Or Condoleezza Rice and Madeleine Albright," Erin added.

Nate got up from his place at the table. He waved again and walked in their direction.

Ben lifted his glass. "I think he's heading over here."

Leta felt desperately shy and totally elated at the same time. She quickly swallowed and ran her tongue over her teeth, praying nothing was stuck between them.

"Hey," Nate said as he neared their table. His mouth curved into a huge smile. "How is everybody this evening?"

Ben stood. "Hey, man. We're good." He extended his hand to the senator.

Troy did likewise. "Yeah, everything's going great. Yourself?"

After shaking their hands, Nate smiled and placed his hand on Leta's shoulder. "Just thought I'd wander over and say hi to a friend."

She felt the heavy weight of their stares. She swallowed. "Hi, Nate."

He gave a little squeeze before moving his hand. "How was your Christmas? Did your mom enjoy the chocolates?"

"She did," Leta said, willing herself to relax a little. "They didn't last long. Especially when she offered one to every nurse who entered the room." She turned to her friends and explained that her mother was in a residential nursing center, and why. "If you guys aren't familiar, Senator Emerson does a lot of work on behalf of people like my mother. He headed up legislation that funded some extraordinary studies."

Troy nodded. "That's pretty cool, man."

Tatum agreed. "Yeah, I'm really glad to hear someone is spearheading an effort to do something that really makes a difference like that."

Erin dropped her fork to the side of her plate. "So, are you going to do it? Are you going to run for governor?"

Troy laughed. "Wow, Erin's going all Katie Couric on us."

Erin threw him a look. "I am not. I'm just bold enough to ask what we're all wondering."

Nate patiently smiled in her direction. "Well, I can tell you this — we're getting really close to making that decision."

"I'd vote for you," Tatum offered.

"Thank you." Nate gave Tatum a wide smile. "I appreciate that. If I decide to go for it and run, it's good to know people like you guys are behind me." He reached in his back pocket and pulled out a small leather wallet and passed out his cards. "In the event I decide to run, we'll be announcing soon. If any of you would like to come on board and help, the campaign would love to have you. We're going to start a grassroots effort, and as all of you likely know, it'll be a tight climb to unseat the current governor. And do me another favor?" He looked across the table at her. "Y'all keep my friend Leta out of trouble tonight. Okay?"

He held her gaze for several seconds before breaking away and moving back to his table.

"Wow, you run in some fancy circles, girl!" Tatum scooped up her fork.

Erin leaned forward. "Yeah, and you might not want to let that untidy piece of information get out at the Ladd Agency. Not sure your connection with Senator Emerson would go over all that big with Jane Ladd and her new client."

16

"So, you know that girl?"

Nate merged onto the turn lane leading to Cesar Chavez Boulevard. "What?"

Tiffany audibly sighed. "At the restaurant."

"Oh, you mean Leta Breckenridge?" he asked as nonchalantly as possible. "Yeah, I met her a while back. She's the girl who backed into my car."

"Oh? I don't believe you mentioned her earlier."

Nate drove west, knowing he needed to choose his next words carefully. He hadn't reconciled in his own mind, let alone explained to Tiffany, his blurred attraction to his new friend and the connection they'd so quickly forged.

He drummed his thumb against the steering wheel and changed lanes, diverting from the lane clogged with traffic. "Her mother suffers dementia and is under full-time nursing care."

"You know," Tiffany said, watching intently out the window, "someone like that could be really valuable to the campaign once you announce."

Nate glanced her way. "I guess I'm not following."

"Think about it," she said. "You'll need a face on the campaign — someone who will personify the issues you most care about. I talked to her in the restroom. She seems nice."

Nate focused on the road. "You talked to her?"

"Yes, in the restroom. Of course, I didn't know you knew her then. Now, what's her name again?"

"Leta Breckenridge. And who said I'm running?"

"Ah yes. That's her name. Leta." Tiffany slowly repeated the name as if tasting a peach to see if it was sweet. She placed her hand on his thigh. "Nathan, I think you should announce soon. There's no point in letting Holiday continue to take front stage. If you time it right, you could capture a couple of key media cycles and grab the spotlight."

"You've really drunk the Kool-Aid on this gubernatorial campaign."

She smiled. "I have, and it's delicious." She gave him an earnest look. "But seriously, do you want Governor Holiday for another term? How many more great bills is he going to block to further his own interests? Worse, do you want him positioned to make a presidential run? Because if he wins this, if no one steps up and seriously challenges his nonsense platform, that is exactly what will happen. You know it, and so does anyone who's paying attention to Texas politics."

"Now you sound like my mother."

"Admittedly, I've got skin in the game." She paused as if she was now the one carefully choosing her words. "I don't like Holiday's approach to offshore drilling. As you know, my firm represents . . . shall we say, opposing interests to the lobbyists funding his well-oiled machine. Pun intended."

"That horse has been on the track a long time here in the Lone Star State."

She nodded. "My point exactly. But many of the issues near and dear to the hearts of my clients are being moved into the federal arena, and we want to tether the governor's pony, if you know what I mean."

Indeed, he knew exactly what she meant. Tiffany Shea was one of the smartest women he'd ever encountered. She knew the angles and how to use every one of them.

He took the exit leading to her exclusive neighborhood.

When he pulled into her driveway, Tiffany tilted her head. "You want to come in? Maybe have a glass of wine in front of the patio fireplace? It's a gorgeous evening."

He decided to beg off. "Nah, I've got a full week ahead."

In Texas, the legislature operated under the biennial system, convening its regular sessions in January of odd-numbered years. Despite it being a bi-year, he had a lot of catch-up to do at the institute. Especially if he was going to launch a campaign soon.

Seeing her disappointment, he threw her a bone and added, "There's a lot of work ahead if I'm going to announce."

His comment hit the mark.

Tiffany's face brightened, and she slapped her palms together. "Yes! I knew you'd listen to reason." She gave him a hug. "This is a good move, Nate. You were meant to shake things up and make a difference. Take things in a new direction."

Nate supposed Tiffany believed her carefully targeted comments had convinced him to move ahead. The truth? Leta Breckenridge was the real reason he'd decided not to hang back any longer.

Her situation with her mother was indicative of so many similar stories he'd heard as head of the institute. Over the course of the past several weeks, he'd given careful consideration and a lot of thought into how he could best serve people like Leta, families who had loved ones needing long-term care and suffered financially as a result. Add in all the other economic and educational needs that had been neglected under Holiday's terms, and Nate knew he could no longer simply rely on the legislative process to effect change.

The real opportunity to make a difference was in creating policy and determining how the laws would translate on a practical level — a level the office of the governor wielded a lot of power over.

He didn't like the idea of someone like Wyndall Holiday circumventing legislative intent with calculated tactics that required challenging in the courts, which tied up any real impact meant for his constituents.

If Nate really wanted to make a difference in brain science research and the care of people with dementia and related issues, if he wanted to ensure Texans' interests were always at the forefront of every decision made in every level of his state's government, he'd need to do it living in the governor's mansion.

As Tiffany alluded to, Governor Holiday had a reputation. To get what he wanted, he'd get down in the mud and wrestle with elephants. He had his sights set on the White House, and he'd dance the two-step with whatever lobby group would get him there.

Key funding for the programs that mattered to the aging and to those who suffered cognitive impairment would no doubt be diverted.

He couldn't let that happen.

Nate moved to open his door so he could walk Tiffany to her house. She kissed his cheek. "No need. I'll talk to you tomorrow. Get rested. There's a lot of strategic planning ahead, and you'll want to be sharp and ready to go."

He watched her walk to her front door. She slipped her key in the lock and turned and waved.

It was then he realized that in the excitement about his decision to run, while saying goodbye she'd strayed from the norm and failed to say "I love you."

Likewise, so had he.

Even more important, he knew why.

17

Leta was taking clothes out of the dryer when the phone in her back pocket began to vibrate. She quickly dumped the load of warm laundry into a basket and slipped her phone out. "Hello?"

"Yes, is this Leta Breckenridge?"

She hesitated briefly before responding, not recognizing the number or the voice. "It is."

"This is Nancy Patrick. I'm calling from the Institute of Brain Sciences. Dr. Emerson asked me to contact you. We're hosting a symposium for families of patients with cognitive impairment. He thought you might benefit."

"A symposium?"

"Yes. There will be speakers," Ms. Patrick explained. "What might interest you even more is the opportunity to connect and interact with a community of people who face issues common to your own. In the past, attendees have reported the time was well worth their while. And it's complimentary, of course."

"Will Dr. Emerson be there?" she asked, trying to mask the extent of her interest.

"Oh, certainly. He'll be one of the main speakers."

Her mind raced. He'd thought to extend an invitation. Obviously he wanted her there. "And when is it? The symposium, I mean."

"Friday night. If you can make it, I'll have a ticket waiting."

"Okay. I'm free that night. Sure, I'll be there."

"Excellent! Seven o'clock at the Omni downtown."

Leta hung up and slowly picked up her laundry basket. She made her way down the hall, pondering what had just occurred.

While she was flattered Nate had extended such a generous invitation and she was thrilled to be going, there were other considerations. Mainly, Bernard Geisler and the fact he seemed to be watching her so closely, especially her interactions with the senator.

She wished she didn't feel like such a traitor. It seemed no matter what she did these days, she was at risk of betraying someone. One could argue that attending the Institute of Brain Sciences meeting was simply her personal business, that she had every right to participate in a function that would provide valuable resources and information relating to her mother's dementia. And that would be true.

On the other hand, she couldn't easily dismiss the fact that she worked for Nathan Emerson's opposition, and it seemed disingenuous to accept his offer knowing that she'd spent the day researching and documenting every statement he'd ever made, publicly or otherwise.

In the end she knew of no way out. She'd consented to go — wanted to go. So on Friday night, she parked her car in the Omni Hotel parking garage and made her way to the elevator that would take her to the lobby.

The Omni was a contemporary venue, the main floor constructed primarily of metal and glass that provided stunning views of the city at night. She stepped into the lobby where the concierge directed her to a conference room upstairs.

The meeting room was nearly full, and most of the rows of seats were already taken. Groups of people gathered at the linen-covered tables lining the wall, where coffee and refreshments were served.

A nicely dressed woman sat at a table near the front door. "Can I help you?"

Leta swallowed. "I'm Leta Breckenridge."

The woman scanned the name tags. "Oh yes. Right here."

Leta thanked her and pinned the small plastic square to her top. She searched the room.

"Leta!"

She turned to find Nate heading her way.

"I'm so glad you agreed to come. I think you are really going to benefit from tonight's speakers."

His eyes told her he was personally glad to see her as well. She couldn't lie. She felt the same.

"Thank you for inviting me," she said, trying to ignore the butterflies in her stomach. "It's good to see you."

"It's really good to see you too." His hand went to the small of her back, and he led her to a seat up front. "Look, I need to go. Duty calls. But please don't leave until we get a chance to talk. Okay?"

She smiled. "Sure."

While others took their seats, Leta looked over the brochure she'd been handed on her way in.

The speaker lineup was impressive. All experts in their various fields, including neuroscience, neurosurgery, psychiatry, and cognitive science. Some had traveled from as far as Washington, D.C.

The woman from the registration table took the podium. "Welcome, everyone, and thank you for coming tonight. I think we have some very interesting information to share."

After introducing Nathan and giving a short presentation about the Institute of Brain Sciences, she welcomed the first speaker, Dr. Grant Luddke. He shared on the latest developments in aging and geriatric research, which Leta found fascinating.

At the end of the evening Nathan took the podium and closed by outlining the plans ahead and the challenges the institute faced, primarily financial. "It is my hope that with the support of both the private and public sectors, we'll end the coming year with astounding success. Again, thank you for coming out tonight."

He looked across the podium and their eyes met. He held her gaze for several seconds before posing for some photographs.

Leta waited over by the coffeepot while those in attendance dispersed. Finally Nate was able to extract himself and headed her way.

"Thank you for staying," he said, a bit breathless. "Sometimes there doesn't seem to be enough of me to go around, know what I mean?" He smiled.

"Tonight was amazing," she told him. "I can't believe all that is being done to reverse my mother's horrible disease. It gives me such hope."

He took her elbow and led her toward the door. "I'd hoped that would be the case." He glanced around, seeming a bit nervous. "I know it's late, but I'd love to buy you a cup of coffee."

"You just did."

"What?"

She pointed back inside the meeting room.

He laughed. "Oh yeah. I guess I did." His eyes held hers. "Can we go somewhere and talk?"

They moved to the bar and ordered club sodas. Minutes later they were seated in a corner of the lobby after finding the bar too noisy to talk.

"Look, I wanted to let you know that I'll be making a big announcement soon."

She grinned. "You're going to run?"

He nodded. "Yes, for lots of reasons. One of the greatest of those circles around what we discussed up in that room tonight. We are on the edge of several major breakthroughs, but the funding just isn't there. My influence has been limited as a member of the legislative branch. I'm hoping I can do more as governor."

Her fingers tightened around her cold drink as she tried to take in all that his decision meant. Of course she was delighted he'd decided to run, but that meant the conflict with her work was only going to intensify.

Suddenly Nate reached out and touched her fingers. A bolt of lightning might as well have landed at that place for the jolt she felt inside.

He quickly pulled back. His eyes darted around the lobby. "I — I'm sorry. That was a little forward of me. It's just that — well, I want us to be friends."

He gave her a sideways look, and Leta couldn't help but admire his brown eyes and the way the overhead light highlighted the strong structure of his face. He was definitely serious-natured, but also soft-spoken and so very smart. He understood things that others couldn't, simply because he took the time to observe. Leta admired him for it. At the same time, it was that aspect of Nate she feared the most. She was afraid that he could see through her with a glance.

"We are friends," she nearly whispered, afraid to let the entirety of her feelings be known. Afraid she was overestimating the meaning of what he was saying.

"No doubt things are complicated. And I have a few key things to sort out." Tiffany's name went unspoken. "But I wanted you to know how often I think about you."

The statement made her unable to breathe. So she simply nodded. "I — I think about you too." It was a silly thing to say, really. But she could barely think. Her mind was dizzy with catapulting emotions.

He seemed to understand because he grinned at her.

Just then, a camera crew headed across the lobby in their direction.

Nathan audibly groaned. He stood and quickly said, "I'll call you." Then he moved to meet the reporters.

Leta held her breath and waited to see if he'd glance back. He didn't.

Which was understandable. He wouldn't want to draw attention to the fact they'd been talking, not any more than what he'd already risked.

It didn't really matter. Like he'd said, they had a lot to sort out. She'd have to figure out the whole Ladd Agency thing and make some decisions. She might have to resign.

But first she'd need to find another job that would support her mother's expenses.

Leta had faith it would all work out. It had to.

Because going forward, she and Nathan Emerson were going to be friends.

She stood and watched Nate and the reporters for a few seconds before heading for the elevator doors. With each step, her heart raced a little faster as she attempted to take in the evening and all that had occurred.

Despite feeling giddy, she forced herself to walk with a steady gait.

But inside, she was definitely skipping.

18

"The first thing you do is choose your color." Katie pulled a peachy-looking shade from the rack of nail polish.

Overwhelmed by all the choices, Leta leaned forward for a better look before reaching for a bottle of nail lacquer. Way fancier than the regular bottles of polish in the bathroom drawers at home. Not wanting to hold things up, she selected a shade called Holy Pink Pagoda and followed her roommate to the back of the salon.

Katie stopped next to a big chair attached to a small tub. "I can't believe you've never had a salon pedicure."

She shrugged. "Wasn't willing to eat ramen noodles for a week to pay for one."

Her friend nodded. "Yeah, I get it. But still."

A cute Asian girl dressed in jeans with embroidery on the pockets handed her a large plastic card and pointed to a menu of services listed. "You choose which."

Katie waved her hand. "The works. We're going to have the works."

Leta handed the menu back. "What she said, I guess."

Within minutes, she was sitting in a black chair with rollers kneading up and down her back, her feet tucked into a warm tub of bubbling water that smelled slightly of jasmine. She couldn't help but sigh. A gal could get used to all this pampering.

She turned to her roommate. "So, you haven't been home much lately. I take that to mean things are going well with Bart?"

Katie's face went soft. "Yeah, really well. I think he may be the one," she confided.

"The one? That's pretty fast, isn't it?"

"I know what you're thinking. But Bart's really different." She pressed some buttons on what looked like a remote control unit, seemingly oblivious to the fact she'd said that before. Many times.

Try as she may, Leta was unable to maintain her scowl. "Well, I'm happy for you. I mean, if he really is different than all the others, like that Jim guy, or . . . now, what was the name of the one with the red bike? Oh yes, Travis. I hope he treats you better than Travis."

As if sensing how badly Leta wanted to

warn her friend how essential respect was in a relationship, Katie was quick to argue Bart was not like any of the guys she'd ever dated. He treated her like a queen. "And there's no other girls in the wings this time," she assured her. "But who are you to talk, oh one who dishes advice but hasn't been in a relationship since high school?"

The comment stung. Especially given what had recently transpired between her and Nate.

"True, but —" She clamped her mouth shut. She wasn't going there.

Katie's eyes sparkled with interest. "But what?"

Trapped, she needed to wiggle out of the conversation. "Oh, not that." In no way could she admit her infatuation with Nathan Emerson.

Sure, she and Katie had bantered about his politics. Katie was even quick to claim he was cute.

But if her roommate knew they'd spent hours talking over coffee, if Leta dared to reveal the way Nate made her feel inside, no doubt her friend would be quick to point out he was a senator and therefore completely out of her league. Next, she'd remind her of the obvious. There was a very real *other woman* in the picture. A highly educated, successful woman who was stunningly poised and beautiful. Everything she was not.

And her roommate would be right.

Except Nate had made a point of telling her how often he thought about her. No doubt they both felt the same attraction and wanted to see where things might lead.

But she couldn't admit that to Katie.

"I'll have you know my social life is improving in multiple ways. I went out with a gal from work. Joined her friends for dinner."

"Get out! You actually spent an evening having some fun?"

Leta nodded. "I did. And guess what? My fun button still works. This new job has freed up time and money and allowed me to push it more often. And the entire evening was just that. Fun, I mean."

"Yeah? Where'd you go?"

The pedicurist lifted her foot from the water. "The Roaring Fork, this trendy little place on Congress."

"In the Intercontinental Hotel?"

"Yeah, that's the one. Great food." Leta's eyelids drifted closed. "The restaurant was surprisingly packed." She took a deep breath before adding, "Especially for a weeknight."

The soothing atmosphere teased her into opening up even more. "And there's something else. I've become interested in politics."

Katie looked at her like she had two heads. "Politics? I think you'd better push that fun button a little harder."

"What? Don't you care about taxes and immigration and all that?"

"No, not really. Besides, do you really think one little vote makes any difference?" Katie shook her head. "Most politicians are crooks. Just looking out for themselves and padding their personal pockets. If you ask me, politics is just a waste of time."

"Not every politician is a crook," she argued, knowing Katie was voicing what had been her own attitude only weeks ago. "There are some who are the real deal. Ones who try to do the right thing."

"Who? That senator you ran into? The one you thought was so nice?" Katie's pedicurist tapped her ankle, and she switched feet. "Is that why you're suddenly interested in politics?"

"No — no, that's not why," she fibbed. Leta's eyes darted around, and she hoped no one had overheard. "Uh — I'm working on a project. Something for my new job. That I can't really talk about. At work."

Katie held up her hands. "Okay, okay. I get it." She leaned back into the rollers and closed her eyes. "Sounds boring to me."

"Oh, I love the work. I mean, you know me. I'm snoopy, and research projects are right up my alley." She leaned back as well, relishing the way the chair kneaded the small of her back. "And once you really understand how politics works, the process is fascinating."

The pedicurist dried off her feet and returned with two see-through bags of warm paraffin wax.

She lifted her head. "Uh, what is that for?"

"Make feet soft," came the woman's reply.

She looked over at Katie, who had a slight grin on her face. "What are you looking at? I've never done this before."

Following instructions, Leta slipped her feet into the bags one at a time. "Anyway, back to what I was saying. Take, for example, a bill that was recently introduced in committee to establish and fund Alzheimer's disease efforts under a single —"

"Ugh, Leta," Katie interrupted. "That is definitely not fun button material."

She sighed and rolled her eyes. "Okay, fine." She'd learned long ago not everyone cared about dementia and the aging issues that mattered to her.

Except Nathan Emerson. He cared.

"Hey, look!" Katie pointed to a television screen mounted on the opposite wall. "Isn't that him? Your senator friend?"

Leta's head shot up. On the bottom of the screen, words scrolled across a banner.

SENATOR NATHAN EMERSON ENTERS RACE FOR GOVERNOR.

She looked around, frantic. "Turn it up. Can somebody please turn that up?"

The pedicurist, who didn't seem to understand much English, smiled and nodded.

Leta scrambled from her chair and immediately felt paraffin wax squeeze between her toes. "Can somebody please turn up the volume?" she repeated, pointing to the television.

Finally, a pedicurist from several chairs over stood and retrieved a remote control from a nearby table and pressed the volume button, just as Nate appeared on-screen, standing at a podium in front of the Texas state capitol.

Good afternoon, everyone. Thank you for taking a few minutes out of your day to hear what I have to say.

I am concerned about our great state of Texas.

Mirroring many of the problems on our

national forefront, Texans have matters of great import before us. Issues relating to our economy, immigration, education, and how we care for our aging.

Like never before, there seems to be a growing aimlessness in the direction of government and its ability to get important business done.

Leta watched intently, barely breathing as he continued.

The evidence is everywhere.

Too often, critical legislation is pre-empted by government wrangling and weakened by obsolete policies that cripple the next generation's ability to prosper.

Too often, young people bursting with idealism soon find themselves playing a game for which they have little heart because our leaders fail them.

Too often, elected officials forget who they serve — and why.

Now is the time for change.

Texas needs a strong leader.

Nate leaned forward ever so slightly and looked directly into the camera.

That is why I am announcing that I will be running to be your next governor. I plan to work hard for your vote, and if elected, I will do everything in my power to make a difference.

Nate ended by thanking the viewing audience again. He gathered his notes and stepped away from the podium, after which the screen immediately turned to the station's political commentator.

"Wow," Katie said. "I see what you mean. Not only is the guy gorgeous, but he certainly has a way with words. I mean, I might even register to vote for him."

Leta nodded in agreement. Nate was certainly everything her roommate claimed.

Gorgeous — check.

Well-spoken — check.

Worth voting for — check, check.

She could barely admit a dawning reality, even to herself. With very little effort, she'd allowed Nate Emerson to wrap her heart in knots.

She thought about him the moment she woke up. His image formed in her mind as she brushed her teeth. While driving on I-35, she mentally conjured up that smile of his and planned what she might say to him the next time they met.

And he'd openly admitted he felt the same.

To borrow from her mother, she'd become smitten with a prince. Only she didn't have a fairy godmother who would wave a wand and make everything turn out in the end. Which meant she'd have to get her job situation settled, and soon, or her glass slipper would be left behind.

Leta looked down at her toes mired in bags of wax.

Even if her feet were now soft and pretty.

19

Amanda Joy Holiday sat in front of the massive bathroom vanity mirror, smiling at how the room's peach-colored walls enhanced the color of her complexion.

Nearly eight years ago, after Wyndall won the election and they'd moved into the historic governor's mansion, she'd fought to make the upstairs living quarters her own. Ridding the bathroom of that horrid burgundy was one of her better decisions, even if her husband balked at the more feminine décor. "Well, Mr. Governor," she'd told him, "I invite y'all to use the guest bathroom, where the colors match your masculine taste."

Thankfully, he'd folded and never pushed her on the idea. But then, that was his way.

"Amanda Joy?"

"In here, dear." She rubbed magnolia-scented lotion into her hands and smiled when her husband's image appeared in the mirror. "Goodness, what's troubling you, Wyndall? You look like someone just trampled your bluebonnets."

He reached for her shoulders and placed a kiss on top of her hair. "More like a bunch of longhorns just relieved themselves all over my grassroots campaign."

She patted one of his dimpled hands. "This wasn't a surprise. You knew he was going to announce."

Her husband frowned. "Yes, but I didn't expect this lovefest with the media. I mean, every pundit on every station is singing 'Kumbaya' and predicting voters under forty will line up around the block to punch this guy's ticket. Meanwhile, my donations are going el busto."

Amanda Joy stood and tightened the belt on her silk robe. "Well, dear, focus on the upside. Now all that speculation is over and you can get on with the business of taking Nathan Emerson and his idealistic worshipers to task."

"Yes, I suppose you're right, sweetheart. But everybody wants that shiny penny in his or her pocket right now. Ethan says Emerson's current poll numbers show unprecedented popularity. I mean, the guy doesn't have a single black mark against him. It's as if he flew into his senate seat with angel wings."

She sighed patiently. "Yes, Ethan and Jane have their work cut out for them, but, dear . . ." This was where she knew to run her fingers through the side of his hair and smile. "Don't forget how well a carefully planned strategy has worked in the past, and it'll work again. Please don't fret." She trailed a finger along his chin. "It's unbecoming of a man with your kind of power."

Before Wyndall's first campaign, when he'd run for Dallas county commissioner, she'd handpicked Ethan Michaels, a brilliant political strategist who was part attack dog, part fixer, and part bridge builder. He'd been indispensable to them in constructing Wyndall's political career.

During the last campaign, when it looked like that horrible woman from Houston might win the gubernatorial race, it was Ethan who got credit for moving the Holidays into this mansion.

Two days before the election, thousands of families across Texas received a mailing postmarked from Houston — specifically the post office nearest the opponent's campaign headquarters — urging them not to vote for Wyndall and his religious wingnut views.

Ethan denied he had anything to do with the huge turnout in their Bible Belt state, most of which voted in their favor, but few insiders believed him.

"Sweetheart, we've assembled the best team possible. Let them do their jobs." She took his tanned puppy-dog face into her hands and kissed him, letting her lips linger on his before her mouth drifted to his ear, where she nibbled slightly.

Her husband simply wasn't on top of his game in this condition. In the coming weeks leading up to the primary, he'd need razor-sharp focus.

Amanda Joy knew from experience that the only way to relieve her husband's stress was to either feed him or ply him with her female ways.

His britches were already too tight from eating. In fact, tomorrow she'd encourage him to make use of the equipment in the basement gymnasium.

In the meantime, as his breath became heavy, she simply smiled sweetly and untied her robe.

"I just got off the phone with Ethan Michaels."

Jane Ladd looked up from her desk and directed her attention to the doorway of her office. "And?"

Bernard stared at her. "He's just authorized us to move forward with Operation Brainchild."

20

Leta settled into a routine of scanning for job possibilities online. She'd even gone for a few interviews, but none of the openings paid what she needed. So she kept looking.

In the meantime, she worked full-time at the Ladd Agency and a couple of Saturdays a month at Central Market. Every Wednesday night and Sunday after church, she'd visit her mom at Heritage House, telling her all about her new life and how happy she was.

"Mom, I'm learning so much about elections." She sat cross-legged on the floor with her iPad. "I mean, like, did you know that Texas has the highest number of NASCAR dad voters in the country? And the lowest number of soccer moms? The only state to have three presidential libraries. And here's something interesting." She slid the iPad to the floor. "For being a primarily red state, we have a surprising number of liberals in

Travis County and around El Paso and the Rio Grande Valley." Leaning back on her hands, she watched her mother's face, knowing it was unlikely there'd be any reaction to the fascinating stuff she'd discovered. "But you know what is really sad, Mom? Texas lawmakers didn't even approve dementia-specific funding until 2005. Thankfully, great strides have been made in grants and studies in the last few years because of the hard work of a senator named Nathan Emerson."

Her mother sat in a chair staring at the television, shuffling her slippered feet back and forth on the floor.

Leta's face broke into a slight grin at the sight. She stood and took her mother's hand. "So, seems you want to dance?"

As they twirled across the floor, she rested her head against her mother's shoulder, taking in the detergent smell of her blouse. She appreciated how well her mom was cared for at Heritage House. Thank goodness she'd landed the job at the Ladd Agency. Now all she had to do was find something comparable to replace it. The sooner the better.

That brought her to thinking about the dilemma foremost in her mind.

The primaries were coming up very soon.

Since both Governor Holiday and Senator Emerson ran on separate tickets, there was no direct face-off . . . yet. Both were projected to easily win their party's nomination, and when that occurred, all bets were off.

Things were already heating up at the office with research projects getting more focused. Just last week, she'd gone to a movie with Erin and learned that up until now they'd been primarily working to collect data that would be useful to Holiday's campaign as they developed strategy.

"But look out after the primaries, when things get real," her co-worker had warned.

"Things?" Despite all the personal study she'd been doing on the topic of Texas politics and the election process, Leta still felt like such a newbie.

"Let's just say it this way — pigs get fat, hogs get slaughtered. And a worm is the only animal that can't fall down."

Leta still didn't know what Erin meant exactly. But it couldn't be good.

And something else wasn't good.

The way she caught Bernard Geisler watching her, like in meetings. And sometimes she sensed someone on the other side of her cubicle wall, only to discover Bernard strolling slowly by.

Never did he say anything. He just looked at her with those tiny dark eyes tucked behind the wire-rimmed glasses.

Frankly, it gave her the creeps.

She had told Erin so and was warned again not to rock any boats where Bernard and special ops were concerned. "Look, that guy gives all the researchers the heebie-jeebies. But if you know what's good for you, you'll keep that little fact to yourself. You don't want to lose this job, do you?"

Now, as Leta's mother began humming softly, Leta squeezed her hand, feeling the soft skin that had so often brushed across her arm to calm her. The same hand that had cooked her dinners and made her bed all those years.

No, she couldn't afford any risks where the Ladd Agency was concerned. Not until she found another job.

In the meantime, she'd just have to rely on what her mother had told her. *Do good and let God do the rest.*

Nate's favorite Bon Jovi song blared from his car radio. With his fingers, Nate beat out the tune on the steering wheel, appreciating his time in the car away from the watchful eyes of the public. Here he could let loose and be himself without judgment.

Ha! No doubt the media would use his taste in music to whittle at his stature, suggest he might not have the ability to grasp the serious business of running for the top seat in Texas.

Losing his privacy was definitely one of the downsides to running for office.

Last week a reporter had crossed over the boundaries. At least in his opinion. "So, many voters find it interesting that at your age you are still single."

He wondered if there was a question in there somewhere. "Well, it's like this. Right now I'm married to this campaign."

Even his mother seemed to evaluate his every move. "Make your mark as Texas state governor, Nathan, and you'll be poised for much higher things — nearly forty percent of our nation's presidents were first governors. And in just my lifetime, three presidents of forty-four were from Texas. You do the math."

While other women of her age and financial means were planning trips abroad or chairing some civic cause, his mother seemed to spend most of her free time calculating how to move him into the governor's mansion, and ultimately the White House. Sometimes he really just wished she would bake cookies.

"Take extreme care not to flip-flop on your positions, Son. That will kill your career, or at least severely wound any aspirations you have to go further in politics," she'd warned after church last week. "I don't need to remind you how Kay Bailey Hutchison's weak position on term limits played in the public eye."

The public eye was a phrase often used by his mother.

Like he'd said, he was already tiring of the scrutiny. Since his announcement, news pundits had opinions about his every move. From stupid things that didn't matter, like whether he preferred sirloin or rib eye steak grilled medium or rare, to his positions on issues that were truly material to his constituents — gun control, immigration, budget, and the state's infrastructure. They'd sifted the keystone to his platform — health issues, especially those relating to cognitive diseases and aging. The media picked through it all and assigned import in relation to the big election ahead.

Later today, he would issue a press release announcing he'd asked Janesa Morgan, a young black woman and brilliant political strategist, to be his campaign manager. Some would criticize that her tactics did not match those of his opponent's manager,

Ethan Michaels. But Nate didn't need a bulldog. He needed someone who deeply understood his philosophies and who could effectively convey those to the voting public. Someone who could fire up the ideals of Texans and bring them on board with him and the changes he proposed.

Wyndall Holiday had a reputation for lounge-chair campaigning — walking in parades, going to spaghetti dinners, even spending money on massive freeway billboards, while Michaels performed his dirty work behind the scenes.

In contrast, Nate's campaign tactics would be social-media driven. He wanted to focus on an open and intelligent conversation about moving Texas forward in the future and creating a thriving place for Texans to live, work, and raise their families.

He didn't take to manipulating voters with scare tactics, or maneuvering the process like elections were some high-stakes poker game where a candidate had to bluff his or her way to victory. Win or lose, he'd much prefer to just show his cards.

Without integrity, he had nothing at all.

The song on his car stereo switched to another of his favorites, "I Still Haven't Found What I'm Looking For" by U2. He turned the volume up even louder.

When forming the planks in his campaign platform, he often thought of Leta, someone who wasn't born with a silver spoon in her mouth, a girl who had worked to overcome adversity, even sacrificing for her mother.

That kind of character was a rarity today. Especially in his generation and younger.

He'd risked a lot telling her how he felt about her. But he didn't regret the move.

He admired how she'd always done the right thing, even when the stakes were high. Many in her situation might try to game the system, look for a free handout. Instead she worked multiple jobs to fulfill her obligations.

He found himself wanting to come to her aid and rescue her. Even just write her a big check. She'd never allow him to, of course.

Many accused him of being idealistic. Perhaps so.

But helping people like Leta satisfied his soul. Research, policy changes, and funding support systems mattered to the individuals and families facing health issues, brain related or otherwise. His work was important.

So he'd give up his privacy and live in the public eye — at least for now.

For all the Texans who needed him.

For Leta.

21

With the onset of summer, temperatures in Austin were really heating up. Nowhere had the climate change been more distinct than inside the offices of the Ladd Agency.

Leta stepped out of the elevator into the office lobby.

"You're late." Elaine charged out from her side of the reception counter and handed her a packet, then pointed toward the conference room. "You'd best get a move on."

Leta glanced at her watch. "Sorry," she murmured, taking the tightly packed manila envelope from the receptionist's hand. In a city often clogged with traffic, she wondered why less than five minutes past eight was considered late.

The conference room was packed. Jane Ladd looked up as she entered. "You must not have gotten my email. Never mind now — just get situated."

Leta swallowed and made her way to where those without seats congregated at the table with the coffee service. "Sorry," she repeated as she found a place to stand.

"Okay, listen up. Yesterday's primaries went exactly as expected. No surprises. Governor Holiday will face off with Senator Emerson in the general this November. Which means we have a lot of work to do." She paused briefly to take a sip from her steaming mug of coffee. "In your packets you'll find our game plan, or at least the one we intend to employ over the next couple of months. As you know, in politics everything can change on a dime. So we don't get too married to any strategy. Success will mean being nimble and ready to court another approach, if necessary."

Across the room, Erin listened intently with her arms folded on the table beside her open packet.

Jane continued. "At this point, it's time for a big shift in our office operations. Three of you will now be working directly with Bernard Geisler and moving to the fifth floor, where we've temporarily leased space. The rest will remain here on the fourth floor and will continue to take direction from me. You'll find everything you need and the answers to most of your questions in the packet. Any issues you need discussed?" She looked across the room as if daring anyone to raise their hand. "Good, then let's get to work."

Leta quickly made her way to her cubicle and held her breath as she pulled the contents from her package. Her heart sank as she saw the words *Geisler* and *fifth floor*.

Erin peeked her head around the divider wall. "Looks like we'll be working together."

She carefully tucked the papers back inside the envelope. "So, what does this mean?"

"It means grab your stuff and I'll meet you up there in five."

She glanced around, feeling confused. Frantic, she stepped out of her cube. "Wait, Erin. Do I pack all my stuff?"

Erin nodded. "Yes — third paragraph in the letter. We won't be working on this floor after today."

"Never?"

"Well, not until after the elections are over. That's a given." Her friend moved on, leaving her to get busy.

Leta noticed two large empty boxes on her floor, labeled with her name. She took a deep breath and tried to ignore the fact her palms were sweating.

Bernard Geisler. Special ops.

The idea was daunting, scary even. The big questions lying heavy on her heart were not answered in that packet of information.

She quickly riffled through the drawers and pulled out all her personal items and her favorite pens. Would she need to take the small stock of office supplies she'd collected and stored in her desk for convenience, or would everything she needed be waiting up there for her — on the fifth floor?

After deciding she'd better skip the risk of not having what she needed upstairs, she scooped most of what was in her drawers into one of the boxes. On top, she placed the framed photo of her mom standing in a field of bluebonnets at the Lady Bird Johnson Wildflower Center. The shot had been taken the day they visited in celebration of Leta's decision to pursue landscape architecture. A long time ago.

She passed the reception desk on the way out. Elaine stopped her. "You'll need this," the woman said, handing her a hard plastic card that looked like a blank credit card. "Don't lose it."

When Leta stepped out of the elevator on the fifth floor, she was surprised to find a security guard who escorted her down a wide hall, then several yards down another narrower hallway to the left. He stopped in front of a nondescript metal door. "Do you have your security card?"

She nodded, shifted the box to her hip, and handed it to him.

He frowned and shook his head. "You are never to give this card to anyone else. Ever." He pointed to the packet in her box. "You might want to read everything again," he warned.

She'd failed his test. Now her gut was really churning. This was like a bad movie or something.

"Yeah, sure. I will," she promised. Following his instructions, she swiped the card in front of a reader box mounted to the right of the door. She heard a buzz, then a click.

The security guard opened the door for her, and she walked inside.

The whole place was nearly bare, like some San Francisco tech start-up might look like — an open, unpaneled ceiling with silver insulation around air ducts, and spray paint on the exposed cement floor to indicate where office furniture would be placed amid slabs of unaffixed carpeting. Half-opened Levolor-style blinds covered windows overlooking the parking lot and Colorado Street below.

Two long counters made up of workstations faced a wall of mounted television monitors. About ten people sat with their backs to the door, tapping their computer keyboards. Each wore large black earphone sets. Some of these people she'd never met.

Erin turned and noticed her. She waved her over. "Your spot is at the end. Down there."

She looked and saw the empty space. "Okay, thanks."

Leta didn't know which was heavier, the box or her heart. At least she could drop the box — and did, giving the guy next to her a start. He glared and went back to typing.

"Sorry," she said, even though she knew the dude wearing a T-shirt and blazer over a pair of jeans wasn't listening.

Over the next ten minutes, she busied herself with the work of unpacking. She placed her pens in a cup and positioned it to the right of the large Apple computer monitor. She nestled the pads of lined, blank yellow paper in her desk and positioned her mom's photo in place.

"Could I have everyone's attention?" Bernard stood at the front of the room. He clapped his hands. "This will only take a moment."

Heads popped up. Earphones were removed.

"Welcome." Bernard looked out from behind those wire-framed glasses, his tone not exactly matching his message. He propped his elbow in one hand and rubbed his chin with the other while he waited for their full attention.

"You have all been promoted to a very special assignment — working on what we call *Operation Brainchild.* Everything that is said, all that is learned and discovered in this room, stays in this room. No deviation. Understood?"

Leta timidly followed the others and nodded.

"Our work will be critical to Governor Holiday's campaign and successful run for another term. It is in this hub that we'll be uncovering and dissecting the mother lode of information. Highly confidential material that could make or break this upcoming election."

With an almost giddy anticipation, he explained that as members of the special apparatus for tracking and research, Leta and the others would be watching hours of broadcasted speeches by Governor Holiday's opponent and reading blogs and online news articles, sifting for any critical piece of data that might catch Senator Emerson flip-flopping on an earlier position, misquoting facts, or generally making snafus that could be spun in the media. They were told to especially watch for anything that would tip a change in strategy in Emerson's camp, even if slight.

"Don't discount anything. Trust your gut. If you think something might be important, it usually is." He slowly removed his glasses and wiped the lenses with a cloth he retrieved from his back pocket. With his frames back in place, he looked over the room. "We'll be working shifts 24-7 and will meet briefly four times a day to download to the rest of the team what we've learned. You'll be provided a written report via a daily email, incorporating data from the night team. Everything on this special server is encrypted, and nothing can be printed or downloaded. Any questions?"

No one raised a hand. The guy next to her looked bored and tapped his pencil against his leg.

Leta wanted to grab that pencil and break it. This was not what she'd planned, and definitely not what she'd signed up for.

With Geisler's back turned, she boldly leaned toward the guy with the pencil. "What's that?" she whispered, pointing to a closed door near the front of the room.

Her work neighbor shook his head. "Read

your packet. You have to have special clearance to have access."

She nodded, feeling even sicker inside. Everything about Operation Brainchild was like a bad John Grisham novel.

Perhaps the broken heel on her first day had been some kind of cosmic warning that what originally looked like a great job was not going to turn out well after all.

While she could justify the research she'd compiled — anyone willing to make the effort could look in the public record and assemble the same — the work she was now expected to do somehow crossed her line of comfort.

In the little time she'd spent with Nate Emerson, she'd learned he was a man of convictions, bright, and determined to help people like her mother. Even her research backed up that notion. How could she now actively work to oppose him in this election? Especially now that he'd shared how he felt about her and she'd admitted she felt the same?

This was a nightmare.

She'd gone to work for a public relations agency. Now she was working for a . . . She didn't even know what to call this floor.

Bernard said to trust her gut. Well, her instincts were telling her that all this secrecy didn't point to anything positive.

Sure, there was always a chance she was wrong. Just not a very good one.

22

Despite the confidentiality paper she'd signed and the strict instructions to keep everything about Operation Brainchild secret, Leta couldn't keep her angst to herself. She had to confide in someone before her mind exploded from the pressure.

Only one person could be trusted — Katie.

"Oh my goodness, you're kidding, right? I mean, I just saw something like this on one of those news shows last week!"

"When did you start watching the news?" Leta frowned as she pulled a can of olives from the grocery sack on the counter and placed it in the pantry.

Her friend stopped painting her nails and looked up from across the counter. "Oh, stop. I watch the news."

She grunted. "Uh-huh."

Katie blew on her nails. "Well, like I was

saying, Miss High and Mighty, there was this program on political opposition organizations, oppos for short, that dig up the political dirt that gets reported on television. I mean, like, there are people who get paid to watch hours of videotaped speeches looking for 'gotcha' kind of statements." She lifted her hand and examined her nails. "How do you think they come up with all those mean things they say about each other?" She shook her head. "Which is why politics and that stuff is nothing but a big game."

Leta stopped putting away the groceries and leaned against the sink. "Maybe so. But why would campaigns spend massive amounts of money and go to all of that effort — even if their tactics are dirty — if politics didn't matter?" She swallowed, trying not to think about her own healthy six-figure salary. "Politics can change the course of lives. Take my mother, for example. Without proper funding, there isn't likely going to be any breakthroughs in research."

Katie nearly huffed. "Maybe private funding is a better answer. For example, my dad says if the church would step up, there'd be less need for all these government programs."

"Well, that may be true, but even if regular

folks suddenly became generous and gave money to worthy causes, it wouldn't eliminate the need for regulations and laws. 'For the people, by the people' and all that."

Her roommate removed the lid on the polish and started on her other hand. "Okay, I get it. And I'm not really saying *no* government, only that the current situation is really broken." She carefully moved the tiny brush across her nail. "Leta, you're naïve if you think all those donations are shoveled into those campaigns so your mom can have a better life. Those rich folks are buying influence and power. That's all."

Katie must have noticed the despair on her face because she quickly added, "Look, here's what you are going to do. You make a decision. Either buck up and keep that big salary of yours, do the work they ask, and don't let all this get in your head . . ."

Leta looked at her miserably. "Or?"

"Or you determine this kind of gig is not for you and you walk away." She shrugged. "I don't see any other alternatives, do you?"

Leta drew a deep breath and willed herself to quit shaking inside as she rapped lightly on Jane Ladd's office door.

"Yes? Come in."

The voice from the other side didn't do

much to lessen her anxiety. She slid the door open with as much confidence as she could muster. "Uh, Ms. Ladd, do you have a moment?"

Jane looked up. "Sure, what's up?" She closed the file she'd been working on and leaned back in her black leather chair. "Have a seat."

Leta crossed the floor to the chair and sat. Despite the fact she'd rehearsed what she would say hundreds of times in her mind, the carefully planned words wouldn't seem to come. "Thank you. Uh, I mean, I know you're busy and —"

"Why don't you just say what's on your mind," the woman staring at her from across the desk urged with a slight look of impatience.

"Uh, yes . . . right." She swallowed. Some people believed employers owed them something just because they came to work every day, but Leta had no illusions about how fortunate she'd been to land this job. She wanted Jane to understand that, which is why her next words were critical. "I so appreciate the opportunity I've been given at the Ladd Agency, and I really enjoy the work. Or, at least I did until recently. But now, well, I'm a bit uncomfortable with what is happening on the upper floor. I'm not sure I'm really cut out for that kind of work."

After talking with Katie, she'd done some research. By everything she could tell, her roommate was right. Operation Brainchild was a political oppo, and she wanted no part in any underhanded tactics meant to be used against Nathan Emerson in his bid for governor.

On top of their budding personal feelings, he was a good and decent man with plans to help people. How could she be involved in some secret activity to take his candidacy down?

Leta folded her hands in her lap to keep them from giving away how nervous she felt. "I'm hoping you might reconsider, and allow me to return to this floor and perform the kind of research projects I was working on earlier."

Jane's eyes turned sphinxlike, as though assessing the situation. "I'm afraid that's not possible." Her voice floated across the desk like the acrid smoke of a cigarette. "You see, you work for me. Those decisions are mine to make. Right now, you are needed upstairs."

A hot flush crept up Leta's neck. Her insides instantly cowered. "I see," she said, her voice breaking.

Reluctantly, miserably, she lifted from the chair and moved for the door. As she briefly looked back, the gravity of the exchange hit her. She had no choice but to balance her mother's needs against everything else. At least for now. "Well, thank you. For your time, I mean."

Minutes after Leta Breckenridge left her office, Jane picked up the phone and dialed.

When the voice at the other end answered, she gazed out the window, where the air was hot and heavy. "Bernard, we have a problem."

23

Leta was on her way home, still berating herself for the bold move that had backfired, when her cell phone rang. She reached in the seat next to her and pulled it to her ear. "Hello?"

"Ms. Breckenridge?"

She slowed for the red light ahead. "Yes?"

"This is Edith Styles from Heritage House. I have a matter I need to discuss with you. Could we make an appointment for you to come by?"

She frowned. "Is everything all right with my mother?"

"Oh, certainly. Yes, all is well where Sylvia is concerned." There was a momentary pause. "We just need to talk about some changes occurring here at Heritage House."

A red car in the lane behind her pulled dangerously close to her bumper.

"Okay, sure," she said, wondering why some drivers were so rude. "I have to work tonight. But I can be there tomorrow, around six?"

"Fine. I'll see you then."

The phone went dead and she tossed it back in the seat, wondering why the director of Heritage House seemed to make everything sound like a storm was about to hit.

She'd had enough turbulent weather to last a lifetime, thank you. Especially after today.

Leta had left Jane Ladd's office with a worried churning in the pit of her stomach. She'd blindly miscalculated the situation, believing she could simply request a reassignment of duties.

From the look in her boss's eyes, her stupidity had cost her.

The light turned green and Leta pressed on the gas pedal, slowly moving forward in line with the other cars. She glanced in the rearview mirror. Thankfully, the rude driver must have turned.

The only thing she could do now was to comply. Katie's suggestion that she simply resign wasn't an option she could consider. Finances dictated she just swallow this bitter pill, even if actively working against Nate made her feel sick inside.

What other choice did she have?

Nate tossed the media file onto the table and leaned back against the deep leather cushioned chair. His eyes burned from hours of reading, and it was only going to get worse going forward into this bid for the governor's office.

He'd let himself forget the energy required to run an effective campaign — endless meetings, war-room strategy sessions, private fund-raising events, meets and greets, and the nagging feeling he was always behind. Not only in his extensive task list, but in the polls.

When in the thick of things, his personal life got shoved aside. No spending leisurely time with personal friends, no movies, no reading the latest *New York Times* bestsellers. Barely time to sleep and rest up for the next day, when everything began all over again.

For all it cost him, everything would be worth it in the end. If he pulled this off and landed on top, that is.

Nate shook his head, pushing the negative possibility of losing the election from his exhausted mind. If he gave even an inch to the idea he might be pushing himself into the ground for nothing . . . Well, best to move on from that type of negative thinking.

To give his everything in order to win, he'd have to stay focused on why he was running in the first place. Losing was no option. Especially with so much at stake.

Especially when *someone* was counting on him.

He hadn't seen or talked to her since the day of the symposium. Just before he'd gone ahead and announced.

How many times had he picked up the phone since that day, only to slip it back in his pocket?

He'd toyed with making a trip to Central Market in hopes of running into her. The time had never been available.

At least that's what he told himself. With everything going on after the announcement, and until he settled things with Tiffany, he thought it best to hold off a little.

Nate got up and walked to the windows and looked out at his pool. His hand slipped into his pocket and he pulled out his phone.

Truth was, he longed to call her. Right now.

What did that say about him?

He thought the absolute world of Tiffany Shea. But the truth was, lying alone in bed at night, he often wrestled with just how he was going to let her know they had no future.

Certainly, there was no doubt in his mother's mind that he should establish his connection with Tiffany permanently, even to the point of engagement. In practical terms, he could easily make that same argument in his own mind.

She was smart, beautiful, and he had loved her. Or, at least he thought so.

Then thoughts of Leta Breckenridge would inch into his mind and delightfully divert his attention. That is, until he realized what a schmuck that made him.

He was running for governor but couldn't even govern his own mind.

Tiffany was far too bright. Soon she'd notice something was different. Certainly, he admired her and never wanted to treat the woman he'd been dating in any manner outside the respect she deserved.

Tiffany had done nothing to warrant anything but the very best from him. She was a woman worth loving and clearly believed her relationship with him was secure.

In fact, she'd dropped over unannounced last Sunday night with a bottle of wine and not-so-subtle intentions.

First, she'd shown up in tight jeans and boots — totally out of character for someone he'd seldom seen out of business attire, or business casual in the rare hours she was at leisure. Her neck was draped with layers of chunky pieces of turquoise set in heavy chains that pressed against milky-white skin exposed by a blouse barely buttoned.

No doubt, she was one beautiful woman.

He'd found himself sorely tempted when she placed her empty wineglass on the table and leaned into his chest. "I think it's time we quit talking about politics for the evening, don't you?"

She smelled of the finest cedar soaked in something sweet, like vanilla. The heady scent had made breathing difficult. Finally, he'd choked out a response. "A wise candidate acts on the wisdom of his closest advisors. And his advisors are telling him he has a very early morning."

Even as he brushed her off, he remembered how he used to thread his fingers through her long brown hair, let the curled twists cascade over his hand as he pulled her even closer. Then the phone rang, forcing the memory from his mind.

Yes, a woman like Tiffany Shea had been easy to love.

So why had he fallen for another? For a

girl who looked at him with adoration, like he was someone capable of holding her entire world in place? Even now, she was there capturing his mind and holding his thoughts hostage.

God help him.

In his wildest dreams, he couldn't imagine what he was going to do.

But he knew he needed to talk to her again.

24

Leta opened the microwave door and pulled out the hot bag of popcorn, poured the contents into a bowl, and made her way to the sofa, where she snuggled up in her mother's old afghan.

Normally, she relished evenings like these, ones where Katie was out on a date and she was left to enjoy *Gilmore Girls* on Netflix. Tonight she was restless. Even cheering for Lorelai and Luke Danes to finally connect was not likely to distract her from the mess churning inside her head.

On top of wondering why Edith Styles wanted to meet with her, her work at the Ladd Agency left her feeling like a traitor.

She'd spent the day watching video footage of a paid speech Nathan Emerson had made at a shareholder meeting of a company that had since been questioned in the media for selling what some claimed to be questionable nutritional supplements.

Bernard Geisler was growing more frustrated with how little negative material there was to find on Nate, and he was grasping at straws.

Nate had easily won his senate campaign by a large margin. His ideas had been fresh and focused on the needs of his constituents. He responded to his detractors with grace and charm, never employing the tit-for-tat politics often seen in the news cycles today.

Governor Holiday had a right to be worried. Still, the end didn't justify the means Bernard was employing. Leta was part of that, and it left her feeling hollow inside.

Leta reached for the television remote. Maybe a funny sitcom would take her mind off the turmoil inside her brain.

She flipped through the channels trying to find a program to watch, finally settling on an old episode of *Seinfeld,* the one where Kramer feeds his horse Beef-A-Reeno.

When the episode had first aired, she'd been sitting with her mother, who claimed the scene where the couple in the horse-drawn carriage began to wave at the sour air was a bit irreverent, but neither one of them could stop laughing.

She settled back and grabbed a handful of

buttered popcorn. She could use a laugh tonight.

Her phone rang, forcing her to lower the TV volume.

She set the bowl on the coffee table and reached for her cell phone. The number wasn't one she recognized.

"Hello?"

"Leta?" The voice was delightfully familiar. "It's Nathan Emerson."

She forgot to breathe. "Uh, yeah. Hi, Nate. How are you?"

"Good, good. We hadn't talked since the symposium." He paused. "I hope all is well."

"Everything's fine. The folks at Heritage House are taking good care of my mom. She seems content."

"That's good to hear. And you?"

She stared at the silent scene playing out on the television. "I've been . . . well, busy working and all."

She couldn't believe she'd just mentioned her work. What was the matter with her?

"Me too. I guess you've no doubt learned my big news? I announced."

"Yes, congratulations! You'll make a wonderful governor." And he would, unless Jane Ladd and Bernard Geisler got their way. "You must be tremendously excited."

"Well, not sure about excited. But I

believe I made the right decision. My heart is to make a difference. The only way to really effect change is to unseat Governor Holiday. But enough about politics. That's not why I called. I really just found myself thinking about you and wondering how you were doing."

So he hadn't only called about her mother. His words tickled her ears and made her feel all warm inside.

"I'd really like to see you again," he continued. "Maybe we could meet for coffee — oh wait, there's someone at my door. Could you hold on?"

On the other end of the line she heard voices but couldn't make out what they were saying. She waited, her heart beating wildly. He wanted to see her.

Still, she had to consider who she worked for. Maybe she should tell him.

"Leta?"

His voice pulled her back into the moment. "I'm here."

"I'm really sorry, I've got to go. My campaign manager just showed up at the door with some data I need to study for a speech tomorrow. But I meant what I said. I'd really like to have a chance to talk again."

"I'd like that too," she ventured, knowing full well the implications she'd face if they were to meet. Forging a friendship under the current situation would not be easy. And likely impossible. Still, despite her reservations she couldn't seem to say no.

"Great! I'll call you. Good night."

"Good night, Nate." She clicked off her phone and stared back at the television.

The reasons to stay far away from Nathan Emerson were stacked high. They were from two very different leagues. As far as she knew, he hadn't broken things off with Tiffany, a woman much better suited to someone like him.

Yet, all he had to do was say her name and her heart skipped a beat.

Of course, there was the cold reality that Nate knew nothing about Operation Brainchild or that she was a part of the effort to tank his campaign.

She'd considered telling him, even if it meant the end of their emerging friendship. Then she remembered the confidentiality agreement.

And she thought of her momma.

This isn't fair!

But then, she'd learned long ago that life could deal some bad cards.

Her mother always said that when things looked impossible, that was when God often showed up and showed off — that nothing was too hard for him. He could turn even the worst things in life around for our good.

Leta believed that was true. Her mother had never misled her. But in this situation, God definitely had a big job before him.

25

"Thank you for coming in, Ms. Brecken-ridge." Edith Styles escorted her down a short hallway and into her office. "I hope I didn't alarm you by asking you to stop by," she said, pointing to a seat in front of her desk.

Leta managed a soft laugh. "Well, I guess I was a little. At first." She briefly toyed with the idea of mentioning she was current on her mother's account and had been for months, just in case.

"You must be wondering why I would ask to see you in person." As she spoke, Edith's smile faded and a muscle twitched in her cheek, as if she were clenching her teeth.

It was at that moment Leta noticed some-thing different. In the few times she'd been in this office, she'd noticed Ms. Styles always kept her desk and credenza neat, but now all the frames were missing. Her gaze strayed to the walls. No artwork either.

She swallowed and returned her attention across the desk.

Edith's arched eyebrows raised slightly. "I'm sorry you were unable to make our quarterly family meeting —"

"Yes, I'm sorry about that. I rarely am able to attend because of my work schedule. I work two jobs."

"Oh yes, dear. I know that. And I was in no way being critical." Ms. Styles folded her hands and placed them squarely in front of her. "Not at all. I simply wanted to share in person the announcement that was made at the meeting. You see, I wanted to let our patients' families know that Heritage House has been purchased."

"Purchased?"

"Yes, which shouldn't affect your mother, or any of our patients, from a practical standpoint. However, it does mean that a new director will be coming on board at the first of next week."

The news took Leta by surprise. Sure, Edith Styles wasn't exactly a warm and fuzzy creature, but she ran a tight ship, and the patients, including her mom, greatly benefited. Her departure would leave a hole.

"I'm sorry to hear that, Ms. Styles. Truly, you will be missed here." She gave the woman a sympathetic look, trying to convey that her words were not just an expected sentiment but that she really would be sorry to see Edith go. "The person coming in after you will have some big shoes to fill."

Edith stood. "Thank you, Ms. Breckenridge." Her chin quivered almost imperceptibly. "That's all I needed to let you know."

The poor woman looked like she needed a hug, but past encounters made Leta believe any attempt to comfort might not be welcomed.

"Okay, well . . . goodbye. And good luck to you, Ms. Styles."

Leta left the office and made her way to her mother's room, wondering about the implications of the news she'd just learned. She supposed these kinds of things happened all the time. But she still felt sorry for Ms. Styles.

She thought of Heritage House as her mother's current home, but in reality this nursing center was a business. And businesses got sold.

"Mom?" Leta peeked inside the door.

Her mother stood by the window, clearly agitated. She turned to the left, then abruptly stopped and turned to the right, while muttering something about the television.

Leta rushed forward and took her mom's

shoulders. "Mom, what's the matter?" she asked, guiding her mother away from the window. "Here, sit here."

"Leta?" she heard someone say behind her.

She turned to the voice at the open door to find Mona, one of her mom's favorite nurses.

"I'm afraid your mother's television went out last night. It was getting pretty old and finally gave up the ghost." Mona moved forward and bent down in front of her mother. "Remember, Sylvia? We talked about that and promised we'd get another one set up for you very soon." She looked at Leta. "Change really seems to stir her up."

Leta nodded and bent as well. "Momma, I'll have a replacement television here by tonight. I promise." Her throat knotted unexpectedly. No matter how much time passed, the blank look on her mother's face made her heart hurt. Thankfully, most of the time her momma still recognized her, not as her daughter, maybe, but as someone who loved her. Today didn't seem to be one of those days.

Over the next hours, she sat with her mom, alone and silent, at the foot of the chair with her hand resting on her momma's arm. Finally, her mom's rocking and murmuring quieted and she seemed to be at peace again.

Leta stayed much longer than normal, not leaving until the nurses showed up to ready her mom for bed.

She kissed her mother's cheek. "I'll be back tomorrow to check on you, Mom." She'd just have to explain to Mike that she wouldn't be able to make it in.

She texted him the message on her way out to the car.

That's when she saw it — a message from Nate.

Been thinking about you and hope all is well. Signed, the future governor of Texas (hopefully!)

Immediately, her spirits lifted.

On a scale of one to ten, her day had definitely been at the low end of the spectrum.

Until now.

Tiffany stopped to admire a terra-cotta pot filled with red hibiscus before following her best friend, Connie Flores, inside the art gallery.

"Oh, look, Tiff!" Connie brushed past her

and headed straight for a giclée print of a longhorn standing in a field of bluebonnets. "C.J. Latta is exhibiting. My dad used to have several of his pieces."

Tiffany wrinkled her nose. "Nate might agree. But something like this is a little closer to what I had in mind for his office." She pointed to a bronze sculpture. "A statement piece."

Her friend nodded. "I see what you're saying. The piece certainly has presence."

She and Connie had become tight friends after attending the same law school in Dallas. Despite their ridiculously busy schedules, both of them looked forward to these getaways to the Hill Country, where they'd browse trendy gift boutiques and art galleries, then spend evenings drinking wine and talking, sometimes into the wee hours of the morning.

Tiffany examined the sculpture a bit closer, admiring the steely look in the eagle's eyes, the authentic-looking feathers. "You're coming to Nate's birthday bash, aren't you?"

"Wouldn't miss it." Connie wandered to a glass case filled with custom jewelry items. "I'm looking forward to meeting his mother."

"You'll love Vera. She is *us* — only older.

I've never met a woman more strategic." She waved the proprietor over. "Sir, how much is this bronze piece?"

When he told her, Connie raised her eyebrows and whistled.

Tiffany lifted her chin, considered the cost. Yes, the piece was pricey, but she wanted to give Nate something really special. "I'll take it."

"That'll look especially nice in the governor's office," her friend whispered.

Tiffany's lips lifted into a sly smile. "Or perhaps the Oval Office someday." A tiny thrill crossed her belly. Few things would cause her to resign her partnership at Shea, Bailey, and Gutteridge. But there was no question she'd turn in her shiny nameplate to be first lady.

Her first official act would be to use her influence with Nate to get Connie, who was currently serving as an assistant district attorney for Travis County, appointed to the US district judicial bench. Even better, maybe she could arrange a Supreme Court nomination. Nate would have to agree her close friend was well suited to serve in either capacity. Connie's Hispanic heritage couldn't hurt their administration's affirmative action either.

But first things first.

She pulled out her credit card, handed it to the gallery owner, and provided shipping information, excited to see Nate's face when he opened her extravagant gift.

Later that night, back in their room at the resort, she sat cross-legged on the floor with Connie, wearing yoga pants and a loose T-shirt.

Connie brought up a more delicate subject. "So, I have to ask. How is this going to go? Birthday bash, election-night party, engagement celebration? Or what?"

Tiffany lifted her wineglass and took a slow, deliberate sip, hiding behind her appreciation of the subtle hint of oak and black currant. When the silence became too heavy, she finally answered, "I'm not sure what you mean."

Connie raised her eyebrows. "Yeah?" She pointed across the plush shaggy carpet to Tiffany's left hand. "No ring?"

Tiff gently swirled her wineglass. "Well, I have to admit I was a bit disappointed when a diamond didn't show up at Christmas. I'm sure Nate will . . ."

"But you're worried," Connie said, finishing her sentence. "I would be too. I mean, what is he waiting for?"

Tiffany took a deep breath. Her friend knew her too well. Still, she wasn't ready to admit she had developed a bit of apprehension. "An engagement announcement could easily draw attention away from the critical issues in this race — especially this early. Nate knows that would be political suicide."

"Or, if timed right, your engagement might endear a great many women voters. Even those with deep pockets. In fact, you could play the Princess Kate card. Did you see how the royal wedding mania played in the media? Just imagine how something similar could keep Nate and his campaign front and center on the airwaves." Connie knotted her hair at the back of her neck. "That entire notion cuts against my fabric, but hey, if it lands a win square in Nate's lap, then I say snip away."

Tiffany looked across the floor at her friend, her confidante, and the only person she really trusted with something this personal. Perhaps it was time to confess the truth.

"Okay, I admit it. I was disappointed when no ring came at Christmas, but not exactly worried. Not until just recently."

Connie frowned. "Why? What's happened?"

Tiffany grew solemn. "This had better never end up on a blog somewhere."

Her best friend crossed her chest with her

finger. "Promise. Besides, you have enough dirt on me to ensure I never talk."

Tiffany reluctantly nodded and downed the last trickle in her glass. She squared her shoulders and took a deep breath, knowing it wasn't going to be easy to admit what she'd done. "I — I looked on his phone."

Connie's eyes widened. "You did what?"

"You heard me. Nate left the room. I was feeling a little insecure, so I acted just like a schoolgirl. I checked his text messages."

"And?"

Tiffany drew a deep breath. "He's been in contact with a girl that has come onto the scene."

Connie frowned again. "What girl?"

"Her name is Leta Breckenridge. From what I can find out, she's nobody, really. Recently landed a job with the Ladd Agency. Never even finished her degree, so she's likely some administrative clerk or secretary."

"Oh, that is a relief. But then, why are you worried?"

Tiffany hesitated. "I saw the way he looked at her."

Ever the optimist, Connie stood and brushed off. "Well, so what? He looked at another girl. Sounds to me like nothing can come of it, even if there is a spark of attraction. No man who intends to be governor can take up with someone like that."

"Maybe. But what should I do?" She hated the way her voice sounded, timid and insecure.

Connie lifted her chin. "Do I need to remind anyone in this room that Tiffany Shea is one of the preeminent environmental attorneys in the state of Texas? Every oil company in the Gulf looks to you and your firm for advice." Her friend smiled down at her. "So here's what I suggest — you need to climb his rig and turn up the pressure. Don't stop drilling until you reach the payoff, if you know what I mean."

Tiffany squared her shoulders. She nodded. "Yes . . . yes, I most certainly do."

Leta pulled a stack of mail from the mailbox in front of her house and riffled through the contents as she made her way up the sidewalk. She climbed the steps and, upon reaching the front door, paused to look more closely at an elegant cream-colored envelope, the kind you'd find in an expensive stationery store. The face was gold embossed, engraved with her name and address, and included a return address she didn't recognize.

Anxious to open it, she hurried inside and

dropped her bag and the rest of the mail on a chair, then made her way to the kitchen, where she grabbed a butter knife and inserted the serrated edge just under the back flap. Puzzled about what could possibly be inside, she carefully opened the flap and pulled out the contents.

Mr. and Mrs. Porter Wyatt cordially invite you to join them at their home for a dinner party birthday celebration for their son, Nathan Emerson. Regrets only. Cocktail casual attire.

With her heart pounding, she scanned the date and address.

A birthday party?

Katie entered from down the hall. "What's that?"

"What?"

"What you're holding, silly." Katie skirted around her and headed for the refrigerator. "Do we have any of that lemon meringue pie left, or did Bart eat it all last night?"

Leta gave her a blank look. "Huh?"

Katie frowned. "What's the matter with you? What's that?"

Without answering, Leta held out the invitation.

Katie took and read it. "Are you kidding

me? You're going to Nathan Emerson's birthday party?"

"I'm not sure I should go."

Her roommate looked at her like she was crazy. "Why not?"

"Have you forgotten what I do for a living?"

"Oh, nonsense, you're going." Katie grinned. "And, girl, we're going to need to go shopping. Unless you have a cocktail dress hanging in the back of your closet I don't know about."

26

"Okay, everybody take a seat." Jane swept into the room with her iPad and an apparent agenda. She waited for a few gathered near the coffeepot to reluctantly make their way to their places before continuing. "Listen up. We've got a lot of work over the next weeks. The election is heating up, and we need to stay on top of every appearance."

Jane's determined nature was not a new phenomenon. Those gathered around the table knew her expectations were high, especially when much was at stake. Governor Holiday's campaign had taken the forefront, shoving every other firm project into the priority basement.

Their boss slid her perfectly manicured finger down her iPad. After carefully examining the screen, she pushed her leopard-print reading glasses up into her hair and looked across the table. "Emerson is appearing at several back-to-back events in Dallas this week — Mothers for Better Childcare Options, a tax symposium at the Anatole, and the Texas Agriculture Council. Dan, those are yours. Elaine has your plane ticket at the front desk." She turned to Mike. "Likewise, I'll want you at his public fund-raisers. Elaine has the details for you in your packet at her desk, along with your travel arrangements."

Bernard cleared his throat from where he sat at the other end of the conference table. "Take careful note of everything said, both onstage and off. We want you to report any contradictory statements, position reversals, slipups, or gaffes that could be spun to Governor Holiday's advantage. In addition, we'll want to distinguish their talking points and work to counter those early. One more critical issue — we need to establish Emerson's surrogates by name." His eyes darkened, if that was even possible. "I want constant contact. Report back to me via text at least every hour, more frequently if schedules allow. And please, people, you are to call if anything critical develops."

Leta mouthed to Erin across the table, "Surrogate?"

Bernard startled her by calling out her name.

She blinked, feeling like she'd been caught talking in class. "Uh. Sorry. Yes?"

"A surrogate is a person who is designated to express views and positions on behalf of the candidate. Often it'll be a spouse, but in Emerson's case, we've not yet determined who his spokesmen are."

She nodded almost imperceptibly. "Oh, okay. I understand." She swallowed stiffly, determined that if she had questions in the future, she'd wait and find someone to ask privately, out from under the scrutiny of Bernard Geisler and Jane Ladd. Both of them seemed to hear and see everything, and that made her extremely uncomfortable.

Strangely, Bernard smiled at her. A first, for sure. A move that made her even more uncomfortable.

She'd told herself that for now she didn't have any options but to follow their program. If she wanted that nice paycheck that kept her mom at Heritage House, she'd have to try not to do anything counter to what they wanted, while still maintaining some level of personal integrity. It would be tricky, but she hoped to avoid contributing in any manner that would impose significant damage to Nathan.

A lofty goal? Perhaps, but she'd spent

many sleepless nights considering her options, and playing along seemed to be the only viable one. At least for now.

In the meantime, she had her eyes out for a comparable job. Maybe she'd break down and call Cassie. At the job fair she'd mentioned she was in HR. Even if Leta didn't make as much, she might be able to make the finances work. Unfortunately, without Jane's recommendation, that might not be an easy option.

"Erin, I'm afraid your assignment is a bit less desirable. But I promise, each one of you will take your turn."

Erin opened a packet of sweetener and poured the contents into her coffee. "What kind of assignment?"

A muscle twitched in Bernard's cheek. "We've connected with an anonymous operative who secured a position with Austin Resource Recovery."

Mike leaned forward. "The trash outfit?"

"Yes," Bernard confirmed.

Jane grabbed her coffee mug. "For a healthy price, we now have a storage unit filled with garbage collected at Emerson's campaign headquarters, his personal residence, and his mother's residence."

Leta's head jerked up.

The idea was appalling, took her breath.

In her wildest dreams, she'd never envisioned how politics were played behind the scenes.

From the look on Erin's face, the idea didn't settle well with her either. "You want me to go through his garbage?"

Jane squared her shoulders. "Yes, this is an essential effort. That storage unit contains valuable intelligence — down to what brand of toilet paper Emerson uses. Somewhere in those bags of refuse is an important nugget that could potentially take down our opponent. Both Bernard and I believe we can count on you to mine the gold."

Erin ruffled, but only slightly. Then, in an unexpected move, she brightened. "Well, I'm here to serve. But I get the travel gig next time," she teased and pointed across the table at Dan and Mike. "And these two get garbage duty."

Jane grinned. "That's fair."

The guys didn't look so sure that they heartily agreed. "Remind me when it's my turn so I can call in sick," one of them teased.

Leta couldn't believe her co-workers were laughing like all this was some party or something. What they were planning was underhanded at best and slimy at worst.

Bernard folded his hands in front of him

on the table. The move revealed starched white cuffs fastened with monogrammed cuff links. He looked directly at her. "From the looks on some of your faces, these practices come as a surprise." He shrugged. "Let me assure you, digging up dirt and highlighting unflattering aspects of the other candidate's life has a long political history."

Jane joined his argument. "How do you think the media stumbled on the story about presidential candidate John Edwards's four-hundred-dollar haircuts, billed at his campaign's expense?" she explained. "Journalists are reluctant to admit they use opposition research strategically slipped to them and rarely say so openly, but I personally can vouch that the practice is utilized often — and by both sides. If the Ladd Agency wasn't providing the dirt for a price, there would be twenty other agencies in town lined up to take our place. It's the way political business is done."

Bernard removed those thin wire-framed glasses and used a tiny cloth retrieved from his pocket to clean the lenses. "And that brings us to our next assignment." He held up the glasses to the light, checking his work. Seemingly satisfied, he positioned the frames back on his face and carefully folded the cloth. "Leta, I understand you've been invited to Senator Emerson's birthday party?"

"Okay, okay — calm down." Katie kicked off her flip-flops and slid onto a bar stool at their kitchen counter.

"Katie, think." Leta raised her voice, her stress so raw it caught her by surprise. "Are you sure you didn't tell someone?"

"No, I didn't. Absolutely did not." Katie pulled her bare feet from the neighboring stool and spun to face her. "I can't believe you think I'd blab something like that! You got a personal invite to the senator's party, and you think your best friend would go around telling everyone when you asked me to keep it quiet? I mean, what's up with that?"

Leta huffed. "Can we focus on the issue here?" She stood in the middle of the kitchen, her emotions swirling like soup about to boil over. Annoyance, confusion, regret. They all churned in her gut.

Katie held up her open palms. "Okay, first things first. You had to have shared the information with someone. And it wasn't me. So who?" Her face went all Nancy Drew, like she was enjoying figuring out the puzzle.

"Look, I didn't share that I'd received an

invitation to that party with anyone but you. Only Mom, and she certainly —" Leta slapped her forehead. "Of course, that's it!"

Katie leaned forward. "What?"

"I told Mom all about the party, not thinking anything about the fact that there was a cleaning lady in her room at the time. That's the only thing it could be." She chewed nervously on her knuckle, then suddenly dropped her hand. "I'm such an idiot!"

Katie slid from the bar stool. "Okay, this sounds like a really bad movie. You think the cleaning person had a connection to that creepy guy at your work?" She shook her head. "You know, maybe you'd better reassess this job thing. I don't like this."

The knot in Leta's stomach didn't ease. "Neither do I."

What were the odds some random worker at Heritage House was acquainted with the Ladd Agency and Bernard Geisler? No, the story seemed far more sinister.

She didn't have all the answers. Obviously, she'd underestimated the people she was working for — the extreme lengths they'd go to in order to find out what they needed. Even to the point of spying on her! Which meant they had somehow discovered she and Nate were friends.

Had they hired her based on that very fact? Perhaps they'd thought she had some in with Nathan, even back then, which didn't entirely make sense. But then none of this really did.

She'd been plain stupid to ignore all the signals.

Leta had admitted to Katie that she'd had reservations about that Geisler guy all along, especially when he showed up at the Hole in the Wall. How he'd watched her with those black eyes. It'd given her the creeps then, and he gave her the creeps now.

Clearly, they'd learned she had a connection to Nate and would stop at nothing to benefit from that — certainly not dirty political tactics — even if it meant spying on her.

Jane Ladd and Bernard Geisler were bent on getting the dirt on Governor Holiday's opponent, and they intended to use her to get it. The question was, when exactly had she become their pawn?

Her back stiffened. Truth was, there was no winning this one. "Katie, I really don't have a lot of options. I'm just going to have to resign."

Her roommate looked at her like she was half crazy. "I agree, but you know what that'll mean for your finances. What about your mom?"

She took a deep breath, feeling miserable inside. "Of course I know. Which is why I initially put Jane and Bernard off by telling them I'd go to that party and report back. But I can't possibly go through with it."

Katie clapped her palms together. "Hey, what's to stop you from returning with a report that says nothing?"

"What do you mean?"

A slow grin formed on Katie's face. "I mean, turn the tables on them."

"You're right!" Her mood immediately lifted. "I can't deliver any dirt that isn't there. And believe me, no one is more squeaky-clean than Nathan Emerson."

Just like Katie suggested, she'd simply go to the party and return with a report that said nothing. She was capable of playing their game. They couldn't force her to damage the senator.

That approach would at least buy her some time, let her shift gears and make a plan before moving forward.

She gave her roommate a big hug. "Thank you! That's the perfect solution. I'll go and do exactly as you said — show up to the office on Monday morning with a report that is primarily meaningless." She grinned. "I've sat across from this man and talked. He's the real deal. Besides, Nathan Emerson is far too smart to say something in public that he doesn't want splayed on all the television networks."

"Exactly," Katie assured her. "Granted, you're playing with the big boys here. You'll have to keep your wits about you — stay sharp. And be careful."

Indeed, Leta would be more than careful.

The plan wasn't without risk. If she withheld anything that would be of value to Holiday's campaign and Bernard and Jane found out, she'd be let go and out of a job. And in that case, there would be no glowing recommendation letter from Jane for future potential employers to consider.

She'd be right back at square one — broke and facing a bleak employment future.

While employed at the Ladd Agency, she'd learned to be smart and resourceful. She'd need those important traits and more if she wanted to swim their shark-infested waters and climb to shore on the other side.

But she could handle this.

She had to.

27

With the help of Google Maps, Leta found her way to the address on the engraved invitation and pulled into a large circular driveway, where an attendant opened the door and helped her from her car.

"Your keys, miss?"

She handed off the keys to her new-to-her Toyota, relieved she was not embarrassed to be driving her old Chevy Blazer. "Thank you."

Leta climbed the steps to the front landing, taking special care not to catch her heels on the beautiful stone. Nate's parents' home was amazing. *Big* didn't begin to describe the size of the expansive structure nestled on a rocky rim overlooking the lights of Austin. She loved the stone and wood architectural elements, the entry flanked by cypress and pots of bright red hibiscus. The house was like something you'd see in a magazine.

Nervous flutters crossed her stomach, and she straightened her skirt.

The dress was a rare splurge, an Adrianna Papell featuring a scooped neckline, cap sleeves, and a full A-line skirt with a scalloped hem. A lucky find on the sale rack at Lord & Taylor in the mall.

She'd left her hair loose and worn her favorite scented Philosophy lotion, even donned some lip gloss in a pretty shade called Iced Raspberry.

After taking a deep breath, she fingered the pearls she'd borrowed.

"Go ahead. Take them," Katie had said, pressing the pearls into her hands. "I never wear them."

Leta hoped they gave her a sophisticated look — in an Audrey Hepburn sort of way.

Another attendant at the door moved forward. "Good evening, ma'am." She granted him a smile as he opened the heavy wooden doors.

Inside, she was immediately greeted by an older man with silver hair and a generous smile. "Welcome, I'm Porter Wyatt. And you are?"

She took his hand. "Leta Breckenridge. I'm a — a friend of Senator Emerson's."

"Oh yes. It's so very nice to meet you, Ms. Breckenridge." He cupped her hand in his and led the way to a big, open area filled with people milling around. "Nathan is in the library." He pointed past the large foyer on their right. "If you care for a drink, a full-service bar is available. Servers are also passing tonight's signature cocktail, the Texas Sunrise." He winked. "My wife's idea," he confided. "By the way, I'm Nate's stepfather. We're so glad you could join our little party for Nathan. I'll make sure he's alerted you are here." He smiled at her again before returning to the door, where more guests were arriving.

So that was Nate's stepfather, the one he thought so highly of. She could see why. He was a very nice man.

She moved across the foyer and into a large living area, trying to take everything in. Soaring ceilings gave the room a feeling of grandeur. The floors were covered with large cream-colored stone tiles trimmed in rough-hewn wood, with rugs and furnishings leading to an entire wall of glass that overlooked an outdoor area with palms and landscape areas beautifully showcased with uplighting.

The entire scene reminded her of the Gaylord Hotel in Dallas, where she'd once visited with her mother. They couldn't afford to stay overnight, but it had been a huge treat to see the indoor gardens and winding waterways, all underneath that huge glass atrium.

Her mother taught her to appreciate nice things, even if they couldn't afford them. And this entire house was definitely something to admire.

She passed by two sixty-something women who were discussing the state's obligation to provide childcare options for single mothers on state assistance. She stood several feet away and listened with interest for a few seconds, then wandered in the direction of an adjoining room filled with people milling around, including several she'd seen on the news.

This room had brown leather sofas arranged along walls decorated with exotic taxidermy mounts. There was even a cheetah on an octagonal table, set among rocks and grasses meant to make the piece look naturalized.

Whoever stuffed that poor thing had done a pretty good job of making the spotted cat look like it was alive.

"Do you like it?"

She grinned and turned toward the familiar voice. "Hey, there you are. Happy birthday, Senator."

He smiled — a warm, welcoming smile

that made her feel a little giddy.

"Why so formal?" He brushed her cheek with a kiss. When he did, she caught the scent of his cologne.

He stepped back, and his gaze dropped to take in what she was wearing. His eyes twinkled in appreciation as he briefly took both her hands in his. "Thank you for coming," he said, looking drop-dead handsome in his tailored suit and tie.

Forgetting to keep her emotions in check, she stared into his eyes. "I was so surprised to get the invite in the mail."

His brows drew together. "You were? Why?"

She shrugged, suddenly feeling like a silly schoolgirl. "I'm not sure, really. But I'm so glad I came."

For all the brave talk in front of Katie, she'd nearly waffled on attending this heady get-together. Not only did she fear the expectations forced upon her by the Ladd Agency, but she was a bit hesitant to throw herself in the middle of such an unfamiliar environment. She rarely went to parties, let alone one so obviously out of her league.

But standing here now — with him — she couldn't be happier that she'd pushed all her reservations aside.

"Let's get you something to drink." He

took her arm and guided her to the bar. "What will you have?"

"A club soda, please, with lime."

"You got it." He turned to the bartender. "Make that two."

With drinks in hand, he guided her into what looked like a game room, with a pool table in the center surrounded by several poker tables. "My stepdad hosts a group of men each week, much to my mother's chagrin." He grinned. "There she is now. Come, I want to introduce you." He handed her the glass of club soda, then took her elbow and led her forward. "Mother, there's someone I want you to meet."

An elegant woman with perfectly styled silver hair pulled away from a small group of men she'd been talking with. She wore light-colored linen dress pants and a flowing, bright tangerine-colored top accented with heavy gold jewelry. The real stuff, Leta imagined. She also suspected this woman was not afraid to be noticed.

"Well, hello, dear. I'm Vera." She reached for Leta's hand. "We're so glad you could join us for this special celebration." She waved at someone outside the open doors leading to a second deck with stunning views of the city lights.

His mother was very attractive for her age.

Nate got his eyes and facial bone structure from her.

A younger woman with dark hair stepped away from a group standing by the sofa and moved to join them. The girl she'd so often seen with Nathan. Tiffany Shea.

Leta couldn't help it. Her stomach clenched.

Early on, she'd researched all she could find on the internet. Who wouldn't have?

A successful environmental attorney from a wealthy family here in Austin, Tiffany had graduated summa cum laude from UT and then law school at Dedman in Dallas, a prominent institution attended by a long list of dignitaries, including judges, foreign ambassadors, and Fortune 500 CEOs. Even Governor Holiday was an alumnus.

Tonight, she wore her pretty brown hair up, showing off large sapphire-colored earrings that caught the light when she turned her head. Wait . . . were those *real*?

Well, authentic or not, the color of the earrings perfectly matched the shade of the flowers in her blue and white sleeveless top. She wore white pants and these really cute wedge sandals in the same blue color. Stylish but not too trendy.

Even in her new dress, Leta felt like a cubic zirconia against this diamond.

Tiffany Shea extended her hand, never breaking her gaze. "Hello, I'm Tiffany. It's so nice to see you again."

Nate's mother's eyebrows lifted. "Again? You two know each other?"

Tiffany flashed a brilliant smile. "Well, we don't actually *know* each other, do we?" She placed the tips of her French-manicured fingers on Leta's arm. "Just a brief encounter in a restaurant restroom. It's Leta, isn't it?"

Nate watched his mother's heavily jeweled hand push at the back of her hair, a signal that something bothered her. Likely she wondered about his new friendship with Leta Breckenridge, why she'd been on his invite list. While his mother was a gracious host, she rarely extended invitations without purpose.

"How do you know this girl, Son?" she'd asked over the phone. "I mean, who is she?"

Like so often, her questions rankled. He squelched the compulsion to explain, reminding himself people were allowed in his life as persona grata. Regardless, his mother would no doubt question his judgment if she knew the truth — that Leta was more to him than simply a constituent with an ailing mother who benefited from his help.

And he'd almost have to agree with her assessment. He could tell himself Leta was simply a friend, but deep inside his feelings edged beyond that. He'd taken a calculated risk in inviting both Tiffany and Leta tonight, but he'd convinced himself the only conflict was inside his own mind. No one else knew what he was thinking or the decision he'd made.

Truth was? He struggled with taking this attraction much further until he found the proper way to end his relationship with Tiffany, a woman he'd once thought he might want to marry.

Yet how could he explain the way he felt every time he encountered Leta Breckenridge?

He stood quietly, listening to the three of them chatter on about him as if he weren't standing near, knowing all he could do was pray his mother didn't look him in the eyes. With very little scrutiny, she had an uncanny ability to silently probe his inner thoughts. She was a master at analyzing every situation, every motive.

What would his mother be taking notice of now as he stood between these two women?

Elegant, smart, and politically intuitive Tiffany — the perfect fit in many aspects.

Few would argue with that.

Yet after only a few hours of conversation in that coffee shop, Leta somehow knew him more deeply than Tiffany ever would. They shared an intimacy born of early loss and mutual deeply held ideals about what really mattered in life. Few people related without masks, and she gave him the gift of two-way authenticity.

And God help him, he couldn't seem to get her out of his mind.

"Tiff, Mom — could you excuse us? I want to introduce Leta to some folks from the institute."

Nate led her out the doors and onto the deck, but not before Leta noticed the wary looks on both his mother's and Tiffany's faces.

"Your mother's place is amazing," she said as they moved toward a small group on the other side of the pool.

Even at night, Leta could see a sparkle in his eyes. "Yes, well, my mother does everything up right." He placed his hand at the small of her back — an intimate gesture that sent a tiny thrill up her spine — and guided her around a table of older men discussing traffic issues. She mentally chastised herself. No doubt she needed to get ahold of her emotions. She wasn't his girlfriend. God willing, she might be someday. But not yet.

The next minutes passed in a whirlwind of names and faces as he introduced her to pockets of his friends and associates. Finally, they approached a smaller group standing together on the other side of the pool. "Hey, everyone, I'd like to introduce you to a friend of mine. This is Leta Breckenridge. Her mother is in a long-term care facility for patients suffering from dementia."

"I'm Hank." One of the guys extended a hand. "Sorry about your mom. That's rough."

A woman who looked about Leta's age gave her a sympathetic look. "Yeah, we know how difficult it is on the families and loved ones."

She and Nate joined in their discussion about the incredible amount of funding it takes to house a patient over years of decline. How debilitating the disease was not only on the patients but also on the families who loved them.

"The work we do at the Institute of Brain Sciences is targeted to slow the progression of these types of diseases, allowing patients to remain in their homes for as long as possible," Nate explained. "Even so, when I'm elected governor, I'll work to make sure the funding is there to help families so they have more choices in care options."

Leta made a mental note. This would be a good piece of information to pass along to Jane and Bernard — innocuous talking points that he'd made public many times. Certainly nothing anyone could turn around and use against him in the campaign.

She tensed, remembering her attendance was serving a dual purpose, one of which she would never want to acknowledge. Not to this crowd, or anyone else, for that matter.

These days it was becoming more difficult to lay her head on the pillow each night and close her eyes believing she'd made the world a better place.

It was definitely time to update her résumé and do everything possible to transition into a new opportunity. Maybe she could come up with some way to explain her short time of employment with the Ladd Agency that wouldn't hinder prospective employers' evaluation of her. The idea lifted her spirits, and for the first time in days she felt clean and hopeful.

She and Nate mingled several more minutes before a man's voice interrupted the gentle music streaming from the outdoor speakers. "Attention, everyone. Could y'all take a moment and give me your attention?" Porter Wyatt stood near the waterfall feature that spilled into the lighted pool. Nate's mother was by his side. So was Tiffany.

"Son, could you come and join us?" Porter scanned the crowd, looking for Nate.

Nathan raised his hand. "I'm here," he hollered, then squeezed her arm briefly and gave her an apologetic look before making his way through the crowd toward them, leaving her with his friends from the institute.

His mother took the microphone. "Porter and I want to again thank everyone for being here tonight. Thirty-seven years ago, on a Tuesday summer night much like this one, a white-capped nurse at University Medical Center handed me a tightly wrapped little guy with dark hair and said, 'See those wide-open eyes? I can tell this one is going to change the world.' " Her voice cracked just a little as she said this. "And now, with the help of people like you, Nathan will take one more step on the path to that destiny."

The crowd applauded.

Nate leaned into the mike. "Everyone who knows my mother also knows she'll turn even a birthday party into a campaign event." She waved him off, and he turned and kissed her cheek. "Let's give a hand to

271

the best host and hostess, and the best parents, any man can ask for."

More applause rang out.

"Seriously, though, you people are my closest friends and associates. The months ahead will be tough. Despite great optimism, pulling off a win is not going to be easy. I hope to make you all proud."

The humility revealed in Nate's impromptu speech was one of many reasons Leta couldn't seem to keep her heart from leaping over the edge. She allowed herself to admit the obvious. Her attraction to this man was in irreversible free fall. Which terrified her. All she could do was hope the inevitable landing would not break her.

Everyone was ushered to a separate outdoor area where they would be dining at linen-draped long tables. Overhead, strings of lights gave the heavy night air a festive feel.

With everyone seated, Nate's stepfather blessed the food, and the meal began.

The woman next to her picked up her salad fork. "So, how do you know the senator?" she asked while scooping a bite of arugula with pine nuts and pears.

Leta smiled at the middle-aged blonde, wondering how exactly to define her relationship with Nate. "We're friends. We met in . . . uh, we met in the parking lot of Central Market over on North Lamar."

"I love Central Market! I shop the Westgate store. They have the best fresh fish you can find around Austin. I'm Barb Franklin, by the way." She turned to the man beside her. "And my husband Neal. We've known the family for years. Since Nathan was in high school with our son."

"Your son and Nathan are also friends?"

A look of pain flashed across the woman's face. "They were. Our son passed away several years ago."

"Oh, I'm so sorry."

Over dinner, Leta learned the couple's son had been a year younger than Nate. Sadly, he'd died at age twenty from a rare disease that affected the cells of his brain.

"Specifically, the disease affects the myelin sheath, the material that surrounds and protects nerve cells," Neal explained. "Damage to this sheath slows down or blocks messages between the brain and the rest of the body."

Barb reached for her water goblet. "Most of these diseases, known as leukodystrophies, have no known cures. The Institute of Brain Sciences is heading up a major research project where they test bone marrow transplantation as a treatment." She

273

reached for her husband's hand. "We're hopeful no other parents ever face losing a son in that manner." She hesitated. "Governor Holiday, on the other hand, cut funding for an annual symposium that had been in place for nearly a decade, a state-sponsored event where some of the most brilliant minds from across the country gathered in a week-long effort to produce innovative solutions to these health issues." She shook her head. "Instead he funded an extravagant effort to boost bass fishing tournaments, including a website and social media campaign. Never mind his largest political donor loves to bass fish."

Neal quickly added, "It's why we've donated heavily to Nate's campaign. He's made these issues a priority, not only in his efforts in the private sector, but he's worked while in government to fund this important research."

"We'd do anything to help him win this election," Barb confided.

"You're not alone in that sentiment," Leta said. "Nate's a remarkable man."

"Yes, that he is." The woman leaned in closer. "And we understand from his mother he may be getting married soon."

Leta's heart skipped a beat.

Before she could respond, Nate's mother

stood at the head table and clinked her glass. "Excuse me, everyone. Before we serve the cake, I have a little surprise." One of the servers handed her a pretty box wrapped in a bright red bow. "No, Nathan. This is not for you, dear. Your gift will come later." She turned to Tiffany, who was seated next to Nate. "Tiffany, could you stand, dear?"

A server motioned to Leta's empty plate. "May I?" he whispered.

She nodded, then quickly turned her attention back to Nate's mom and Tiffany. An uneasiness formed on Nate's face, like he had no idea what his mom might be up to.

His mother handed the package to Tiffany. "Dear, I want you to have this."

Tiffany's eyebrows lifted. She smiled broadly and took the gift, thanking Vera profusely.

"Open it," Vera urged. She smiled widely back out at the crowd.

Tiffany did as she was instructed and busied her hands untying the bow. When she opened the tiny box and saw what was inside, her hand immediately went to her mouth.

Nate's mother grinned. "That diamond brooch has been in my family for generations, given as an engagement gift to my great-great-grandmother, one of the founding members of the Daughters of the Republic of Texas, or the Lone Star Republic, as it was known back then."

The scene playing out up front left Leta gaping. From the looks of things, if Nathan's mother had her way, the next invitation she received might very well be to Nate's wedding.

Beside her, Barb's hand went to her chest. "Oh my. Isn't that endearing?"

She nodded, never taking her eyes from Nate standing up there next to Tiffany. "Yes, that's . . . um, really nice," she answered, and was happy to hear that her voice came out calm and even.

28

Nathan turned after shutting the door behind the final guest. "Mother, what were you thinking?" he exploded, not caring to hide his anger. "That move was wholly inappropriate." He'd never spoken to his mother in that tone, but this time she'd gone entirely too far.

Porter rubbed his chin. "Dear, I have to say I agree with Nathan. That stunt was clearly designed to imply Tiffany will soon be part of the family, and we both know Nate has not told us he's ready to make that move."

Vera lifted her chin, unrepentant. "Oh, you both know I only implied the inevitable."

"How do you know that?" Nate argued. "No one but you has claimed my marrying Tiffany is inevitable. Never have I made that assertion, nor am I ready to." He shook his head, dumbfounded that his mother would put him in such a tenuous position, especially at such a critical juncture in his election bid. "Tonight you created not only a political nightmare but a personal one as well."

He'd seen the look on Leta's face. A look that may have explained why she'd left the party soon after, bidding him a wooden goodbye.

Porter diplomatically placed his hand on the small of his wife's back. "You've got to see the boy's point, Vera. Can't you see he's not ready to commit?"

His mother waved both of them off. "Tiffany Shea is from a good family and has extraordinary connections. You've been seeing her for several years. Clearly you think a lot of her. Nathan, what more could you possibly need to make this fine woman your wife?" She walked across the foyer, removing her earrings.

Nate clenched his fists. There was simply no getting through to her. "I need to know I love her!" he nearly yelled.

His mother startled as if he'd just shattered her favorite heirloom bowl. She kicked off her heels and took a deep breath, a frown etched across her face. "Oh, I see," she said slowly. "Well, all right then, I apologize. Clearly you'd not made your feelings under-

278

stood prior to this evening. Son, you've sent a very mixed message — not only to me but to that lovely girl who obviously believes you've reached clarity in this relationship and are ready to commit."

He sighed, knowing her passive-aggressive move was the best he was going to get. He'd made his point and knew there was no need to belabor his position. Still, he demanded a clear understanding going forward. "Mother, I appreciate all you and Porter did this evening. The party was thoughtful, and you know I love you. But this is a line you are never again to cross. Do you understand?"

Porter looked at her too, waiting.

Her body stiffened beneath the flowing orange-colored top, a sign she wasn't ready to give in entirely. "Son, I accept your need to sort out your feelings for Tiffany. But you know me better than to skirt the edges of an issue. Let's talk about the real problem here." She let herself fold into the cushions of a nearby sofa. "I'm truly exhausted, but this is a conversation that must not wait." She patted the seat beside her, and he sat. "Porter, be a dear and get me some ice water with lemon. I'm parched."

Without any hesitation, his stepfather did her bidding.

His mother placed her heavily jeweled hand on his arm. "Nathan, who is this girl who has suddenly come into the picture?"

"I don't know what you're talking about, Mother." He felt her watching him, the same way she did when he was a boy. Only he was not a child and he wouldn't be coerced into a discussion he wasn't prepared to have. "You are clearly deflecting, wanting to turn the glare of the spotlight in another direction," he told her, smiling for good measure. He wasn't born yesterday. And he was far too tired to have this conversation.

She slowly pulled her arm back. "Nathan, I want to show you something. Come with me."

She stood. Without waiting for him to answer, she made her way to the sweeping staircase and hurried up, despite her age and bare feet. Near the top, she turned and looked down. "Well, are you coming?"

He sighed, wondering what he'd done to deserve this punishment. Regardless, he lifted off the sofa and followed.

To the right of the door leading to her and Porter's bedroom suite was the entrance to her private study. She waved him inside.

"What about Porter?" Nate asked. "Didn't you send him for water?"

"My husband didn't go for water," she

said simply before moving behind her desk, where she opened a drawer and retrieved what looked like a small photo album. Her fingers flipped to a certain page with little effort. "Here, take a look."

He took the album. "What's this?"

She waited while he looked over a black-and-white photograph of a man in cuffed dress pants and a white shirt. Despite the casual way his sleeves were rolled up, his demeanor was serious, like the world had landed on his shoulders and he was bound and determined to hold up under the weight.

"Who is this?" he asked, his curiosity getting the best of him.

"That man was to be my husband."

Nate's eyebrows shot up. "Your husband? What . . . ?"

Her fingers went to the back of her hair. "Yes, I was engaged prior to meeting your father. His name was Ben Simpson."

"Ben Simpson? Of Simpson Media?"

His mother nodded. "Yes, that one."

Nate drew a deep breath, trying to assimilate the information he'd just learned. His mother had been engaged to the owner of the largest news conglomerate in North America. He'd died . . . what, only about five years back?

"You were engaged to Simpson?" he asked again, just to clarify.

"Don't be a bore, Son. You heard me the first time."

He ran his hand against the side of his face. "Why are you telling me this now?"

"Sit." She pointed to a chair. "I'm not the kind of woman to kiss and tell, even after all these years. All that is apropos to this current situation is this: It was August 12, 1972. I had a ring on my finger and a local seamstress was already altering my white gown when I let a girlfriend talk me into going to see a concert at the Armadillo. That night, Willie Nelson walked onto the stage in front of a crowd of rednecks and hippies, and Austin's musical landscape changed forever. More importantly, it was the night I met your father."

Nate wanted to sound lighthearted, tease her — ask which camp his father had fallen into, hippie or redneck. The pallor of unease etched across his mother's face drove him to simply ask, "What happened?"

"The details are not important." She stood and moved to the window. After gazing out at the darkness for several moments, she slowly turned. "I want you to know I loved your father." Her lips grew tight with purpose. "But there have been times I

282

wonder how different things might have been."

"Mom —"

She held up her open palm. "No, this is important, and you need to hear it." She squared her shoulders. "One slight turn, one momentary decision, can alter your course. One type of existence exterminated and replenished with another without any conscious design."

"What do you mean? Dad loved you. Now so does Porter. You have a good life," he argued.

"Ah yes, I do. But different than what might have been, nonetheless."

She seemed to be on the verge of saying something else, but Nate stopped her by shaking his head, signaling she was being completely ridiculous.

But of course his mother wasn't being ridiculous at all. "Son, choices matter."

In those few words, they both knew she'd sliced to the very heart of the matter.

"Tiffany's a strong woman. She'll recover from a slight indiscretion of the heart. But you might not." His mother's face softened. "Infatuation is fickle, Nathan. And when early attraction wears off — and I promise you whatever you currently feel for this new girl will wear off eventually — you may well realize that the two of you have very little in common." She placed her hand on his arm. "Tiffany is a smart woman. She'll soon see what I've noticed, if she hasn't already." She gave him a pat and guided him to the door. "In life, there are rarely do-overs. Choose wisely, Son."

Nate gunned the gas pedal, appreciating the feline purr of his car engine as he rounded a bend on the way home from the party.

With the top down, there was nothing between him and the clear night sky filled with stars. He only wished his own thoughts were as unclouded.

While his mother had been dead wrong in her approach, he couldn't escape her wisdom. She was entirely correct about one very important matter.

No doubt it was time to convey to Tiffany he'd made a choice — and the sooner the better.

He picked up his cell phone and dialed Leta's number.

When she answered, he swallowed his sudden case of nerves. "Leta?"

"Yes?" She didn't sound that surprised to hear from him.

"Look, I need you to understand something." He paused, trying to find the right words to convey his jumbled thoughts. How could he possibly make her understand what he had only recently dared to comprehend himself? He swallowed and rushed on. "Leta, I really like you."

"We're . . . uh, friends. I like you too."

"No, I — I mean, we're more than friends. I don't want you to misunderstand what went on tonight. With Tiffany, I mean."

His mother's words rang out in his mind. *Choose wisely.*

"I'm not sure I know what it is you're trying to tell me." She sounded confused.

Indeed. He too was confused.

"Look, we need to talk. Alone and in person. I'm scheduled to leave in the morning for Dallas, but when I get back, can we meet somewhere? Talk?"

Say something, he thought.

After several agonizing seconds, her voice finally came through the phone. "Sure, I'd really like that."

29

"That should do it," Jane said from her place at the head of the conference table. "We all have a lot of work ahead this coming week."

A heaviness settled over Leta as she gathered her notes. Monday morning staff meetings were always a bit grueling, but never more than today, as she knew what was ahead. Despite her jangled nerves, she tried to focus on the information that had been reported back to the entire team that morning. Bernard took copious notes, like a bony dog hoping for any morsel to gobble.

Thankfully, Bernard and Jane seemed to buy the sanitized information Leta had reported this morning. She'd handed over a partial guest list, repeated some overheard conversations that were of no real consequence. It gave her no small amount of pleasure to pass on Nate's magnanimous speech. The grimace on Bernard's face was priceless.

There were, of course, things she didn't reveal.

Even before receiving that surprise telephone call from Nate, she'd decided Friday night at Nate's party that she could no longer remain connected to an organization planning on hurting his campaign. Not after talking with the Franklins and hearing the story of their son. Not when considering her mother's rapid decline and the pain she shared with so many families just like her. And certainly not when she'd learned how Governor Holiday's priorities were so skewed on these critical health issues.

Her mother always said that if you did what was right, God would do the rest.

While doing so felt like jumping off a cliff, deep inside she knew she had to resign. Not to do so at this juncture was far too risky — politically and personally.

But first she wanted to say goodbye to Erin. Of all her co-workers, she was one Leta would really miss. She didn't have many girlfriends because of her compact schedule, and Erin was certainly someone she'd enjoyed getting to know.

Back on the floor that housed Operation Brainchild, she made her way down the space in between two long tables lined with keyboards and monitors, stepping over bundled cables taped to the floor, until she stood at her friend's workstation. "Hey, Erin."

The woman startled and pulled the head-phones from her ears. "Goodness, Leta. You shouldn't sneak up like that."

"Sorry," she whispered, feeling her stomach tighten. "I just wanted to let you know I'm heading down to Jane's office to resign."

"Quit? Why would you do that?"

Erin's curt tone took Leta by surprise.

"It's too long a story to go into right now," she explained, keeping her voice low. "But I hope we can go to lunch sometime soon. Maybe then I can explain a bit more."

"Yeah, sure." Erin quickly glanced around before slipping her earphones back in place. She briefly nodded and returned her attention back to a speech Nate had given last week at a Flag Day celebration in the VA Medical Center in Amarillo.

Leta tried to justify Erin's slight as she rode the elevator to the fourth floor. By resigning, she would no longer be part of the team. Her decision also signaled a rejection of Operation Brainchild and its mission. Of course those factors would alter her relationship with Erin.

Still, she felt the loss.

Leta stepped off the elevator and into the reception area, remembering months earlier when she'd done the same and broken her heel. A lump formed in her throat. Despite knowing she was doing the right thing, she'd had dreams of a bright future with the Ladd Agency. Now those dreams were dashed.

The receptionist looked up from behind the counter and immediately smiled. "Welcome back, Leta. How's the upper floor treating you?"

She shrugged and tried to hide the fact that every cell in her body was shaking from nerves. She only wanted to get this over with.

"Could you check and see if Jane is available?"

Leta felt Elaine's scrutiny as the woman's gaze moved to her face. "Anything wrong?"

She tried to appear nonchalant. "I just need a minute or two."

Elaine continued to stare as her fingers went to the phone set. "Jane? I have Leta Breckenridge here to see you. Are you free?" She looked across the counter and nodded in Leta's direction. "You can go back."

Leta summoned all the courage she could muster and walked down the hall and lightly tapped on Jane's office door.

"Come in," she said when Leta peeked her head inside.

She willed her knees to quit shaking as she came forward. She slid her security badge and parking tag across the desk.

Jane raised her eyebrows. "What's this?"

Leta swallowed what felt like shredded wood. "I'm afraid I'm going to have to resign. While I've loved working for you and the Ladd Agency, I'm just not comfortable with the work I'm now being asked to do as part of Operation Brainchild." Before she could lose her nerve, she hurried on. "You see, I know Nate — Senator Emerson. He's a friend. I thought I could go to a party like the one over the weekend and report back, but frankly, I now realize my conscience just doesn't line up that way."

Jane leaned back in her chair and steepled her fingers. "I see," she said slowly.

"Even more, I support Senator Emerson's political endeavors. I can't see fit to spend my days trying to hurt that effort."

Jane's eyes narrowed. "Anything else?"

The woman's abrupt manner was not exactly unexpected, but a part of Leta's insides melted just the same. Jane had extended an offer for employment at a time when Leta was in real financial trouble and had no job prospects. She'd felt so validated when this woman had praised her work.

"Jane, please know how grateful I am for the opportunity you gave me," she said, trying to soften the impact of her resignation. "The compensation was extraordinary, and I'm truly sorry to have to move on."

When Jane didn't respond right away, she felt compelled to add, "Thank you for everything. Really."

"You're making a mistake." Jane's voice was now filled with undeniable disdain. "Opportunities like what I granted you don't just fall from the sky. You are absolutely correct. I took a risk on someone off the street with no degree, no work history to speak of. I believed you might have the ability to foster thoughts and ideas well beyond what is normally seen in someone of your age and background. This decision of yours shows I clearly miscalculated your intellect." She stood. "Believe me, you are throwing away a career that might have taken you far."

Jane's demeanor turned hard as cement. "I will remind you of the confidentiality agreement you signed. Your work with Bernard is of an extremely sensitive nature. We can't tolerate any violation of that agreement without instituting legal ramifications."

"I understand," Leta confirmed, feeling like she might throw up at any minute. "I won't be disclosing anything about my work."

"Or that Operation Brainchild even exists."

Leta sobered considerably. Of course they would have this concern. She should have thought about that and addressed the issue up front. "You don't have to worry."

Jane shifted her gaze away from Leta and lifted a file from her desk. "We'll have your final check in the mail. That's all."

And with that, she knew she was dismissed.

"Okay, yeah. Thank you again." Leta let out the breath she hadn't realized she'd been holding and headed out the open door.

Elaine never looked up as she moved for the elevator.

In the parking lot, she tilted her head toward the sky now dark with storm clouds. As she crossed the sweltering asphalt, she tried not to second-guess her decision. She'd done the right thing, and she would land on her feet again, she told herself.

In the meantime, Mike had told her he'd load her up with hours at Central Market. "I can't guarantee forty hours every week, but I'll keep you busy. And maybe I can up your salary a bit. How's that?" he offered.

"Thanks, Mike. I appreciate anything you can do. Just to be on the up-and-up here, I will still be looking for another career-level position. Is that okay?"

"That's fine," he assured her. "You just tell me what you need and I'll make sure the schedule allows for you to have time off to interview. Customers love you, and the department always makes a profit when you're running the shop. We're glad to have you for as long as you can be here."

Thankfully, she'd saved a considerable sum in the months she'd worked for the Ladd Agency. That, coupled with her small raise at Central Market, would allow her to meet her obligations until she could land something else, especially now with her mom's account at Heritage House current. She'd just have to be really careful financially and not spend a dime over her budget.

True, she'd likely never land a position that would replicate her salary at the Ladd Agency. At least not anytime soon. But in the big scheme of things, that didn't matter.

She could now look herself in the mirror without feeling shame.

Jane Ladd threw the file she was holding across the room, scattering the contents.

She balled her fists and punched out Bernard's extension on her phone set.

A click sounded, then his voice. "Yeah?"

"We have a problem."

There were a few seconds of silence. "And?"

"We miscalculated Leta Breckenridge and her need for financial security."

"What do you mean?"

"I mean, the girl's conscience kicked in."

Bernard coughed. "Not entirely unexpected." Before she could argue, he quickly added, "Which is why I have a contingency plan."

30

With the primaries over, Nathan's run for governor took center stage, as did the need to be out on the road selling his ideas for change to Texans.

Unlike his earlier bid for a senate seat, which had been limited to District 14 and Travis County, a statewide election would encompass much more travel and personal appearances at events across the state.

Nathan clipped up the steps into the campaign bus, feeling buoyed by the response of a crowd of veterans and their families at an event held at VFW Post 7835. These supporters clearly connected with his narration that government leaders needed to be men and women of deep character, that the climate of the state and even the country was plummeting because of a severe deficit of principles in politics.

They all agreed his was a very important voice that needed to be heard.

As he entered the bus, his staffers broke into applause. Janesa Morgan grinned and waited several seconds before she stood and held up her hand. "Okay, everyone. That's what we're talking about." His campaign manager had to project loudly to be heard over the high school band that played outside the bus windows. "This is only the beginning of the political earthquake that is going to shake Wyndall Holiday and his tired and predictable malarkey out of the governor's office."

This met with enthusiastic nods from those sitting at the tables and sofas, armed with iPads and Bluetooth devices.

People didn't like to think of elections as armed combat, but of course they were. Make no mistake, Nathan Emerson had declared war on the Holiday era, and the people on this bus were his foot soldiers. Janesa Morgan, his general.

In the early stages of forming his campaign strategy, it was Janesa who assembled a think tank comprised of the best talent she could find to create a brand that would connect with Texas voters. These creative minds came up with a winning salvo.

NATE EMERSON — A HEART AND MIND FOR TEXAS.

Each time he walked across a stage to a

podium and microphone, in the background played "Deep in the Heart of Texas," including the soundtrack *clap-clap-clap-clap.* A bit corny, but an immense hit with focus groups from the key voting sectors across the state.

These epistles were meant to convey his integrity and sense of wanting to make Texas a better place to work, play, and raise a family. Together with his past voting record, these strategies had polled well and would hopefully march him up the steps of the state capitol and into the office of the governor.

Fund-raising was headed up by a former college buddy. Colin McElroy could be trusted to handle his mother, who would no doubt be attempting to supervise every aspect of his campaign, but especially the money. Behind the scenes, of course.

Nate grabbed a Dr Pepper from the bus refrigerator and slid into a seat opposite Janesa. "Okay, so what's on the agenda for Dallas?"

"I've loaded your specific talking points." She handed him an iPad. "You'll notice a slight difference in the message for Tarrant versus Dallas County, primarily economic focus. Except for that adjustment, just keep to our general theme and we'll have a repeat of what you just pulled off here in Granbury."

He nodded and checked his watch.

"You have time to catch a quick break. Why don't you go back and try to sleep? I'll make sure to wake you in plenty of time to get ready for the rally. We have a full few days ahead, and you'll appreciate the rest, even if brief."

"Yeah, the high is wearing off, and I am growing tired." He patted her shoulder as she returned to her Mac, her fingers already clicking away on the keyboard. "Catch you in a few."

He retreated to the back of the bus where a full-size bed awaited. Good intentions of refreshing himself with some sleep were short-lived, however. As soon as his head hit the pillow, his mind raced forward.

After his speech at the American Airlines Center, he would be taking Tiffany to dinner. She was in Dallas for a deposition, which conveniently allowed them some time together.

He'd texted her after the birthday party, but their schedules had crisscrossed and this was the first time they'd been able to connect in person.

While he hated to admit his mother was right, he'd done a lot of thinking and knew he needed to officially end their relationship.

He did need to make a choice.

About Tiff, certainly.

More importantly, he needed to finally admit that he couldn't seem to chase Leta Breckenridge from his mind.

The Friday night crowd at Five Sixty was loud and happy. Conversation flowed easily as patrons enjoyed the panoramic views of the Dallas skyline from the top of Reunion Tower.

He'd much prefer a good steak and baked potato, but he remembered Tiffany had raved about this place after the last time she'd stayed in Dallas, how she'd loved the Asian-influenced cuisine and the illuminated glass bar and lounge area.

Tiffany glanced across the table at him and frowned. "What's up with you tonight, Nate? You've barely cracked a smile since we got here."

"Finally able to quit smiling," he explained with a forced brightness in his voice. "I've been cheerful since five this morning."

"I hadn't thought of that." She reached a manicured hand over the polished enamel table and touched the back of his hand. "I've missed you."

She was such a great girl, he thought wistfully. Early in their relationship they'd been together in the greenroom of KVUE, the local ABC news station in Austin. She was scheduled to do a segment on the Austin city council's proposed Climate Protection Plan and how the targeted levels of emission reductions would affect local businesses.

Her passion was contagious, her advocacy sharp and well thought out. He remembered watching her on the monitor and thinking she was incredible. And beautiful.

Apparently, she'd been as interested in him.

He finished his interview and left the hot lights of the studio to find she'd waited for him.

"If you feel that impassioned about your health cause, you need to do something about it."

"Excuse me?"

"You heard me. It's easy to spout political views, but a whole other thing to actually step up and do something that changes the way government funds are allocated," she challenged.

"I beg your pardon. I do a lot." He pointed back at the studio door. "I happen to be really good at influencing and changing the way people think. It's really a matter of education."

She grinned. "Oh, phooey. Real change happens when you insert yourself into the process, when you position yourself as a decision maker. It's why lobbyist organizations pay hundreds of thousands to get in front of elected officials — the ones who decide how everything is run by wielding power the rest of us don't have."

"Is that so?"

Her eyes twinkled. "Don't believe me? Run for office and prove I'm wrong."

The truth was simple. He wouldn't be running for governor today if it hadn't been for Tiffany.

Even so, he fought the urge to pull his hand back. Instead he cleared his throat and simply moved past her comment about missing him. "How'd the deposition go?"

She gave him a hesitant look, withdrew her hand from his, and leaned back in her chair. "Well, this is one where I wished I was sitting on the plaintiff's side of the table."

Nate reached for his water goblet. "How so?"

"It's clear that opposing counsel is setting up to seek class action status. Frankly, I think the complainants would be awarded a favorable ruling. While we have seismologists who will assert an existing fault line is to blame, the timing of the gas drilling in the area certainly suggests the actions of our clients may be a contributing factor. I think the whole case will come down to allocation of liability."

He pulled the goblet to his lips and paused before taking a drink. "Sounds like protracted litigation."

Tiffany shrugged. "Not exactly a bad thing," she said with a slight grin. She leaned forward and picked up her menu. "Are you going to let me order for you?"

"Do I dare?"

Ignoring his remark, she waved over a waiter. "I think we're ready here." She handed off the menu to a man in a crisp white linen jacket that was buttoned down the front. "We'll start off with some salt and pepper calamari and pot stickers with dan dan sauce. Follow that with orders of your lacquered Chinese duckling and lapsong sausage fried rice." She turned to Nate. "Do you think we'll want dessert?" Before he could respond, she turned back to their waiter. "I think we'll end our meal with a chocolate martini in lieu of anything off the dessert menu, but check back with us. Okay?"

Their waiter nodded. "Yes, ma'am."

She looked back at Nate then. "What?"

"Do you always know exactly what you want?"

She tilted her head. "I'm not sure what you mean."

He groaned inside. "That. Is there ever a time you feel unsure of yourself? Ever not know which direction to go, what to say, where to turn?"

Tiffany looked at him like he was crazy. Which gave him his answer.

He'd meant to wait until after dinner, but he'd just opened up a discussion he couldn't pull back from.

She seemed to sense it too and picked up her chopsticks as if they were weapons. "If you have something you want to say, I suggest you be direct."

He heard her attorney voice, but not before he noticed her fingers tremble slightly as she tightened her grip on the sticks. While he'd wrestled with what he wanted to say, even rehearsed exactly how he would begin, his carefully chosen words failed him now.

This time he was the one who reached across the table. He took her hand in his. "You know you matter to me —"

She pulled back, the look in her eyes so raw it took him by surprise. "But?"

He swallowed. "But I don't think I'm being entirely fair."

The waiter reappeared at their table, his arms laden with small platters. He placed them on the table. "Your entrées will be out soon."

Nate thanked him while Tiffany simply stared out the windows. The setting sun filled the vista with color, a hue similar to that of orange sherbet.

"Tiffany," he said, trying to return to their earlier discussion.

She held up her palm. "That girl, Leta Breckenridge. Did you know she works for Holiday's camp?"

He stopped short. "What?"

"It's true. She's employed by the Ladd Agency, which is really just a front for Holiday's oppo machine."

Now it was his turn to stare. "Why are you bringing up Leta?"

"Why am I talking about Leta?" The look in Tiffany's eyes sharpened. "Are you serious?"

"I'm not sure what you're implying, but—"

"Don't Clinton me! This girl may not be an intern in a little blue dress, but somehow she's pulled a Monica. You keep this little infatuation up and she'll take you down.

You're not as bright as I thought if you somehow missed that fine point."

He tossed his napkin to the table. "Now you're being ridiculous!"

"Am I?" She pulled her iPhone from her bag and worked her thumbs furiously over the face. "Here. I'm forwarding Bernard Geisler's number." She huffed and pushed the phone back into her purse. "Next time she's looking at you with those doe eyes, I dare you to ask how she knows him."

"Tiffany —"

She stood. "Goodbye, Nate." Without saying anything more, she turned and walked away.

31

Leta parked her car outside Heritage House and made her way to the entrance. Inside, the lobby was festooned with red, white, and blue bunting and miniature flags. Every season was celebrated here at her mother's residential center, and none more than Independence Day. Perhaps because freedom meant so much when contrasted with those trapped inside their own minds.

Lucy waved from across the lobby. "Hey, Leta."

She waved back at the red-haired nurse and moved in her direction. "Lucy, do you have a minute?"

"Sure thing, sugar. What's up?"

Leta placed her hand on the arm of the woman's uniform smock printed with tiny pink flamingos and guided her away from the noise of a running vacuum.

"Is everything all right?" Lucy asked with a concerned look on her face.

"Oh yes," Leta assured her. She leaned close and lowered her voice. "I was just wondering, have you guys hired a new cleaning lady lately?" The identity of the person who had infiltrated her world and reported back to Bernard Geisler might not change anything, but Leta had a deep desire to avoid her sharing anything more with that man.

"Cleaning personnel? Hmm . . . let me think. Well, yes. Now that you mention it, we hired a woman a few weeks back. She didn't work out, though. Quit after only a couple of days."

Leta took a deep breath. "So she's gone now?"

The nurse nodded. "Yup. Heard she never even showed up for her check."

"Oh, okay. Thanks. That's what I needed to know." Leta couldn't help but still be a bit worried. The fact she'd been spied on was no small thing. She turned and headed in the direction of the hallway that would take her to her mom's room.

"Uh, honey . . . we had to move your momma."

Leta turned. "Move her? Where?"

"New management made some changes. All patients are now doubled up." As Lucy neared, she leaned close and whispered,

"These folks are very profit-driven. Doubling up the rooms allows for more patients — and more revenue," she confided.

"They didn't check with the families first?" Leta thought about how any change of environment created havoc for these patients. Especially in her mother's case. "Not even a phone call?"

Lucy slowly shook her head. "They're even trying to cut our salaries."

Leta patted the woman's arm in a show of solidarity. "Oh, Lucy. I'm so sorry. That's not right."

The red-haired nurse squared her shoulders. "You got that on the nose. I love working here at Heritage House, but it's a lot of heartbreak. You know? Patients like your mother become like family to us. Their struggle is hard to watch sometimes." She glanced up at the security cameras in the lobby and shrugged. "But what are you gonna do?"

Leta gave her another pat before moving to the receptionist at the front desk. Someone new. "Can you tell me what room Sylvia Breckenridge is now in?"

A young brunette looked up from her computer. "Who?" The bored-looking girl went on chewing her gum.

"Sylvia Breckenridge. My mother." Leta

tried not to let her impatience show while wondering what had happened to the former receptionist who did such a great job.

"Just a minute." The girl clicked on her keyboard.

"Uh, you're new here, aren't you?"

The brunette shrugged. "Yup, just started Monday. Oh, here it is. Room 5C. Fourth floor, south wing."

Leta made a mental note and headed for the elevators, not particularly liking all the changes around here. Everyone, including the staff, had always been so proficient and friendly. If wages had been cut, good people would be forced to seek employment elsewhere.

The elevator dinged and the doors opened.

Inside stood an older woman with short-cropped white hair and a square jaw. She wore a tailored black pantsuit with a name tag that read *Penny Murdock, Director.*

Leta greeted her with a smile and joined her. "Hello," she said with her hand extended. "You must be the new director?"

The woman's hands remained clasped in front of her. She frowned. "Excuse me, but where are you going?"

Leta blinked. "What? I — I'm going to visit my mother. Why?"

"Not without a visitor pass." Ms. Murdock jammed at the bank of buttons to the right of the doors and waited for them to slide open. "Come with me," she ordered.

Leta didn't have a choice. The new director placed her hand on Leta's back and nearly shoved her back to the front desk.

"You let a guest upstairs without a visitor's pass?"

The brunette looked up. "Oh, sorry. Yeah, I forgot."

Ms. Murdock's face morphed from stone to granite. She reached over the counter and snatched a clip-on tag from a basket. "What's your name?"

"Uh, Leta Breckenridge."

"And the patient you wish to visit?" she demanded.

Leta rubbed the back of her head. "Sylvia Breckenridge. She's my mother," she added for good measure.

Apparently the information was sufficient because the woman thrust a pass in her direction. "Clip this on, and don't forget to turn it back in before you leave the premises." Ms. Murdock turned back to the receptionist. "And you. Get your things. You're relieved of your duties."

The girl frowned. "Relieved of my duties? What does that mean?"

The director sighed and looked at the ceiling. "Your employment is terminated."

"I'm fired? Man, that's not fair." She stood and slammed a file across the counter. She grabbed her purse from a drawer. "This place sucked anyway."

The new director looked back at Leta. "Anything else?"

"Uh, no. I'm good." She slowly backed away and headed toward the elevators for a second time, wondering again about the changes she was seeing. Edith Styles had been a no-nonsense woman, but she'd never acted like a drill sergeant.

Despite Ms. Murdock's unfriendliness, Leta hoped her fastidious nature would serve the patient population well. If that were the case, Leta could overlook a bit of rudeness.

When the elevator doors opened onto the fourth floor, Leta stepped out and glanced around, not sure which direction to go. A directory on the wall showed her mother's new room was to the left, so she headed that way and within minutes stood before a door marked 5C. She tapped lightly before slowly moving the door open and peeking inside. "Mom?"

Immediately, she was met with gunfire blaring from a television mounted on the

311

wall. While the room was dark, Leta could make out that an episode of *CSI* was being broadcast with a volume far higher than needed.

An elderly woman in a pink housecoat sat in a rocking chair, gliding back and forth at a rapid pace. "Wheeee . . ." She clapped her hands every time a gun fired in the chase scene.

Leta quickly moved for the remote on the table next to her. "Do you mind?" she shouted over the loud commotion and turned down the volume. The rocking woman didn't seem to notice.

Leta quickly glanced around the darkened room.

That's when she saw her.

Against the far wall, her mother was huddled in her bed with the covers tucked tightly against her chin. As Leta drew closer, she could hear her mom mutter her name over and over. "Leta. Leta. Leta. Leta."

Leta's gut wrenched. She dove for the bed and wrapped her arms around her mother's quaking shoulders. "Momma, I'm here. It's okay. I'm here." Angry tears burned in her eyes. "Shhh . . . shhhh. You're okay now. I'm here, Momma."

■ ■ ■ ■

Katie's eyes grew wide. "You're kidding, right?"

Leta shook her head. "No. I'm not."

Katie frowned. "That's outrageous. What did you do?"

Leta took a deep breath, remembering how she'd calmed her mother and then made a beeline for the administrative offices. "I cleaned that new Penny Murdock's clock, that's what I did."

"Who's Penny Murdock?"

She explained how Edith Styles had been let go when Heritage House had been sold to a new owner and told her roommate how the new director's personality could best be described as coarse, and that was on a good day.

"Did you know that place was even up for sale?"

"No, not prior to Edith telling me." Leta paced the kitchen. "You know, something's not right. I feel it in my gut."

"But you've always said such great things about where your mom lived and the people who cared for her."

"I know, but everything seems to be changing. Mona, our favorite nurse, isn't

there anymore either. They said she quit."
Her gut twisted. "I didn't even like leaving
my mom. But I didn't have a choice." She
chewed on her thumbnail.

Katie folded onto the sofa and tucked her
legs up. "Okay, but it's possible what you're
seeing is just a transition phase, and this
Murdock woman will eventually get everything straightened out. I mean, she fired
that receptionist on the spot when she let
you up without the proper security measures."

Leta shook her head. "You may be right. I
mean, it's possible. I guess time will tell."

The following day, Leta woke plagued by
the small sense of dread she'd wrestled with
while trying to get to sleep the night before.
What Katie suggested made sense. Heritage
House could simply be going through some
transition as the new owners and the director took over. Sure, profit was always going
to be a consideration. But she couldn't seem
to get Lucy's comments out of her mind —
about how profit-driven measures were
adversely affecting the patients and even the
staff.

She found herself wishing she could talk
all this over with Nathan. He'd been out on
the road campaigning since his birthday

party, and she missed him. It was crazy the way she'd allowed herself to feel toward him, especially after his phone call. They had connected easily and seemed to be able to talk for hours. She remembered how he looked at her, and the tiny thrill she felt every time their hands brushed against each other.

When he'd invited her to his birthday party, her spirits had soared, and she knew that their connection was not solely in her mind. She was indeed more than just his friend. Only time would tell where all this might lead, but she knew where she hoped their relationship would land.

She sighed. Her thoughts all sounded like a silly romance novel. And until she and Nate talked again, she wasn't entirely sure her story would have a happily ever after. Though she was delighted they seemed to be taking steps in that direction.

Even so, she'd done the right thing in resigning from the Ladd Agency. The move had cleared her conscience and left her free to join the efforts to elect Nathan as the next governor of Texas.

In fact, Nate might have insight into what was going on at Heritage House. He'd likely share her concern over finding her mom so frightened and unable to adjust to such sudden changes. He might even have some ideas on how to handle the matter.

Certainly, her outburst with Ms. Murdock had not won her any points.

Before she started contacting potential alternatives for her mother's care, Leta decided to call and ask Nathan's opinion. When he didn't answer, she left a message.

"Hey, Nate. It's Leta. Look, I know you're in the middle of a lot right now, with the campaign and all, but could you call me? I need to talk with you about something. It's kind of important. Thanks."

With just a little research, Leta learned there were seven facilities registered to care for Alzheimer patients within the Austin metro area and about half a dozen in nearby communities. Most of those were thirty or more miles away, so for now, Leta crossed those off her list of possibilities.

By noon, she'd made initial calls and learned only two of the seven had openings for new patients. Both were cost prohibitive, with fees that nearly doubled what she currently paid. Even with her mother's Medicare benefits, the cost was simply out of reach.

She was able to get on the list for a new facility scheduled to open next fall, at a cost she might be able to handle if she took on a second job again. That wouldn't solve the current situation if what she suspected were true and the changes at Heritage House extended past a simple transition period. If that ended up being the case, she'd need to have an alternate plan.

She closed her phone, trying not to think about how she'd left a six-figure salary behind. How she'd felt such elation when her life started turning around, and how her own integrity had forced her to leave her job at the Ladd Agency. As of right now, she was back where she started — needing a good job to support her mother's care.

Somehow, after she'd had a taste of what life could be like, facing a financial shortfall was worse this time around. It was as if she'd sampled fine escargot but was now back to eating canned tuna.

She glanced at her phone again, curious as to why Nate hadn't called her back. Anxious to reach him, she put caution aside and texted him.

Hey, I left a voice mail but not sure you got it. Could you call me when you have a minute? It's important.

By the following evening, she still hadn't heard from him. Which was strange, given the last time they'd talked.

Perhaps his campaign events had not allowed for a break. Maybe he couldn't catch any privacy to call her. She supposed his battery might be dead, or a number of other excuses could be at play and might answer for why he hadn't contacted her when she'd reached out.

A fragment of concern niggled at the back of her mind — what if there was a remote possibility he'd connected her with Bernard Geisler and Operation Brainchild?

If that were so, her worries would certainly extend much deeper than canned tuna.

32

Nate campaigned out on the road for nearly three weeks straight before he could finally return to Austin, where he'd be the guest of honor at a large Fourth of July barbeque sponsored by the Friends of Texas.

Hundreds attended the annual event held in Zilker Park, and this year would be no different.

Red, white, and blue bunting decorated a massive dais with the Colorado River as a backdrop. Media trucks lined Lou Neff Road, tucked behind rows of bright blue porta-potties.

On the opposite end, closer to the entrance, two eighteen-wheelers emblazoned with orange flames and decorated with longhorns stood nearly thirty feet tall. On board the trailers were open kitchens, each equipped with ten grills and a custom wood-fueled smoker large enough to cook two whole hogs and three hundred whole chickens. Enough to feed a hungry crowd.

Nate and his campaign staff hoped those attending would be just as hungry for what he had to say about budgets, the economy, and immigration issues.

Despite promising otherwise, Nate couldn't help himself. He scanned the crowds for a sign of a young woman with soft blonde hair and hope-filled eyes. A hope that had been phony, as it turned out.

He still could barely believe what he'd learned. Reluctantly he'd brought the news Tiffany had shared to his campaign manager. Janesa shared his concern and followed up.

Yes, Leta Breckenridge worked for the Ladd Agency.

She may have been a down-on-her-luck gal who needed help, but from all appearances, she'd been playing him like a chessboard, carefully maneuvering their encounters to gain access to private information, which she could then report back to some guy named Bernard Geisler to later use against him.

Leta had cashed in on her connection with him, and that betrayal changed everything.

Rarely did he misjudge someone's character. Certainly, this was an exception.

Janesa reported she'd recently resigned.

Perhaps she'd changed her mind.

It didn't matter. He had no business talking with Leta Breckenridge ever again. He only wished someone would clue in his heart.

The notion he could've fallen so easily for her was still a surprise. For several nights, he'd lain in bed and rehearsed the night they'd met, how vulnerable and upset she'd been after running into his car. She had no way of paying for the damage, and the haunted look on her face had drawn him in, causing him to want to erase her despair.

Could all that have been a ruse as well?

When they'd become friendly in the months following, he'd felt a profound connection to this girl. They had much in common, despite the fact their lives were so different. No one seemed to understand his heart more than she.

Nate shook his head.

That was what made him the most angry and hurt. He'd opened up and shared something of himself he'd not allowed many to see, especially no woman. Well, no one, really.

The very thought shook him to the core and nicked at his confidence. If Leta Breckenridge could dupe him, he was gullible to every person he met. Who could he even trust?

It often seemed everyone had disguised motives. Even his mother.

Yes, she loved him. He knew that. But a part of her was manipulating him, moving him to perform like a circus monkey. She lusted for power, the kind that came from high political places.

Her first husband, his father, had failed to come through for her before his life came to a tragic end. Now she'd shifted her expectations onto her only son.

Without meaning to, Tiffany had also created a lot of pressure, even promising to line up wealthy oil clients to endorse him as an enticement to get him to run.

While Tiff's recommendations were well researched and her efforts would've no doubt benefitted him politically, she'd never really understood the real him, even after nearly two years of dating.

He needed to shake all this off and focus on his campaign. A campaign that was not about winning to gain prestige. If elected governor, he wanted to use the position to make life better for his constituents.

That was the only reason he'd put himself through all this.

While it seemed those closest to him failed

to get his message, in a few minutes he'd climb the steps of the dais and position himself in front of the microphone, hoping to convey that very sentiment to a growing crowd of strangers who would soon cast their ballots.

With any luck at all, he'd win their votes.

Leta picked her way through throngs of people gathered in Zilker Park, hoping to catch a glimpse of Nate before he took the dais. She'd phoned and texted him, even left messages to call her — and nothing.

She worried he'd learned she hadn't been truthful with him about her involvement with the Ladd Agency, and that thought killed her inside.

A million times she'd tried to convince herself to just move on. Perhaps it was far better to part with a misunderstanding still between them than to try to insert herself into a world where she would never quite belong anyway.

The people in Nate's world were highly educated movers and shakers, and she was an ordinary girl who had never even finished college. For a short time she'd considered herself astute, but she wasn't. Not really. She'd even been gullible enough to believe Jane Ladd thought she was skilled, when the woman only wanted to use her to get information on Nathan.

Less than a year ago, she'd never given politics a minute of thought. Elected officials were simply voices on television.

Her encounters with Nathan had been brief, yet they'd changed the way she thought about her responsibility to get involved in the system that determined so much about her daily life.

More, he'd changed her ability to hope that someday she might even fall in love.

True, there was no way to know for sure whether or not Nate was upset with her. But it was entirely out of character for him not to respond to her attempts to contact him.

Her stomach tightened when she considered Nate might believe she'd broken his trust. She needed to find him and explain. Make sure he understood the full story — that she'd never shared anything that might hurt him or his campaign. She'd never cross that line. He meant too much to her.

Once she had a chance to clarify what had really happened, he'd understand and they could pick up where they left off.

At least she prayed that was possible.

The day had really warmed up, with temperatures expected to be in the high nineties. Typical of an Austin day in July, but the heat didn't seem to be a deterrent for the people crowding into Zilker Park, proving the old adage, "If there's free food, they will come."

A slight breeze carried the intoxicating bouquet of spices, smoke, and roasting meat. The smell made her hungry.

She was also dying of thirst, so she made her way to one of many tents where teams of men and women were serving complimentary lemonade and sweet tea. She got in line behind a young couple. The woman pushed a stroller with a toddler inside, a cute little blond boy who grinned when Leta winked at him.

As the line inched forward, the man placed his broad hand on the small of his wife's back. The intimate gesture made Leta feel lonely inside.

She wanted a family someday with a man who adored her.

With iced lemonade in hand, she made her way toward the dais, appreciating the talent of the band playing on a raised stage to the right. She knew from the promo spots on television that the band was called Late Eternity and had been featured at the Austin City Limits Music Festival last fall.

Two little girls in patriotic-themed sundresses and sandals ran in front of her, blowing soap bubbles. A harried-looking mother chased after them, not far behind.

Leta smiled and waited for them to pass.

Then she saw him.

Nate was standing about ten feet from the dais, shaking hands with a small crowd. An eager young dad thrust his chubby-cheeked baby into Nate's arms, which made him laugh. He smiled as the father clicked photos with his iPhone. After handing back the little one, he placed his hand on the guy's shoulder. She couldn't make out what he was saying, but from the look on the guy's face, Nate was definitely connecting.

To his right stood a very attractive young black woman, his campaign manager, Janesa Morgan. Leta had met her at Nate's birthday party. She held a clipboard and was extricating Nate from the small group he was talking with. With a determined smile, she led him toward the steps to the dais and they huddled, apparently getting ready for his big speech.

It appeared Leta had missed any opportunity to catch up with him until after he finished his address, so she found one of the few open spots on the grass and sat with her legs crossed, anxious to hear what Nathan had to say.

Minutes later, a man took the podium and introduced himself as the director of Friends of Texas. "Good afternoon, everyone! Thank you for coming out for our little party."

A roar of applause swept through the crowd.

While he continued talking, Leta watched intently as Nathan pulled at his cuffs. He smiled and nodded to a staffer, patted a security guard on the back.

"And now, without further ado . . . let's bring up the man of the hour, the one who, with all our help, will be the next Texas state governor!"

Nate climbed the steps up to the dais, waving to the crowd. He wore light-colored khakis, loafers, and a white button-down open at the collar. He smiled widely out at the crowd, then held up his open palm, quieting another round of applause. He stepped to the mic. "Hello, Austin, Texas!"

In what was likely a carefully calculated interruption, the band started playing a rendition of "Deep in the Heart of Texas." People clambered to their feet and clap-clap-clapped in unison.

Leta couldn't help but get swept up in the passion. For the first time, she considered that Nathan really could be the next governor of Texas.

"Thank you, boys," Nate said to the band members when the music finally wound down. "I am a huge fan and appreciate y'all being here with us today." Then to his crowd of supporters, "And thanks to all of you for showing up and joining us for this little barbeque!"

Over the next twenty minutes, Nate shared his vision. He was a gifted orator and conveyed his ideas with a sense of passion and purpose that definitely had this crowd fired up.

"This is not about a simple stopover on the way to the White House. My campaign is about serving the people of Texas. And so, with all of your help, we'll get this done. We'll change the landscape of what is ahead for our great state. Together, we'll make a difference! God bless y'all and God bless Texas!"

The crowd immediately went to their feet, and applause roared across the park. Behind the dais, red, white, and blue balloons were released, and seconds later fighter jets roared overhead with red and blue plumes of smoke trailing behind.

Leta watched as Nate posed for photos with various supporters and constituents. She hung back and glanced around at the crowd of people who were now making their way to the barbeque trucks and lemonade pavilions. People from every walk of life — families, seniors, and teens — all prepared to rally behind a candidate they now believed in.

While the media stormed forward, hoping to get an exclusive with Senator Emerson, Leta picked her way through the remaining people standing between her and the man who up until recently had been her friend.

She needed to talk to him. If she could only get a couple of minutes alone with Nate, she could explain.

The anchor from a Dallas news station held out a microphone. "Senator Emerson, over here. Sir, could you tell us the key way voters can differentiate you from your opponent, Governor Holiday? I mean, you both say you want more border security, and each of you is highlighting the need for better health options. You want better funding for neurological compromised patients, an issue dear to your heart. Holiday has his pet issues as well, like capping punitive damages in high-stakes litigation cases and subsidies for highway improvement. Why are all these people gathered here today going to be better off if Nathan Emerson becomes their next governor?"

Nate drew a breath, ready to answer. That's when he saw her.

Leta stood only a few feet away, looking at him like he had the ability to make the sun come up in the morning.

He forced himself to focus back on the news anchor and cleared his throat. "Dwight D. Eisenhower may have said it best when he claimed the supreme quality for a leader is unquestionable integrity. He asserted that people with good intentions make promises, but people with integrity keep them." He let his gaze slip back to his former friend, sadness building in his heart as he struggled to reconcile the girl he'd been so drawn to and her betrayal. "Integrity is everything. I can't speak for Governor Holiday, but I can promise Texans that I am not one man on that stage and another in private. You can count on me always being a man of my word."

She was still watching him, and for a second he let his gaze meet hers. A hopeful smile nipped at the corners of her lips.

He had a decision to make.

As much as it hurt, he took a deep breath, knowing he had to be sensible. Despite the trust he'd placed in her, she hadn't been honest. So he did what he had to do.

He turned away.

33

Katie pulled into the parking spot in front of Central Market. "Look, you need to quit beating yourself up over this thing with the senator. I mean, yeah, he was becoming a friend and all, but what kind of friend just assumes the worst? Why did he never let you explain?"

Leta didn't have an answer. Neither could she say why Nate's attitude toward her felt like a razor slicing at her heart. She'd barely acknowledged to herself that she had romantic feelings, let alone believe those feelings might be reciprocated.

She had no business thinking that way. She'd watched enough *Downton Abbey* episodes to know that the upstairs people shouldn't mingle with the downstairs folks.

He was from a very influential and wealthy family and had accomplished more in his thirty-plus years than most people in an entire lifetime. Nate was destined for great things, especially politically.

She, on the other hand, had very little to show for her years on this earth. She loved and cared for her mother, and that was important. She'd have it no other way. But no one was going to show up with media trucks to report her successes to an adoring public.

All other factors aside, there was the bottom line here. She'd messed up by hiding that she was working for the Ladd Agency in fear of losing him, when he was never hers to lose. Not in that way.

And now not in any way — not even friendship. She wished she'd just been honest from the minute she learned what Jane Ladd and Bernard Geisler were really all about. Sadly, she couldn't turn back time.

"Yeah, I suppose you're right," she told Katie as she gathered her purse and lunch sack. "Thanks for dropping me off. My car should be ready by four, if you want to pick me up then."

"No problem, I'll see you at four." Her friend waved. "And quit worrying about this misunderstanding thing — let it go."

She moved inside the store and made her way to the break room, where the employee lockers were located, sensing that in some regards she had indeed turned the clock back in time and was right back where she started. After having her high hopes dashed at the Ladd Agency, she'd returned to Central Market, still lacking a job with any real future. While considerably better than before, the financial needs for her mother's care still prodded her worry buttons.

She sighed and stored her personal belongings, locked them up, and made for the floral department, determined to put the negative thoughts aside. This was her life, and she could choose to be happy despite the disappointment.

A delivery had arrived earlier this morning. In the cooler, she found tall stems of larkspur in pretty shades of blue, pink, and white. Buckets filled with delicate rosebuds competed for space with highly fragrant stargazer lilies. There were brightly colored gerbera daisies and poppies in soft hues of coral and yellow. Gorgeous blooms filled the cooler — and her senses.

A memory formed of the bright, sunny day that had inaugurated her love for flowers and nature.

As was her custom when Leta was small, her mother had pulled her from under the covers and scooped her into her arms. "Good morning, princess. Mommy has a surprise for you. What do you say we skip school today and I'll take you out to the Lady Bird Johnson Wildflower Center?"

Leta frowned. "A bird lady?"

Her mother smiled. "No, baby. Lady Bird was President Johnson's wife. She was our first lady back in the sixties. She loved flowers and opened a botanical garden where they work to preserve native plants and landscape features, particularly those native to Texas. Would you like to go, princess?"

She scrambled from her bed, not believing her good fortune. "Oh yes, Mommy!"

They'd packed a lunch and headed about ten miles south of Austin, pulling into the visitor area by midmorning, before the sun got too hot. Over the next several hours, she and her mother examined more species of plant life than she could count.

Even now she loved to spend time out at the center admiring the bluebonnets, Texas paintbrush, and pretty purple winecup. When she found the time, that is.

She carefully unpacked a box of foliage and clipped the ends before placing the stems in a bucket of fresh water, then busied herself with making arrangements to fill the nearly empty display case.

Twenty minutes or so later, she reached for a shell-pink rose and heard her name.

She looked up, shocked to find Nathan

standing in front of the counter.

Nate had told himself he was going because Central Market was the only retail outlet that carried his favorite Ossau-Iraty, and no other cheese would do.

He'd argued that chances were slim she'd be working, and he could easily avoid meeting up with her even if she was in the floral department. Nothing good would come of an encounter. He was a candidate for governor and couldn't risk any confrontation. Every move was carefully scrutinized by the media. Even now, customers in the store recognized and watched him.

Yet here he stood.

"Nate?" She looked genuinely puzzled. "What are you doing here?"

There was now no turning back. He swallowed, feeling more like a kid who'd been caught skipping school than a candidate for governor. "Hello, Leta. I — I, uh, could you take a break? I'd like to talk."

She hesitated only briefly before nodding. "Sure. Let me grab my bag and clock out. Wait here?"

She said this like she believed he might bolt. And that wasn't so far from the truth. This was a dumb idea, and he couldn't believe he'd taken such a step.

The truth was, now that his early anger had dissipated a bit, he just couldn't stand not knowing why she'd betrayed him.

Leta reappeared in less than a minute, appearing a bit flustered and out of breath. He noticed she'd put on lip color. He liked that.

"It's about lunchtime." He pulled a loaf of crusty sourdough bread from his shopping basket and held it up. "Do you have time to catch a quick bite? Central Park is walking distance."

She nodded. "Okay, sure."

He paid for the items, and they walked outside in polite silence. He glanced around the parking lot. "Where's your car?"

"At the shop. The drive belt went out." She walked with him toward the path leading to the park.

"Didn't you just buy that car?"

Leta shrugged. "Yeah, it was used." She said this like he was a bit out of touch, and perhaps he was. He'd never purchased a pre-owned vehicle.

The path circled to the right. They climbed a small knoll that opened up to a pretty grassy area with a pond and waterfall. He pointed. "Will this work?"

She nodded and followed him to a bench next to the water, where he opened a package of salami and a jar of Kalamata olives while she cut slices of bread and cheese using a paring knife he'd purchased.

A voice in Nate's head warned he'd made a colossal mistake. Did he expect her to be honest now, when that was the very reason their budding relationship had withered? She'd hidden the fact she was working for his opponent. The very idea had the power to make him mad all over again.

He tossed the lid to the Kalamata jar onto the bench next to him before he could lose his nerve. "Look, I don't know any way around this. You lied to me."

Leta visibly bristled. "That's not exactly true. I mean, you don't know the full story."

He shook his head in disgust. "Please don't tell me you're one of those."

"Those?"

"I live in a world where people justify shading the truth, folks who believe the end justifies the means. But that idea is just crap." He was startled by his passionate word choice but needed her to understand. "The sharp edges of the truth can't be rounded to ease how it rolls. The truth is simply that — the truth."

She squared her shoulders. "So you didn't come to listen and understand? You only wanted to bawl me out and make me feel worse than I already do?" Her face frosted over. "I don't need you to be my conscience. I have God for that, thank you."

"And God lets you lie?"

She balled her hands into fists. "I didn't lie. I just didn't announce the horrible situation I found myself in to the world, and especially to you. Do you know what it was like to learn I didn't work for a simple publicity firm, that I'd been duped? That instead of Jane Ladd being impressed with my research abilities, she was only using me to get to you, the target of their opposition research? Yeah, that was fun!"

When he didn't respond right away, she went on. "I suppose you think it was easy for a person in my financial situation to give up a six-figure salary — so I could look you in the eye without feeling like scum?" She started to tear up. "If you no longer want to be my friend, then fine. But I am *not* a liar!"

Her outburst took him back. He rubbed his forehead, trying to take everything in. "Okay, now wait. I don't understand."

"You're right. You don't understand. So quit judging me."

"Wait —" he stumbled, surprised at her ardor. There was a brief silence. "All right, look," he said, his breath coming in a rush. "Can we just start over here?"

338

There was a hesitation. "Okay, what do you want to know?" she asked, clearly still feeling stung.

He tilted the open jar of olives in her direction. "Everything."

Despite any reservations she felt about the confidentiality agreement, Leta relayed the entire story from beginning to end. She told Nate how she'd desperately needed a job, even disclosing the pressing financial need at the time. She laid everything out — how Bernard Geisler showed up at the Hole in the Wall, creeping her out. The warning from Erin that made her nervous. The way Jane Ladd had made her feel like a superstar.

She helped him understand how she'd come to realize the publicity firm was nothing but a front for something far more, how she'd not been smart enough to decipher what was up — until it was too late.

"And you quit? Because of me?"

She waited until his gaze met her own. "Yes."

Leta could see Nate's self-righteous outburst deflate before her eyes. His eyes turned soft, and he reached for her hand. "I'm sorry, Leta," he said, his anger seeming to shift. He managed a tiny smile.

Now it was her turn to apologize. "Before you think I had no culpability, I did attend your birthday party knowing about Operation Brainchild and fully aware I was expected to return to the office on Monday with some sort of scoop that could manifest into dirt to use against you. I should have come clean then, but I talked myself into believing I could weasel around the situation and play the players, know what I mean?" She shook her head. "It was foolish of me. And because I allowed you to learn about the situation from someone else, it nearly cost our friendship. I hope you'll forgive me, Nate. I never meant to betray your trust."

"I'm an idiot," he said, his voice heavy and sad. He stared out at the waterfall, blinking away emotion. "I should have known you wouldn't. I'm the one who is terribly sorry, Leta."

She lightly touched his arm. "Please tell me we can be friends again."

He turned to face her and smiled. "Yes, of course. Friends."

She smiled too. Somewhere in the deep creases of her mind — the folds where hope gets caught — she believed in the two of them again. And that made her very happy.

Suddenly, her phone buzzed in her pocket.

"Sorry, let me get this," she said, pulling out her iPhone. "Hello?"

"Is this Leta Breckenridge?"

She frowned, not recognizing the voice. "Yes."

"This is Penny Murdock. I'm going to have to ask you to come right away."

Leta's good mood immediately shattered. Her heart pounded. "My mom — is she okay?"

Ms. Murdock cleared her throat. "I'm afraid she's missing."

34

"I'll drive you," Nate offered. He crammed the remains of their mini picnic into the bag and grabbed her hand. "Let's go."

Leta tearfully nodded and followed him back to the car. She gave him directions as he started the engine, trying not to think about the danger her mom might be in. Even so, endless possibilities marched through her head. What if her mom met up with a stranger with ill intent? What if she wandered into traffic?

Terror filled her at the reality of the situation. "Please hurry," she urged.

Thanks to Nate's driving skills, they made it to Heritage House in record time. Penny Murdock was waiting. "We've alerted law enforcement, and they are watching for Sylvia. In addition, we have staff members scouring the area on foot and in cars."

Leta nodded. "Thank you. I appreciate all that, but I don't understand how she could possibly have walked out of here without anyone noticing." She realized her voice sounded sharp, but she'd apologize later. Right now they had to find her mother.

Nate pulled his phone from his pocket. "How long has she been gone, and do you know what she was wearing?"

Lucy stepped forward, looking completely flustered. "We discovered her missing when we went to get her for lunch."

"And before that?" Nate asked. "When did someone last see her?"

Ms. Murdock looked at her clipboard. "She was bathed and clothed this morning, taken down to breakfast, and returned to her room at nine thirty. That's the last record." She struggled to maintain her composure, clearly aware she was address-ing a senator who may soon be governor, and at a time when something horrible had happened under her watch. "We maintain meticulous care records."

Nate nodded and punched out a number on his phone before stepping back to place his call.

Lucy placed her hand on Leta's back. "We told the authorities she was wearing blue slacks and a yellow top." She shook her head. "Honey, we are so sorry."

Tears pooled in Leta's eyes. "We've got to

find her."

"She can't have wandered far. We'll locate Sylvia soon," Ms. Murdock assured everyone. The worry in the director's eyes betrayed her confidence.

Nate shoved his phone back into his pants pocket. "Good news. A woman fitting your mother's description was spotted by some runners out on the Shoal Creek Greenbelt near the trailhead on 35th."

"At least she's not out on the MoPac Expressway with all that traffic," Leta said, somewhat relieved. She turned for the door. "C'mon, let's go."

"I'll alert the staff that she's been spotted," Ms. Murdock said, already turning for her office.

Nate grabbed Leta's hand, and they rushed by foot across the park in the direction of where her mom had last been seen. While hurrying toward Shoal Creek, Leta called Katie and rallied her help, then asked her to let Mike know she wouldn't be back at the store and why.

"They lost your mom? How can that possibly happen?"

Her roommate voiced what was in her own mind. "Seems so. Look, I've got to go. I'll let you know if we find her."

Shoal Creek ran right down the heart of

Austin. At times the far northern portions resembled little more than a drainage ditch, widening considerably the farther south you went. Where her mom was spotted was about a mile away from Heritage House.

As they neared, Leta cupped her hands to her mouth. "Mom," she called out several times. Her mother wasn't likely to respond, but she hollered again anyway, "Mom!"

A recent rainstorm had left the creek flowing at near capacity, and while it was not to be compared to the Colorado at the south of town, Leta conjured an image of her mother slipping on the banks and falling into the water.

Panicked, she frantically turned to Nate. "We've got to find her."

Nate clasped her hand and pulled her along the trail toward a stand of trees known as Seiders Oaks. "We'll find her. I promise. There are a lot of people looking."

She couldn't help it. She choked up. "You don't understand. She's all I have. Without her, I'm all alone." She knew she sounded like a frightened child, but she didn't care. She'd never been this scared.

Nate's phone rang, and he quickly grabbed it and pulled it to his ear. "Yeah?" He stopped walking.

Leta fumbled back a step and watched his

face, her heart pounding. *Please, Lord, don't let that be bad news.*

"Okay, yeah. Got it." He turned to her, grinning. "They've found her."

"Is — is she all right?"

He nodded and returned his phone to his pocket. "Yes, your mother is safe and sound."

She couldn't help it. Her knees buckled, and she crumpled to the ground with her face in her hands. "Oh, God. Oh, God, thank you!" she sobbed, grateful the Lord had answered her prayers.

Nate's arms folded around her. "Shhhh, it's okay. Everything's all right."

She buried her head into his chest, clinging to him in tears, letting the terror she'd experienced drain from her soul.

He held her tightly. "It's all right. I'm here."

After several minutes, she pulled back and looked up at him, a bit embarrassed. "I — I'm sorry. It's just that —"

"Please don't apologize," he told her, his voice tender. "I understand."

She took a deep breath and tried to collect herself. "Nate, I need to hurry and go be with her. She's likely frightened and confused."

He nodded and helped her stand. "C'mon,

I'll take you to where they're waiting for us."

Minutes later, he pulled in front of her house. Two officers waved at Nate.

On the front steps sat her mother, smiling, in a yellow top and blue slacks.

Leta pulled the bedcovers up around her mother, leaned over, and brushed her forehead with a kiss. "Sweet dreams, Momma."

Lucy folded Leta's mother's clothes and placed them neatly on top of the bureau. "I've worked here a lot of years, but I'll never quite understand what happened today. Sylvia can't remember her own name or how to dress herself, but somehow she pulled off the feat of making her way back home, nearly three miles away." She shook her head and turned for the door. "Never seen anything like it."

Nathan followed them out into the hallway. "That's not that unusual. Brain chemistry is very complex. Neurological deficits can sometimes be temporarily reversed to some degree when certain factors are in place. Often light and exercise sharpen the mind, which is why it is so important that residential centers incorporate these elements into patients' living regimens."

Lucy walked alongside Nathan as they headed for the elevators. "But still, all that way."

"I agree, it is extraordinary. But the light, coupled with the walking, may have fostered her brain's ability to function at a higher level than normal. At least temporarily."

The information both elated and depressed Leta. She loved knowing her mom had some moments of lucidity but hated that she'd missed it. Maybe her mom had gone looking for her? Hard to say. But she'd found her way home, and that was amazing.

"Leta, are you all right?" The concern in Nate's voice pulled her back to their conversation.

She nodded. "Yeah, just wish I'd been there to see it."

An incident report was prepared. Leta signed it and was promised there would be a full investigation into what had allowed a patient to leave the premises unattended. "I assure you we'll institute any and all proper remedies," Penny Murdock promised.

On the way home, Nate asked if she was hungry.

"I am, but I'm just not up to going out. Know what I mean?" She leaned back against the headrest. The tension of the day had left her wrung out.

"Tell you what." Nate looked across the seat at her. "Why don't we stop and pick something up and you can eat in."

"But you'll stay?"

"Only if you want me to."

Of course she wanted him to! She was tired, but being with Nathan somehow buoyed her spirits. She was so happy he'd shown up at Central Market. Not only had they worked out their misunderstanding and were now friends again, but he'd been there when she needed him the most.

Still, there were plenty of reasons why she still needed to guard her heart. For example, how did this romantic inclination toward Nate fit in with his relationship with Tiffany?

She supposed that would all get sorted out. Nate was her friend again. That's all that really mattered.

35

Nate left Leta waiting in the car while he ran inside EZ's Grill for a brick oven pizza. After placing an order for a Hawaiian barbeque chicken thin crust and a salad, he moved to a table to wait.

His phone was filled with anxious messages. He shot off a quick text to Janesa, apologizing for being off radar. Despite knowing what it would do to his tight schedule, he alerted his campaign manager that he would not be available for the rest of the evening.

While he had no events that particular evening, she'd no doubt wonder why he'd take a night off when he had such a tight itinerary, including an early morning appearance at the local CBS station.

The rest of the messages would have to wait, including the dozen or so from his mother. She'd been particularly vigilant after he'd distanced himself from Tiffany, hovering over him and his campaign. Likely she too wondered about his judgment. Despite the fact she'd encouraged him to make a choice, he knew she was surprised he'd not taken her counsel. Especially if Tiffany told her what she suspected about Leta and her involvement with the Ladd Agency.

He couldn't really blame his mother for any concern she might foster. He'd immediately thought the worst too. But he'd been terribly mistaken.

Outside the window, Leta sat in his car with her head resting against the seat back, her eyes closed. She looked so sweet, so vulnerable. He'd been there when she needed him today. The hollow spot inside him filled with something pleasant.

In some ways it was as if he wore a hero's cape when he was around Leta, that he had the power to make everything right in her world. As much as he was reluctant to admit it, that feeling was intoxicating.

For the first time, he actually understood why Rhett Butler craved affection from an unlikely Scarlett, why Indiana Jones chased more than the lost ark across the desert, and how Superman fell in love with Lois Lane faster than a speeding bullet.

And Nate also knew he was totally smitten.

When the pizza was ready, he gathered the flat box and the sack with their salad and carried them to the car. When the door opened, Leta lifted her head and smiled. "Mmm, smells good."

"Good thing. Because I ordered a large."

Minutes later he pulled up in front of her house for the second time that day.

Leta lived in a modest Craftsman-style home typical of those in this part of the Brentwood area. The front porch and steps were painted brick red, as was the front door. Pots of brightly colored flowers adorned each of the steps. Everything neat and tidy.

This house fit her — modest in stature, yet beautiful in its simplicity.

Inside, she invited him to have a seat while she got out dishes and utensils. "Let me help," he told her.

Leta shrugged. "Sure, okay."

He took plates from her hand and moved to the table. "This you?" he asked, nodding toward a framed photo on the bookshelf.

Her face flushed. "Yeah," she said, laughing. "The pigtails were a nice touch. Don't you think?"

Nate leaned in to get a closer look, not

able to suppress his own chuckle. "Pretty Pippi Longstocking, but cute." The next photo was of a man and woman on their wedding day. "And this must be your parents?"

She joined him and lightly brushed her finger across the image. "Yes." She pointed to another. "And that was my father."

"I see a strong resemblance." He pulled his wallet from his pocket and flipped to a tiny snapshot. "This is mine."

"Oh my goodness, that could be you!"

Their eyes met, and understanding passed between them. A shared moment that needed no justification.

Nate noticed something pass through her eyes. "You all right?"

"What? Oh, sure. I guess today's events are still playing in my mind a bit. She was one remarkable woman, you know?" She fought to keep from choking with emotion. "I mean, before everything changed."

He nodded, wanting to thread his fingers through hers.

She turned to him. "I have to admit, I barely remember my father. I was only four. But my mom, she was my world. You know?"

"That kind of connection is a special gift," he told her, realizing his own heart longed for the same. Perhaps that's why he'd taken a risk and showed up at Central Market earlier. There was a missing spot in his life, and he suspected this girl had the ability to fill it.

He gave in and squeezed her hand.

She smiled back at him, and they moved to the table and sat.

Leta lifted a piece of pizza from the box. "I remember this one time I was home sick with the chicken pox. I was miserable for days. Mom stayed right by my side the entire time, dabbing calamine lotion on all those red spots with a cotton ball to ease the itching. And later, when I started to feel a little better and boredom set in, she gathered a cardboard box and transformed the thing into a stage, complete with curtains and lights — which were really just the string of holiday bulbs."

He watched her face grow animated as he filled his plate.

"Together we cut scraps of material and made costumes with superglue and sequins and dressed an entire box of plastic spoons. These became the cast — Cinderella and her prince, the wicked stepmother and stepsisters. Oh, and the fairy godmother!" She smiled before turning her attention to her plate. "It was our favorite story."

Leta seemed lost in thought for a moment before she looked across the table, her eyes filled with emotion. "I don't know what I would've done had we not found her today."

"But they did find her," he reminded her. "And she's warm and safe in her bed tonight."

"Yes. Thank God prayers were answered."

Over the next couple of minutes, they ate in silence, buried in their own thoughts.

Nate took a bite of his pizza and considered how a strange thing happened every time he was with her. His vision got a little sharper, music a little sweeter, colors a little brighter, and the air a little more crisp. Never before had a woman affected him quite like Leta Breckenridge. She had the power to turn his pewter existence to dazzling gold, and he was only now completely recognizing that fact.

"Leta?"

She dabbed at her mouth with a napkin. "Yes?"

"I have something I need to tell you." The moment the words left his mouth, he knew he was about to take a very important step, move in a new direction. He would not be turning back. The thought both elated him and shook him to the core.

His heart pounded as he pushed his plate

aside. "I — I broke things off with Tiffany."

Her eyes widened. "You did? When?"

He nodded, anxious to convey what was in his heart. "Weeks ago. I didn't feel right about continuing our relationship when I had feelings for someone else." In a bold move he reached for Leta's hand and lifted her from her spot at the table. "For you."

He focused on the way her hair cascaded over her shoulders like a slow-moving river. Her skin milky soft.

He caught her chin with his fingers, tilted her face so he could look deep into her eyes. "What do you say to that?"

She gazed back, a slow smile nipping at the corners of her lips. His move had no doubt surprised her. He liked that.

The girl before him sparkled with innocence, a deep well of pure motive he'd nearly missed by believing the worst.

She looked back at him with adoration. "I'd say I now know what Cinderella felt like at the ball."

The room shifted a little. His stomach tightened as he bent and covered her mouth with his own.

Her lips were soft and warm.

Nate pressed his kiss lightly and then with a surprising urgency. He could have imagined this moment a thousand times and would have never been able to guess exactly how it felt — the moment she turned his entire world upside down.

The moment he no longer felt alone.

36

Jane Ladd stepped from her car and crossed the parking lot to the boat launch, wishing she'd thought to change shoes first. Of course, until the text of thirty minutes ago, how could she have imagined she'd be walking along the banks of the Colorado nearly out in the middle of nowhere?

She picked her way across a gravel path toward the shade of a large oak along the shoreline, a respite from the blistering sun. A fly buzzed near her face, and she swatted the nasty thing away.

Why couldn't Holiday just meet in her office, for goodness' sake?

Suddenly, a small white motor yacht came into view. The governor waved from the deck as the driver eased the vessel up to the wooden dock.

Surprised, she waved back, feeling a little rivulet of moisture trail down her spine.

"Come on board," he bellowed. "You look

like you're about to melt."

The boat came to a stop, and Ethan Michaels, Holiday's campaign director, stepped forward and offered her a hand. "I hope you didn't have to wait long."

"Not long." She trailed Ethan and Wyndall inside the impressive cabin. While it was small compared to some boats that traversed the waters of Lake Travis outside Austin, the interior was tastefully decorated with high-glossed tile flooring and caramel-colored leather furniture, accented with rugs and pillows in shades of sand and ocean blue.

Amanda Joy slipped from behind the bar and handed Jane a frosted stemmed martini glass filled with a blue concoction. She smiled widely. "That's a Desperate Housewife, sans the alcohol."

Jane thanked her and took the glass, wondering what the point of a cocktail was if you served it without any alcohol. But then, not everything was as it initially appeared with the first lady of Texas.

"Please, sit." Amanda Joy motioned to a sofa nestled beneath a long window that ran the length of the cabin.

The engine revved, and Jane felt a slight forward motion as she sank into the cushions. "So, what is this meeting about?"

Governor Holiday and his wife sat on a sofa on the opposite side of the cabin. His arm went around her shoulders. "Well, Janie, it's like this. It's nearly halftime, and we're behind on the scoreboard."

Ethan moved to a side chair and took a seat. He was dressed casually — khakis and a white shirt left unbuttoned at the collar. The sleeves were rolled to the elbows. He leaned forward, his elbows on his knees, his expression anything but casual. "It's time to carry water to a thirsty team," he said, cutting to the chase. "As you are aware, a great deal of money is being funneled your direction, and so far the campaign has little to show for the investment."

Jane swallowed tightly. "Excuse me for being a bit bold here, but while I appreciate a good sporting event, people don't just grab a hot dog and some popcorn and head off to the polls." She lifted her chin slightly. "As you know, Ethan, timing is everything. The most critical news cycles are still ahead. You have my guarantee that voters' confidence will deteriorate significantly once our intelligence is released."

A grin appeared on Governor Holiday's face. He squeezed his wife's shoulders. "You can assure us Emerson will be sidelined?"

Jane downed the too-sweet drink, stood,

and handed off the empty glass to Amanda Joy. She then pulled a folder labeled *Operation Brainchild* from her bag and handed a copy of a thick, stapled report to each of them. "I'll let you be the judge."

Jane sat quietly as the others read the findings.

Outside the windows, thick foliage at the water's edge grew anemic as the Austin skyline gradually came into view. The engine slowed as their vessel neared the Congress Avenue Bridge, where brightly colored kayaks floated in the water near a shoreline crowded with spectators waiting for that magical moment at dusk.

Jane glanced back at her detractors, watching as they turned the pages of the report with great interest. "So?"

Ethan looked up, his eyes glistening. "Well done."

Governor Holiday nodded in agreement. "I almost feel sorry for the chap."

Amanda Joy held up a glossy photo. "Yes, this is superb. I recognize this girl. Didn't I see her in your office?"

Jane felt tension drain from her shoulders. "Yes. We had an .... uh, unexpected change of plans when she resigned. But as you can see" — she paused and grinned in her clients' direction — "the Ladd Agency knows how to turn a fumble into a first down."

The governor exchanged glances with his wife. He smiled. "Well, it certainly appears we miscalculated you, Jane."

Ethan nodded. "Yes, we've placed our trust, and our funds, on the right side of the stadium, so to speak."

The governor tossed his copy of the report onto the sofa and quickly herded them toward the deck. "Hurry, everyone, it's time. We don't want to miss the big moment."

Feeling extremely gratified, Jane followed her hosts out into the heavy evening air, knowing she'd pulled off yet another dead cat bounce. Governor Holiday was a performer, a guy better suited to *Dancing with the Stars* than running the state of Texas. But that didn't matter. There was much more at stake than a simple election.

She let a slow grin form on her face. She had an affinity for pork, and if Holiday pulled off another election, they'd all be eating out of that barrel for a good long time.

Amanda Joy pulled her sweater down from around her shoulders. "Goodness, it's sweltering out here."

Wyndall took his wife's hand and led her to the railing. Ethan followed.

Standing shoulder to shoulder with her clients, Jane joined hundreds of onlookers and watched as over a million tiny black bats launched from underneath the bridge and spiraled into the sky.

Leta walked the hiking path along the Colorado River, enjoying the unusually warm evening, when suddenly a black cloud formed in the sky above the Congress Avenue Bridge in the distance. Even from here, she could hear the tourists applauding as the bats took flight, thrilling the crowds.

Katie wiped her brow with a bandana before tying it around her forehead. "That never gets old, does it?"

"No, it doesn't." She stopped and gazed upward at swarms of bats making their way across the skyline overhead. "In fact, no matter how many times I've seen that crazy phenomenon, I still find it absolutely amazing."

That wasn't the only thing she found amazing.

These days, the sky was a brighter shade of blue. Flowers smelled sweeter. Music chords resonated more deeply. She even found the mailman's jokes funny.

Was that what it felt like to be in love?

She closed her eyes, still feeling Nate's

lips against her own — reliving his kiss. That wonderful, astounding, sensational moment when everything changed and the world suddenly became a much better place.

It took every ounce of inner strength not to holler to the handholding couple passing by that they weren't the only ones in love. She too knew what it was like to feel your heart race, your skin tingle, at the sight of a man. Her man. For the first time in a long while, her heart was completely full.

Yet she couldn't tell anyone. If word got out, it could hurt Nate's campaign. She hated not sharing her delightful news with Katie, had a hard time answering for the constant smile on her face. Her roommate knew something was up, but Leta didn't dare give in to the impulse to give a minute-by-minute account of that wonderful encounter and her new relationship with Nate. Not even to her best friend.

They'd agreed to keep their budding relationship under wraps temporarily. At least until the campaign developed a plan to officially release the news, which would be soon, Nate promised.

Now that she was romantically connected to a prominent public figure running for governor in a very heated race, every move she made would need to be sifted through the campaign and postured in consideration of the voters.

If Nathan got elected, there would be a whole other set of issues to face. But none of that really mattered. She was in love.

Katie pointed her water bottle toward the street. "Hey, is that lady waving at us?"

She looked in that direction. "What lady?"

"The one standing next to that big black car."

Leta squinted, trying to make out the woman's identity. "Uh, look, why don't you go on ahead?"

"Without you?"

She nodded. "Yeah, I'll catch up with you later. Meet me at Banger's Sausage House." Without explaining further, she jogged toward the car.

Nate's mother glanced around. "Thank you for coming over." Her driver opened the door. Mrs. Wyatt motioned Leta inside, then circled the back of the car and entered from the opposite door, sliding in next to her.

Mrs. Wyatt straightened her skirt. "I'm sure I have you puzzled. I just wanted to talk with you — privately."

Leta nodded, not sure what to say exactly. "Okay."

"Nate does not know I'm here talking with

you. I'd prefer to keep it that way, but of course I can't dictate to you in that regard."

She swallowed. "I — I'm not sure I want to keep any secrets from him."

"Yes, as it should be, I suppose." Despite her verbal agreement, her face looked a bit pinched. "You and I met briefly at his party, of course. But let me officially introduce myself." She held out her hand. "I'm Mrs. Wyatt, but I'd like it if you would call me Vera. Especially now."

"Now?"

"Yes, now that you are seeing my son."

The fact Nate had shared their relationship with his mother hit her with unexpected force. "So, you know?"

"I make it my business to know. He's my son."

Frankly, this woman was unnerving. Vera must have sensed how uncomfortable the discussion was making her because she reached across the seat and placed her hand on her arm.

"Few know Nathan better than me. I sensed some time ago that he was developing feelings for you. And I was right. It appears he thinks very highly of you."

"The feeling is entirely mutual. Nathan is amazing."

"Yes, much like his father, my Nate is easy

to love. And I suspect you will make him happy." She gave Leta a quick pat on the arm. "Unfortunately, love and politics make strange bedfellows, as they say."

Leta frowned. "I'm not sure I'm following you."

"Hear me on this. It is not easy being a politician's wife. Nate's poll numbers are high, much higher than we really expected at this juncture. He has a very real chance at being the next governor of Texas. I'm not sure you know what that will mean." She smoothed her skirt again. "You see, Nathan is much like his father. Very idealistic and not always in touch with the dirty underbelly of electioneering and what it takes to juggle the affairs and interests of competing parties in a manner that leaves him on top." She lifted her chin. "While Nate's father was the face of the office he held, and no one built the rapport with the public better, I was behind the scenes maneuvering and staging the less desirable aspects — always through a third party, of course. A good chief of staff is invaluable, but make no mistake, no one will be as equipped to protect Nate more than you, in the event this relationship builds and you become his wife."

"His wife? I — I mean, that's presuming a

lot at this early stage."

Vera's eyes turned impatient. "We both know where this could end up, don't we, dear? That brings me to my second point." She touched the back of her neckline. "You worked for his opposition research team. You better than anyone know the tactics they employ. Given the opportunity, Holiday's camp will utilize any unflattering ammunition to shoot down Nathan's reputation in the voters' eyes."

Vera looked at her full-on, and Leta found herself peering back, worry building in her gut. "What exactly are you saying?"

"In the event I'm unable to get through to Nathan, I can only hope you understand the import of these matters and are able to set emotions aside and do what is right for my son, for his campaign." Her eyes narrowed. "As any future wife would."

Leta swallowed. She tried to ignore the thoughts whipping through her brain, but they were insistent.

No matter what this woman might believe, Leta had no illusions about what Nate deserved. He was a smart and generous soul who had earned the right to ask the voters of Texas to consider placing him in the office of the governor, where he could continue to serve and act on behalf of the ones who needed him most — those with compromised health issues who needed a strong advocate in their government. He did not warrant a media circus.

Still, Leta's disappointment was almost palpable, and her chin dipped toward her chest as if she couldn't quite bring herself to hold her head up.

"If you continue seeing each other romantically, it is only a matter of time before news breaks and he will take a major hit. Nathan will no doubt argue that the public has no business in his personal life. But we both know the fact he ended a long relationship with a highly influential woman in this town and started up another with you will create a media stir — a diversion from Nate's very important message. Undoubtedly, his numbers will suffer at this very critical stage. He may not recover."

Vera gazed at her intently as though to see if she understood. "Perhaps you should consider placing your romantic feelings on hold — temporarily, of course. The election is only a relatively short time away. Once Nathan has secured the election and is governor-elect — well then, the two of you can make the happy announcement that you are a couple at that time, when the risk has passed. If staged properly, your budding relationship will garner even more connection with his constituents." Vera paused briefly, letting her words sink in. "This is your first test, dear. If you fail to take my advice and your relationship with Nathan is discovered and leaked to the press, Holiday and his camp will take every opportunity to run both of you through the mud. No ugly stone will be left unturned. And if they can't find a dirt-sodden boulder, they'll create one and roll it over the campaign. Believe me on this — you do not want to be standing in its path and not see it coming."

37

Leta bent and fastened the bag of floral clippings. In an online video, she'd learned that clipping all the stems each morning controlled product shrinkage, one of the biggest challenges of keeping a floral department profitable. The result of her findings raised her bottom line by nearly thirty percent, a fact that thrilled Mike. The information also served as a tiny distraction from the turmoil whirling in her mind.

Nate had been campaigning in El Paso for the past two days, appearing at a symposium of business owners wanting solutions to the growing drug trafficking issue along the border in that part of the state. A mounting problem that definitely needed to be addressed.

Another more urgent problem was his mother's warnings. Leta needed to talk to Nate as soon as he got back, tell him she agreed that they were taking a risk he couldn't afford. What would it hurt to wait to make their relationship public until after the election?

Leta picked up the overstuffed bag and headed for the back of the store.

While Nate's campaign would try to control the narrative, she recognized that Bernard Geisler would not play nicely. He was a playground bully who was used to employing nasty tricks.

On the back landing, Leta tossed her bag on top of several others to be hauled away, then turned back inside, wishing she'd taken a lunch hour after all. Her stomach grumbled in protest as she passed the break room, but Leta didn't waver. She wanted to clock out early so she could watch the news and reaction to Nate's press conference after his talk in El Paso.

She recollected a recent article that claimed young people were less apathetic and more interested in public issues and current affairs than was commonly supposed. But politicians — along with the word *politics* — were widely seen as boring, irrelevant, and an immediate turnoff.

She could certainly attest that attitude had been true of her — until she met Nate.

Suddenly, she was watching poll numbers, laughing at political memes in the newspaper, and switching off old episodes of *America's Funniest Home Videos* to opt for *Face the Nation* instead.

She'd learned how Texas voters felt on many important issues — the health issues she cared about, but also economic and moral matters that caused controversy among political factions.

There were a lot of places for Nate to trip up in his bid for the governor's seat. She didn't want to be one of them.

Which is why when she returned to the floral department minutes later to find Nate waiting for her, she was both elated and concerned.

"Nate! What are you doing here? I thought the bus wasn't scheduled back until tomorrow."

Ignoring the fact there were security cameras and people who might see, he brushed a kiss on her cheek. "The bus will arrive in Austin in the morning, but I took a charter flight back. I wanted to see you."

She couldn't help it. A tiny thrill scattered across her stomach, the same feeling she'd had as a child seeing all the presents under the tree on Christmas morning.

She lowered her voice. "I'm glad to see you too." She glanced around, afraid they might be overheard, even though there was no one within fifteen feet of where they stood.

Nate's face broke into a smile. "Look, the need to hide our relationship is being taken care of as we speak. When the bus gets back, Janesa will have a press release ready to go. We'll announce the news and get ahead of anything that might cause problems."

"Are you sure that's a good idea? I mean, maybe we should wait until after the election. It's not that long and —"

"Don't worry," he assured her. "I have everything handled. And I don't want to hide in the shadows any longer, looking over our shoulders to make sure no one sees us together."

She opened her mouth to protest, but he held up his hand. "What time do you get off?"

She gave in and smiled, pushing his mother's dire warning from her mind. "I can leave in about an hour."

His expression brightened. "Great! Meet me at my place. Here's the address." He slipped a piece of paper into her hands. "I'm already counting down the minutes."

The drive to Nate's neighborhood took about twenty minutes from downtown Austin. The exclusive community located southwest of the metro area offered amazing views and amenities, including Barton Creek running along the landscape.

Leta tried not to think about how Nate's lifestyle contrasted with her own as she pulled in front of his address and cut the engine. Even so, his house was not as grandiose as many of the ones on his street.

A wide brick walkway wound across a beautifully manicured lawn to a covered entry. Large wooden doors with leaded glass and ornamental black wrought iron were flanked by carriage lights, which were mounted above pots containing beautifully spiraled topiary shrubs and vinca in delicate shades of pink and rose. The exact look she would've selected had she designed the landscaping.

She took a deep breath and rang the doorbell, wishing she'd thought to refresh her lip gloss in the car.

Before she could give the matter another thought, the doors swung open. Nate caught her arm and pulled her inside. He swiftly kicked the door closed and immediately pressed her against the wall, molding his lips against her own.

When he finally released her, she managed a soft laugh. "Well, hello to you too."

Nate grinned. "You have no idea how

much I missed you while I was out on the road."

She straightened, basking in the way every cell in her body tingled. She put her hands on his chest and stared into his eyes. "Maybe you should show me again."

His fingers traced along her cheek. He bent, slowly this time. His kiss lingered, and she closed her eyes, letting herself be swept up in how he smelled, like a fresh shower mingled with spicy cologne.

He grabbed her hand. "C'mon, I thought we'd stay in and cook tonight." He pulled her through an expansive room with gorgeous wood flooring, a high-beamed ceiling, and a fireplace made of Austin stone. Arched windows overlooked an outdoor seating area similar to one she'd seen in a Pottery Barn catalog last week. "You hungry?"

"I'm starving," she said, trying to take it all in. "I love your house, Nate. It looks like you."

He grinned and guided her into the kitchen. "I hope you like steak. H-E-B had a special on rib eyes."

Besides his concern for people like her mom and his extraordinarily generous spirit, she loved that Nate never thought too highly of himself. He wasn't above doing his own shopping, his own cooking, even though he was a candidate for governor of one of the largest states in the nation. He was intelligent and handsome and had garnered respect in prestigious circles. His humility endeared him to her heart even more.

She rubbed her hands together. "Love steak."

"Great! I have them marinating in soy and garlic. Want to help me with the salad?"

She nodded and watched as he moved to his refrigerator and opened one of the doors. He retrieved an armload of vegetables and unloaded them on the granite countertop.

He handed her a knife. "Okay, so I'm dying to know if you saw channel seven last night."

She slid onto a bar stool and reached for a cucumber. "Channel seven?"

He laughed. "Yeah. Seems one of their reporters walked in on Holiday while his handlers were finishing his makeup. They got photos."

"He wears makeup? Are you kidding?" She sliced through the cucumber's slick, dark-green skin.

Nate shook his head. "No, not kidding. And that's not all — that prompted a whole segment on how much he spends on, shall we say, cosmetic enhancements."

"Ouch!" Leta sliced up the cuke, then reached for some mushrooms. "That had to have hurt."

He turned to the sink to wash the radishes. "Yeah, I almost felt sorry for the guy. The media can be your best friend or your worst enemy." Finished, he returned to the counter. "Here you go." He handed the radishes off to her and went to work on a head of romaine, tearing the lettuce into pieces and dropping them in a large silver bowl.

"That's what your mother's afraid of." She paused, letting her words float across the room until they landed.

He scowled. "My mother? What do you mean?"

She spilled, told him how his mother had shown up that day and about the concerns she had expressed. She stopped short of telling him Vera wanted her to put the relationship on ice until after the election.

He circled the counter, and his arm went around her waist, drawing her close. "You let me worry about my mother and the voters. I'm not going to alter who I am, or hide who I'm with, to get elected."

"But —"

"But nothing. Listen, I hate being on the

378

road without you." He took her hands in his own. "Which is why I've come up with a great idea."

"Idea? What idea?"

"Quit your job at Central Market. Join the campaign. We certainly have plenty for you to help with."

Leta shook her head. "No. I don't think that's a very good idea."

"Think about it. You've done oppo research. You can help vet Holiday's positions. I mean, we don't intend to play dirty politics. Not my style. But it's fair game to take ole Wyndall to task on his positions. Especially when he changes direction more often than the wind in west Texas."

"I know you think you can put out a tidy press release and none of this will get messy, but —"

He gave her a reassuring look. "Janesa has already assembled a focus group, and the findings were favorable."

She found the notion almost comical, that there'd been a group of people in a room deciding how their relationship would play with voters. "Well, that'll certainly make your mother feel better."

"Come to work with us," he urged. "We need you — I need you."

Nate cupped her face in his hands and

looked at her with a longing that matched his words, causing her own heart to surge with feelings no words could adequately express.

She reached up and kissed him softly, letting her lips linger.

There was no greater intimacy than revealing your broken places to another and still being wanted.

He lived in Barton Creek, and she lived in a tiny house in north Austin. But in the depth of his eyes, she'd seen early on that they shared a deep loneliness, a vacancy of spirit born of loss. They both knew that some holes are hard to fill.

He had a way of erasing all her fears and insecurities. No matter what came, she knew he'd be by her side. The joys, the sorrows, life's great disappointments — he'd share all of it.

She desperately wanted to do the same for him.

Nate trailed a finger lightly across her shoulder and down her arm. The gesture wasn't overt, but she found his touch conveyed her own craving.

"You are amazing," he whispered against her hair.

An unexpected feeling hit her with such impact, her knees nearly crumpled. This wasn't about sex. Yes, his kisses were amazing. But this was more. He warmed her in places that had been cold for a very long time. When she was with Nate, she felt safe. *Known.*

She was no longer alone.

Leta's embrace left Nate feeling shaken and a bit unsteady. She had an uncanny power over him, the ability to break through all the performance, the roles he played. She saw him without judgment or expectation. Giving and rarely taking.

No one made him feel as large in life, as able to move mountains.

Certainly, Leta Breckenridge was not his first infatuation. But this time his feelings were so much more. He couldn't imagine finding anyone better suited to share his life. He was falling hard, and in some ways that scared him.

Never had his emotions been this out of control. Yet he couldn't bear not to move forward and see where this relationship would take him. Even if doing so held great risk to his campaign.

Okay, so he hadn't been entirely honest with everything the focus group reported. There was a significant fraction of participants who felt like adding a woman no one had even heard of to the mix at this late stage would muddy the water. More importantly, Janesa felt it might cause the media to go off message, and that was never good.

The debates were coming up, and then the election. They needed every voter focused on the issues that really mattered — not on his personal life.

Even so, he wasn't willing to push the pause button. Not when this girl was the very reason he'd decided to run in the first place.

He'd get over losing an election.

He'd never recuperate if he lost Leta.

38

When Leta resisted joining the campaign, Nate made a hasty decision and pulled back from going on another road trip. He explained to Janesa and his team that he needed to prepare for the upcoming debate, and that was the truth. At least in large part.

Right now he was up in the polls by a comfortable six-point margin, but they all knew his standing would deteriorate if he failed to connect during those critical minutes in front of the television cameras.

His campaign wasn't about beating up his opponent but about winning the minds, hearts, and trust of the people of Texas. He had to be bigger in appeal, better at listening to voters, and bolder in his ideas.

If he did all those things, he'd have done his very best — win or lose.

The campaign office was located on the seventh floor of the Capitol Center building on Congress, a modern open space divided into several sections, including a large space for data collection, an area for the press team, and another for administration and finance. To the right of his private office, a tiny conference room overlooked Congress Avenue. An entire wall was covered with whiteboards with scribbled notes from strategy meetings.

Nate was pouring himself his third cup of coffee when the phone buzzed.

"Yes?"

The receptionist's voice filtered through the speaker in the ceiling. "Your mother is here to see you."

He stirred in powdered creamer and grabbed a glazed donut, vowing to eat better after the election. "Send her on back."

Seconds later, his mom appeared in the doorway. "Hello, Son. I hope I'm not interrupting."

He placed his mug and donut on the table and moved to give her a hug. "When has that stopped you?" he teased and offered her a chair.

His mother placed the sunglasses she held into her bag. She grinned and looked across the table at him. "Point well taken."

"Can I get you a cup of coffee, Mom?"

She shook her head. "No, and by the way, you should eat better, you know."

"Point well taken," he bantered back while sliding into the chair next to her.

"Look, dear, I know you can only spare a few minutes, so let me get right to the point of my visit. I have something important I want to talk with you about." She straightened. "By now, you likely know I approached Leta Breckenridge and voiced concern about the timing of this budding relationship in light of your campaign. Your bid for the governor's office is at a critical juncture, as you are no doubt aware."

He lifted his steaming mug of coffee. "Look, Mother. You have nothing to worry about. Janesa and our press team are getting ready to release a statement. I'll take questions at a press conference, and the sizzle will quickly dwindle."

"But, Son — it's only days before the debates. Please don't be foolish."

He took a sip of his coffee and leaned back. "You're not seeing the possible upside to the timing. If the media focuses on my personal life in the days leading up to the debate, Holiday is also robbed of screen time and the opportunity to cement his positions in the minds of Texas voters."

His mother's face took on a look of dismay. "Oh, Son. You've severely misread this one. You are opening yourself up to an attack you can't control. Please believe me on this."

Nate fingered the rim of his coffee mug. "What do you propose I do, Mom? I can't very well roll back how I feel about this girl. It's possibly more dangerous to try to sit on the news that Leta and I are involved romantically. We don't need any 'gotcha' reporting." He shook his head. "No, I've built this campaign on my integrity. What message is conveyed if I try to hide this relationship and spring it on the public only after the election is over? I realize you are trying to protect me, Mother. I hope you'll understand that this time I just can't take your advice."

"Are you sure you really know this girl?" His mother was nothing if not direct. "Leta used to work for Jane Ladd . . . and there's significant risk she can't be trusted."

"I'm sure you had her investigated. What did you find?" He paused, waiting for a response.

When his mother remained silent, he squared his shoulders. "Exactly as I suspected. There's nothing." Nate had to tell himself not to be angry, that his mom meant well. "I invited her to quit her low-paying job and join the campaign as a salaried employee. She wouldn't."

"Smart girl — at least she's using her head. Which is more than I can say for you right now."

"Please, Mom. Back off this one. I'm not changing my mind. I've never felt like this about anyone, and Leta Breckenridge is going to be part of my life. Regardless of what the pollsters say."

She sighed, gazed at him several seconds, then stood. "I want you happy, Son. But once again you are much like your father. Stubborn as a hungry longhorn, heading without caution into tall grass filled with copperheads. I only hope you don't get bit."

Nate brushed a kiss against her cheek before walking her to the door. "Well, I guess I am like my father. He was never afraid of snakes. Neither am I."

She suddenly turned. "Please, Nathan, consider holding off on the announcement. Only until after the debate, a mere week from now."

Governing was all about compromise, and he supposed it wouldn't hurt for him to bend a little here. Especially if it made his mother feel better.

If his relationship with Leta developed as he hoped, she could easily be his wife in the future. He didn't want her to experience any unnecessary friction with her future mother-in-law.

He nodded. "Look, I'll think about it."

His mother's face immediately brightened. "Good decision. You won't be sorry, Son."

Twice a year in Austin, artists and craftsmen set up booths on the historic district along Sixth for the Pecan Street Festival, displaying their wares to crowds in the thousands. Open-air music venues and a children's carnival rounded out the fun.

Leta and her mother had attended every year until no longer possible. On this occasion, Leta agreed to go with Katie and Bart. The way she figured things, feeling like a third wheel was better than staying home alone, wishing she was with Nate while he was busy preparing for the upcoming debate.

It'd been less than a week since he'd made her dinner at his place, but the time felt much longer. Since that special night, she couldn't seem to get him out of her mind.

Keeping busy didn't help. She went to work, visited her mom, and cleaned the refrigerator. Still, every minute without him by her side was as painful as waiting for the blooms on a Madagascar palm, which flowers only once every one hundred years.

Okay, she was exaggerating, but only a little.

Thankfully, they'd see each other very soon. And once the debate was over, Janesa would issue the press release and their relationship would be out in the open.

Bart looked up. "You know, it's really a shame all the modern buildings in downtown Austin are overtaking these gorgeous historic structures."

Katie stopped walking and gave her boyfriend a pointed look. "That's a bit funny coming from someone who makes their living in commercial real estate."

"No, I mean it." Bart pointed ahead. "Take the Littlefield Building up ahead. That beauty was built well over a hundred years ago, an exemplary example of the Beaux Arts style of that era."

"I don't think you have to worry about any of these buildings," Leta injected. "This entire area is on the National Register of Historical Places, or at least that's what the sign on the lamppost says."

"Yeah, I get you. I know that. But I work in this business, and if that Holiday guy is elected again, these kinds of places are going to be in more danger."

Leta stopped at a booth and picked up a soy candle and brought it to her nose, taking in the sweet scent of lavender. "Yeah, how so?" She hoped her voice didn't betray her conscious effort to sound casual. Anything related to the upcoming elections was of special interest to her now, but she still couldn't disclose the fact, or why.

"The governor's a real jerk when it comes to these things. That guy's political coffers are padded by special interest groups and their lucrative development ventures. I see evidence often in my dealings. I'll guarantee you, in Holiday's book, money trumps every time."

Katie slipped her hand in his. "Enough about politics. That's boring. Let's go see what they have to eat." She pulled him along. "How about a turkey leg? Or some fried dill pickles?"

Leta laughed and shook her head. "How in the world do you eat like that and stay looking so good in those jeans?"

Bart kissed the top of his girlfriend's head. "I agree, Leta. She does look great in those jeans."

Up ahead, four street jugglers tossed brightly colored clubs back and forth to a backdrop of jazz and the laughter of children running and playing nearby.

Even with the slight breeze, Katie fanned herself. "Could it get any hotter out here?"

In an attempt to get out of the sweltering temperatures, they stopped by a food vendor tent with cooling water misters and a menu offering fried pies in a dozen or so varieties. She ordered peach, her favorite. Bart had cherry. As usual, Katie couldn't make up her mind. Finally, she chose a banana with pineapple and coconut. "What?" she asked when they stared. "I like the tropics."

Minutes later, with pies in hand, they continued down the row of displayed wares.

"There she is. Over there!"

The loud yelling distracted Leta from examining an oil painting of longhorns standing in a field dotted with oak trees. She frowned and turned in that direction.

Her heart clenched.

A woman rushed toward her with a microphone thrust out in front of her, followed by half a dozen more reporters also carrying microphones. Men with cameras hoisted on their shoulders, trailed by others lugging cords and battery packs, followed close behind.

"Leta! Leta Breckenridge!"

Katie looked alarmed. "Are they calling *your* name?"

Before Leta could respond, the reporters circled her like wolves. "What exactly is the nature of your relationship with Nathan

Emerson?" one reporter snarled only inches from her face.

They crowded in, pinning her against the vendor's tent wall. So much so, she was afraid the entire structure might collapse.

Bart held up his forearm in an attempt to shield her from the flashing cameras.

"Hey!" Katie yelled. "Back off!"

Another reporter held out two large glossy photos, one of Nate and her alone on that bench the day her mother went missing. Her arm was on his, and they were looking into each other's eyes. The second was taken at night, a shot of him opening his front door to her. "Would you confirm you're romantically involved with Senator Emerson?"

Before she could temper her response, she reacted. "That's none of your business!"

The woman holding the photos bared her teeth in a wide grin. "You're mistaken. Nathan Emerson is running for governor. Your relationship is everyone's business."

39

"As you know, Susan, this is very surprising news. Until recently, Nathan Emerson, candidate for governor of Texas, has been linked with an Austin attorney, Tiffany Shea of Shea, Bailey, and Gutteridge — a highly successful environmental firm headquartered in Austin, with offices in Dallas and Houston."

"Yes, Bill. The news breaking this morning is quite shocking when you consider he's now romantically involved with another young woman, a floral department clerk at Central Market who never even finished college. And he's been having secret trysts with this woman, keeping their relationship hidden from the public."

"I don't know, but my gut tells me Texas voters might take pause in knowing . . ."

Nate slammed his palms on the conference room table. "Shut it off!"

Janesa stood and grabbed the remote. She turned to the head of Nate's press team, Jim Perry. "You're recording all the networks, right?"

He nodded.

Janesa pointed the remote and muted the sound. "Look, we already ascertained this was a possibility. Sure, we'd wanted to get out in front of this and break the news ourselves, but even then, there would be news pundits serving as Holiday's attack dogs. What we're not focusing on is that there's an upside here."

"Yeah, what's that?" Nate sank into a chair. "Because all I see is that they are painting Leta with Sarah Palin brushstrokes in front of the entire state, making her out to be some simpleton who doesn't belong in political circles and surely isn't fit to perhaps become first lady of Texas. Leta didn't sign up for that," he said miserably.

He was a big boy, could handle the bomb throwers, the e-fluentials, and the downright nasties who loved to bring down anyone currently on top. Sadly, that's how politics worked.

With her first foray onto the public scene being a scandal of this nature, surely he wouldn't blame Leta if she thought twice about their relationship and ran the other direction.

"No, listen to me," Janesa said. "There's a way to spin this. Yes, there is a huge amount of constituents in heavily populated metro areas who are image snobs, and this relationship might give them pause. But there are also a number of registered voters who will see this as a positive. If we play this properly, they will view this story as proof that you really are one of them and not sitting off in the governor's mansion, out of touch and not caring about the common folk — the everyday voter."

Nate buried his head in his hands. "Nice try, Janesa."

Jim tossed several newspapers on the table. "That's not the biggest issue. These photos make you look like a two-timing dog in heat. Especially with shots of you and Shea taken only months ago printed side by side with these clandestine 'gotcha' pics of you with — uh, I'm sorry, what's her name again?"

Janesa gave him a scalding glare from across the table. "Her name is Leta Breckenridge."

Nate held up his palms. "Okay. I get what you're saying. We all have to concede none of this is good. We'll take a big hit in the polls, which the opposing side will play up big-time. Especially with the debate only days away. The timing couldn't be worse."

For the first time, he doubted his own judgment. He'd not listened when warned, and because of that, he'd placed the entire campaign in jeopardy. Worse, he'd let down his constituents, those who counted on him to serve and protect them and govern in a manner that kept their interests in the forefront of every decision made.

His shortsighted disregard for how deadly political oppos could turn a campaign on its head, using whatever sleazy means available, had placed the woman he loved in harm's way. He'd have a hard time forgiving himself.

Suddenly, there was a commotion outside the door. His mother barged into the conference room, trailed by a bewildered-looking Leta. A woman he didn't recognize, dressed in a suit and carrying an expensive-looking leather attaché, followed close behind.

Before he had time to react to the unexpected interruption, he was faced with yet another surprise among the unexpected visitors.

Tiffany Shea.

Now was definitely one time Leta envied her mother's addled inability to comprehend reality. She'd almost rather be cognitively impaired than to face walking into a conference room filled with these smart and important people staring at her.

No doubt they were all wondering why someone as politically astute as Nathan would place himself in this precarious situation in the first place. Admittedly, after all those news reports, she'd wondered the same.

She was a political nobody. Worse, a liability. What could possibly have enticed Nate into falling for someone like her? Especially when he'd been warned against doing anything that might hurt his campaign.

"Okay, everyone. We have a lot of work ahead of us." Nate's mother untied a scarf from her neck and laid it over the purse she handed off to a guy standing at the table. "Take these, would you, Jim?"

"Mother, what are you doing here?"

"Protecting the interests of my political action committee and its numerous donors." She softened momentarily, placing her hand on Nate's shoulder. "And those of my son."

Without waiting for a reply, Vera nodded toward the woman Leta had only just met in the car on the way over to the campaign offices. "Everyone, this is Carolyn Hawley.

She's with the Hawley Moxell crisis management firm." She turned and faced her son. "Carolyn's father, Bob, helped with the matter concerning —"

"My father," Nate said.

"Yes," she confirmed while moving to pour herself a glass of water from the pitcher on the table. "And I brought Leta and Tiffany along because we all need to be on the same page as we address Holiday's attempt to distract voters from the real issues."

Janesa appeared relieved that help of this nature had arrived on the scene. "Have we confirmed it's Holiday and not some PAC or well-intentioned crony?"

Carolyn moved forward, not a dark hair out of place in her neatly constructed bun. Large gold hoops dangled from her ears as she tossed her bag to the table. "Yes. Apparently an insider named Erin Robertson texted Leta to warn her, but she failed to see it in time."

Nate moved next to Leta, touched her lightly on the forearm. "I'm so sorry about all of this," he said quietly.

Tiffany took a seat across the table. She wore the brooch Nate's mother had gifted her at the party.

Nate nodded in her direction. "Thank you

for being here, Tiffany."

"Anything to help. Allowing Governor Holiday another win is certainly not in my firm's best interests."

Leta couldn't help but admire her flinty determination, the way Nate's former girlfriend was able to keep any emotion from her face. Especially given the fact she was also being splayed across the media.

Carolyn dug in her leather case and pulled out a small stack of stapled papers. She passed them around the table. "Here is our official response. I recommend this go out on the wires immediately. I've also included talking points and have scheduled a media blitz of our own." She looked at Leta. "We'll take her shopping. It's important that we create a visual that will pivot the mental image the press has planted in the minds of voters."

"Leta," Nate said.

Carolyn glanced in his direction. "Excuse me?"

"Not to get off to a bad start here. I appreciate all your help. But her name is Leta."

Vera frowned. "Son —"

Carolyn held up her hand. "No, Vera, he has a point."

Leta felt the heat of everyone's gaze as Carolyn quickly added, "Leta, please accept my apology."

She nodded. "Thank you." What else was she supposed to say? She wished Nate wouldn't have even brought the matter up. It wasn't as if she could feel any worse, really.

Carolyn turned to Janesa. "We're going to paint this as a bunch of sleazy creeps hiding in the bushes with cameras — the very opposite of the character and integrity Nathan Emerson projects." She placed her hands on the table and leaned forward. "Leta, it's important you never, ever apologize. Not for your relationship with Nate, and certainly not for your education level or job. You are a smart, kind, and motivated young woman who dealt with life's blows the best you could. Frankly, the sacrifices you made for your mother are to be admired." She glanced around the room. "The only way the opposition wins on this one is if this camp lies down and lets them walk on your backs. The counter to that is to stand tall and claim you have nothing to atone for — absolutely nothing." She stood square. "Got it, Leta?"

She nodded, feeling buoyed by the woman's confidence and energy.

Nate nodded his approval as well before returning his attention to the printed messages he held in his hands.

"Tiffany, your job is to convey how your relationship with Nathan was over long before he started up with Leta. That there are no hard feelings and you remain friends with both Nate and Leta. Defuse any drama."

Nate stood and moved to the window. He looked out over the street below. "Do we really have to impose on Tiffany to help clear this up?"

His mother answered. "What we face extends beyond anything personal, Son. As Tiffany said, her firm cares very much who lands in the governor's mansion."

Despite her earlier performance, Leta could see from Tiffany's eyes that notion wasn't entirely true. Of course this was personal.

Of anyone in the room besides her, Tiffany had a significant emotional stake in what was being blasted across the television screens. She was being depicted as the highly accomplished woman tossed aside for an uneducated twit. Of course she'd want to alter that impression, given the opportunity.

Still, the disdain Tiffany Shea felt toward the unfortunate situation, and most likely Nate and Leta, would remain hidden. At least when she was in public.

"Vera's correct," Tiffany said. "I have a vested interest in making sure no one acts in a reckless manner going forward. It's imperative we do everything possible to end the sensationalism as quickly as possible."

Seeming satisfied that everyone was on board with her plan, Carolyn rubbed her hands together. "All right. We all have our marching orders. Let's get going."

An image of Jane Ladd and Bernard Geisler formed in Leta's mind. She still couldn't believe they had sunk so low as to use her to bring down Nate's campaign. Although she shouldn't really be surprised at all. If she'd learned anything while working for the Ladd Agency, it was that Bernard, with those dark crow-like eyes tucked behind the shiny wire-rimmed glasses, was capable of this and more.

40

Despite Carolyn Hawley's carefully planned glass-jaw approach, the media story was not easily clamped down.

In addition to local outlets, the media-created scandal made the front pages of the *Dallas Morning News* and the *Houston Chronicle,* including several photographs of Nate and Leta together. The thought that cameramen were hiding and watching them completely creeped her out.

Pundits on the popular *Inside Texas Politics* broadcast out of Dallas debated whether or not a man who traded girlfriends so quickly could just as easily flip-flop on important issues like immigration and economic commitments important to the state. Did the fact he so carefully kept his key relationships hidden mean he was hiding other matters Texas voters cared about? And what kind of first lady would an uneducated grocery store clerk make? Could

Leta Breckenridge even understand the issues and speak intelligently in front of the cameras?

Everyone seemed to have an opinion and felt free to share.

Sadly, the story had hit at a time when there were no other dramatic stories to fuel ratings, and the networks milked this one for everything — and more.

The story headlined every news program for nearly a three-day news cycle, and even then there were no signs of the story dying down.

The inability to shift focus left everyone a bit testy, none more than Nathan.

Leta knew none of this could happen at a worse time than when he needed to have a clear mind to prepare for the debate.

"Don't forget to smile," Janesa admonished. "You don't want to appear angry in front of the cameras. Especially when you're talking about compassion for immigrants contrasted with the need for reform."

"I know." Nate immediately seemed to regret his sharp response. "Look, I'm sorry. Maybe we'd better take a break."

Leta made her way to his side. "You okay? Want to go for a walk or something?"

"And have cameras flashing the minute we step outside these doors? No thanks."

She followed him down the hall. "Are you mad at me?"

Nate stopped and turned. "What? No, baby. No. I'm not mad at anyone. Just frustrated, that's all." As if to punctuate his proclamation, he slipped his hand into her own and squeezed.

She squeezed back. "I'm not an expert here when it comes to campaigning, but it seems to me we did everything we could to adequately respond to this mess. Your mom hired the best crisis management firm money could buy. Carolyn Hawley came up with a brilliant strategy. We can't control the public's lust for gossip. That's all this is, really."

They went into his office, and he closed the door. "Gossip that has the power to hurt a lot of people."

She buried her head against his chest. "My mother used to tell me if you did the right thing, God would do the rest. I think all we can do now is believe that will be true."

Nate kissed the top of her head. He circled his desk and sank into his chair. "I just can't help feeling like I made a severe miscalculation and let a lot of people down — including you."

Leta took a deep breath. "Look, Nate. I

really need to say something. Something I believe you desperately need to hear — especially before you head in front of those cameras tomorrow night." She paused and let her words sink in. "Listen to me. The world does not rest upon your shoulders. There is no finer man with any more integrity than you, Nate. You've offered voters a choice, an opportunity for change. If the majority of the electorate fails to get that, if instead the masses choose to believe slimy charlatans who hire people like Bernard Geisler to assure a win, using any level of dirty tactics — if that ends up being the case — frankly, the people of Texas get what they deserve."

Surprisingly, Nathan said nothing. Instead he stared out the window.

"You stood in front of those cameras and said what was on your heart. You explained your relationship with Tiffany, and me. How love doesn't always play by tidy rules."

His eyes filled with emotion. "Leta Breckenridge, you are a remarkable woman. I want you to know that if I could turn back the clock, I would choose to fall in love with you all over again."

She moved into his arms. "What? You've fallen in love with me? I don't think I got the press release," she teased.

Nate traced her jawline with his finger. "It's not a talking point, Leta. I knew very early that you were special. I love you."

Her heart pounded with emotion. She was on the verge of telling him she loved him as well, but a knock on the door interrupted. Still, she couldn't let the moment pass, so she mouthed the words.

He smiled.

Nathan Emerson loved her.

She felt like a schoolgirl who had gotten a valentine from the most popular kid in class. No matter how many years they had ahead, she would never forget the tiny thrills chasing up and down her spine, how her palms had turned sweaty when he said those words. How no amount of media hullabaloo could shrink her euphoria.

He loved her.

Leta hummed as she made her way to the entrance of Heritage House. She couldn't wait to tell her mom, even if she couldn't really comprehend the meaning of the news.

A siren in the distance grew closer, more insistent.

Leta glanced around, saw nothing. She shrugged and scurried up the steps and through the front door, and immediately into a scene of controlled chaos.

Lucy nearly knocked her over as she passed by and ran for the door. "I see them. They're coming!" She opened the doors and waved.

"What's going on?" Leta asked, alarmed.

An ambulance pulled into the parking lot and slammed to a stop under the front portico, the revolving blue lights and dwindling siren casting an eerie sense of distress.

"They're here," Lucy announced. She raced to the door and called out to the EMTs, "Hurry, this way!"

Leta took in the emergency scene. "What — who is it?"

Behind her, two EMTs pushing a gurney blasted into the front lobby.

A look of relief passed over Penny Murdock's face as she tossed her clipboard on the receptionist's counter. "Okay, everybody. Stand back!"

Lucy quit wringing her hands and pointed to the bank of elevators. "Room 5C, fourth floor."

Leta's head jerked up. "That's Mom's room."

Without another word, she dashed after them, ignoring that Penny Murdock called out her name. Her hands slammed against the elevator doors as they closed behind the EMTs. Frantic, she looked around and sprinted for the door leading to the stairwell.

Taking the stairs two at a time, she rushed up several floors until she hit the fourth level. Winded, she struggled to open the thick, heavy metal door and then raced down the shiny tiles to her mom's room just as the EMTs wheeled the gurney inside.

"Mom!" Leta cried, racing for the door.

One of the EMTs stopped her. "You'll have to wait here."

"But that's my momma!" She pushed forward.

At the same moment, Penny Murdock exited one of the elevators with Lucy close behind. "Honey, it's not your momma," Lucy assured her. "It's her roommate, Mrs. Hunt."

Leta's hand went to her mouth, emotion washing over her. For a minute, she thought she might be physically sick with relief.

Thank you, Jesus.

When the EMTs finally wheeled Mrs. Hunt out into the hall, Leta quickly brushed past them and made her way inside the room. Her mother sat in her chair, staring blankly at the muted television screen. She gently rocked back and forth, seemingly unaware of all the excitement happening around her.

Leta knew from all the literature and

websites she'd studied that this was a sign her mother's disease was advancing, her mental state deteriorating. Even so, Leta felt nothing but the need to wrap the older woman in her arms.

Tears streamed down her cheeks as she sank to her knees and buried her head in her momma's lap.

If not today, someday that scene would play out and it could easily be her mother. The thought terrorized her.

Her mother's hands sifted through her hair. Leta didn't move, savoring the feel and remembering what life used to be like, when her mom could communicate and comfort her.

She hated dementia.

Perhaps it was too late for her own mom, but she couldn't help but pray that Nate won this election. As governor, he would make sure more studies and programs were funded to counter this horrible affliction, which was critical as funding options became more limited in the current economy.

How long before her mother dribbled from her mouth, had trouble swallowing and even breathing? Someday her brain function would simply give out — and the end would come.

Until then, she intended to cherish every

moment of the time she did have with her mom.

Leta stood and gently took her momma's hand in her own. "Hey, Mom," she whispered against her ear. "I brought your glass slippers. You want to dance?"

41

Despite the fact that prior to the media fiasco Leta had greatly anticipated watching the debate from her designated front row seat, some on the team now thought she shouldn't be present. Focus group predictions indicated any sign of her would refuel newsmongers' gossip and direct the focus off critical differences between the candidates.

She couldn't help but agree. Besides, the last thing she wanted was to have a camera swung her way and a microphone thrust in her face. She had answers ready in case she was accosted in public, thanks to Carolyn Hawley and the campaign team, but why risk testing her ability to follow their carefully constructed talking points?

In the end, however, Nate insisted she be there. "While I appreciate the findings, the only way this campaign can stop rumors and defuse this media frenzy is to remain as open and transparent as possible. Given that, we won't hide but will face these matters head-on."

So, instead of watching from home with her legs tucked up on the sofa and a large bowl of buttered popcorn within arm's reach, she now sat nervously next to Nate's mother, Janesa, and Carolyn, holding her breath and praying Nate did well, that this debate would move voters to elect him as their next governor.

A black woman with a warm smile and easy demeanor took the stage. "Good evening. I'm Susan Hart, managing editor for KERA, your public television network. For the next hour, I'll be moderating as this station brings you the debate between the leading candidates for governor. I'd like to invite our viewers to tweet your thoughts using #TexasDebates."

Wyndall Holiday and Nathan were seated behind microphones mounted on tables draped with blue tablecloths and skirting. Gold curtains served as the backdrop, with a large Texas state seal the size of a giant medallion centered between the candidates.

After the viewing public was welcomed, strategically placed monitors aired a quick segment on the candidates' political bios, segued with music and flashy graphics.

Wyndall Holiday had grown up in Huntsville and graduated from Texas A&M, where he was a linebacker for the Aggies. He helped deliver three consecutive Southwest Conference championships before he graduated. For a short time, he worked on an oil rig for a company in which his daddy owned a majority share and then went into politics, working his way into the governor's mansion over the course of several elections.

An image of Amanda Joy Holiday appeared, the first lady looking stunning in perfectly styled hair and makeup. They had met in college and married shortly after. They'd proudly raised two boys, both of whom served in the military.

Next the camera zoomed in on Nate. He smiled and gently nodded while a long list of professional accomplishments was reiterated for the viewers.

Before winning his current seat as state senator, Nathan had enjoyed a lustrous climb to being considered one of the top neuroscientists in the nation. He started and served on the board of the Institute of Brain Sciences headquartered here in Austin, which was committed to advancing the fields of brain and cognitive science through original research that strengthens understanding of the brain and mind.

Mr. Emerson was currently single.

Next to Leta, Vera tensed as a smattering of quiet snickers drifted from behind them. If such rudeness had occurred anywhere but here, his mother would likely turn and verbally reduce her son's detractors down to the size of their manners. Frankly, Leta would be happy to assist in that process.

The moderator smiled. "Good evening to both of you. Tonight the eyes of Texas are on you, and everyone sitting in front of their television screens is wondering where you each stand on key issues. So over the next minutes, let's clarify for the voters exactly what your positions are."

Each candidate took turns answering questions regarding education, immigration, and economic matters. For the most part, Holiday and Nate were cordial.

Halfway through the debates, everything took an ugly turn.

The moderator leaned into the microphone. "Thank you, gentlemen. Now let's turn to health care. Senator Emerson, we'll start with you. Obviously, this is an issue you care very much about. In earlier public statements, you've hinted rather strongly that you believe changes are needed in the way health research is funded. Would you care to expound on that for the voters to-night?"

Nate cleared his throat. "Yes, I would. Thank you." He looked into the cameras. "The biggest challenge to keeping medical research properly funded is rampant fraud. Sadly, there are unscrupulous medical providers and even those placed in positions of trust who bilk the system, depleting and diverting funds from much-needed research to pad their personal pockets."

"How do you intend to fix that?" the moderator challenged.

"Well, there will be those who do not agree with me, but the solution for dealing with the problem is not to create a gigantic and expensive bureaucracy like my opponent has often suggested, but rather to apply a stiff deterrent. I would advocate maximum penalties for this kind of fraud, such as loss of one's medical license for life, no less than ten years in prison, and a requirement for full restitution, even if it meant the loss of all of one's personal possessions. This would result in a severe disincentive and would curb illegal pilfering of donations and government funding."

"And you, Governor Holiday? Care to rebut?"

"Well, I think on this one, the senator and

I aren't so far off in approach, not near as much as he tried to suggest here tonight." He grinned at the camera. "Yes, there are those who are on a first-name basis with the bottom of the deck. But I can assure Texans that all appropriate measures are already in place to deal with these crooked corkscrews. Just ask our Enron friends who are living in their concrete apartments with bars on the windows how we Texans take to their shenanigans." He relaxed his posture to look like he was simply chatting and not in a heated debate. "Some time back, Mrs. Holiday and I personally created a 501(c)(3) fund to subsidize residential nursing care in order to equalize access for those who couldn't otherwise afford these types of services. While my friend here at the table with me tonight is all about research and data, I'm all about action."

The governor leaned back in his chair. "I've been elected to two consecutive terms and believe Texans are anxious to honor me with a third opportunity to serve them. Obviously, there's no slack in my rope. Over time I've come to understand what is truly and deeply important to Texans. I'm proud to reflect those in my campaign motto: 'Faith, Family, and Freedom for Future Generations.' " He paused. "Of course, my opponent's slogan also has deep meaning. Nathan Emerson claims he stands for the heart and mind of Texas." Holiday tilted his head, grinning. "Voters might now believe Mr. Emerson should consider using his mind a little more when it comes to matters of the heart."

Laughter spread across the venue from the governor's supporters sitting in the audience.

Leta felt more than actually saw the cameras turn in her direction to catch her reaction. She took a deep breath, lifted her chin, and forced a slight smile. Just as she'd been trained.

She did, however, note how Nate's jaw twitched ever so slightly. She also knew from sitting in on all those strategy meetings what was coming next.

"Senator Emerson?"

"Thank you, Ms. Hart." Ignoring Holiday, he looked into the camera. "In politics, there's a commonly employed distraction strategy that was illustrated in the 1997 movie *Wag the Dog.* In a nutshell, the tactic involves attempting to distract voters from the important issues by sensationalizing a separate matter and preoccupying media attention. Taken further, a desperate candidate might even go so far as to pull the fabricated drama into an important exchange of ideas such as we're trying to have tonight."

Nate turned and spoke directly to the governor. "Texans are worried about paying their bills, educating their children, fixing the roads they drive to work each day. If asked, they'll tell you they care much less about who I'm giving roses to. Texans do care about placing a man who embodies the heart and mind of his constituents in the highest office of this state." He turned back to the camera. "In only a few weeks, voters will make a very important choice. They'll do the right thing and place trust where it belongs."

"How could the right thing not matter?" Janesa moaned from back at the campaign offices. "Are you sure those are the numbers? Check again." She placed her hand across her mouth and watched several guys stationed at a bank of computers furiously work their keyboards.

One swiveled his chair. "Denton, Dallas, Tarrant counties. All up."

Nate slapped his hands together. "That's good. That's good."

A young guy with long dark hair shouted over his shoulder, "Down in the Houston districts. Panhandle too."

Another let out an expletive. "Holiday's pulling away in eastern Texas. By double digits."

Nate's mother paced the floor of the campaign headquarters. "What are we showing in Austin?"

The first guy shook his head. "Down by eight points."

Janesa moved to the conference table, grabbed the phone, and punched several buttons.

"Yes, Miss Morgan?" the receptionist asked over the speaker.

"Can you beep Carolyn Hawley and ask her to join us here at headquarters as soon as she can? Thanks."

Nate folded his arms behind his head. "I don't get it. We're down, and that simply doesn't make sense."

The first guy held up a finger. "Wait, wait. Look at central Texas. We're climbing."

Janesa leaned over the monitor. "Go down to Galveston. Looks like we're inching forward there as well."

He shook his head. "Nah, that's old data." He punched a few keystrokes. "See there? Not good."

Leta fingered her glass of water from the far end of the conference table, watching the tense scene unfold. She'd like to catch

Nate's attention, wanted to give him an encouraging look, but he was focused on his dropping poll numbers.

Frankly, she didn't get it. From her vantage point, Nate had aced the debate.

How could the numbers be going down when he'd expressed such bold ideas? Such integrity? Governor Holiday, on the other hand, came across as cocky and overconfident. Like he had nothing to lose.

Like he knew he couldn't lose.

Her mind drifted back to Bernard Geisler, to Operation Brainchild and the fifth floor of her former office building — to their political devices as acrid as the stale coffee smell in this room.

There was little doubt it was Jane and Bernard who had carefully leaked the photos to the media, leaving Holiday looking clean in the dirty deed.

Something inside told her these dropping numbers could be tied to their underhanded tactics as well.

But how?

She pushed her water glass back and stood. With her bag in hand, she moved to Nate and kissed his cheek. "Look, I'll catch up with you later."

He frowned. "Where are you going? It's late. Wait and I'll drive you home."

She shook her head. "No, you should stay. I've got something I need to do."

42

"I don't understand why you needed to borrow a wig from my mom." Katie pulled an auburn mass of curls from her bag and tossed it on the bathroom counter.

"Thanks." Leta finished applying a thick layer of mascara over her heavily lined eyelashes. "I need to be incognito, which is getting more and more difficult with my photographs flashed on the nightly news."

Her friend gave her a puzzled look. "So you're going to go out looking like Molly Ringwald in a bad eighties movie?"

She nodded. "Yup, that's the plan."

Leta could understand why her friend looked at her as if she were crazy. Her idea was a bit off the map. But a couple of things she'd heard Governor Holiday say at the debate bothered her.

Much was at stake. People across Texas had donated personal funds and worked hard to elect a candidate who would represent them with honesty and integrity, which seemed rare in today's politics. Operation Brainchild was clear evidence of that.

She could only hope her gut was right. While she was filled with anxiety over whether or not she could pull off what was ahead, she held to her mother's motto.

Do good and let God do the rest.

The James Earl Rudder State Office Building was located on Brazos Street, just a short distance from the Texas state capitol. Before she'd had to leave UT, she had passed by the historic building on her way to classes.

Inside, the five-story structure featured eighteen-foot ceilings and terrazzo and marble flooring, which created a bit of a hollow echo sound as she searched for the appropriate door.

Thankfully, there was no line this early in the morning.

A tall, lanky man wearing a white short-sleeve shirt with a green bow tie looked at her from behind black-framed glasses. "Can I help you?"

Leta stepped forward. "Uh, yeah. Thanks. I need copies of some corporate documents."

"Do you have an account with us?" he asked.

"An account?"

"Yes. We charge twenty-five cents a page for Xerox reproductions. If you need any official document certified, that's another two dollars. Per page."

She dipped her hand inside her bag and retrieved her wallet. "No need. I have cash."

"We don't accept cash."

"No cash? Well, maybe a credit card?"

"Only if you have an account," he reported.

Leta nodded. "Okay, understood. How do I create an account?"

He pointed to a row of computers on a counter against the wall. "You have to do that online."

She nodded again. "Okay, yeah. Sure." She turned in that direction when his squeaky voice stopped her.

"You should be warned. New accounts can take up to two days to process."

She whirled back. "Two days? But what if I need those copies now?"

"Sorry." He held up his hand and beckoned a man who had followed her in to step forward. "Next."

"No, wait!" She leaned across the counter, imploring him to reconsider. "I really need that information today."

The clerk looked at her, his eyebrows raised. "I'm afraid the only thing I can recommend is entering the required data and opening an account." He pointed. "Over there."

She sighed and tried to remain polite. "Fine." Frustrated, she rubbed her forehead and stepped back.

The process to start an account took less than five minutes. After the final entry screen, a warning came up, just as the clerk had said.

New accounts could take up to two days to process.

Leta growled silently and tried to think of a solution. She simply didn't have two days.

She needed to pull an Erin Brockovich move.

She approached the counter. "Excuse me?" She paused and looked at the nameplate. "Arrio, is it?"

He nodded.

"I just wanted to thank you for all your help. I know you don't personally set the rules."

"No, I don't." He gathered a stack of papers and lightly tapped the edges on the counter to create a neat pile. "I don't make the rules, but I must carry out the instructions of my superiors."

She tipped her head slightly to the side. "You know, Arrio? You look really familiar. By chance, did you attend UT?"

"Yes, I did. Graduated two years ago."

She slowly nodded. "Thought so. I think I used to see you on campus. What was your major?"

His hand went to his tie, and he straightened the bow. "Management Information Systems — School of Business."

Leta did her best not to smile. Of course he was an IT geek. She leaned her elbows on the counter. "Wow. Impressive! You landed a great job. I bet the state has excellent benefits."

From the way his eyes gleamed with pride from behind those glasses, she knew she'd hooked him. Now all she had to do was carefully reel the line without losing him. "I work in a grocery store. We get next to nothing compared to those of you smart enough to land a state job."

"State benefits are great. 401(k) retirement, health, dental, vision." He pointed to his glasses. "These babies alone would've cost close to five hundred dollars without insurance."

She shook her head and fingered the fake curls next to her ear. "I know. Everything is so expensive these days."

The clerk stealthily glanced around the empty room. He leaned forward. "Look, maybe there's something I can do to help you," he offered in a lowered voice.

Leta's face broke into a hopeful smile. "Really? I mean, that'd be so great. I really need those copies today."

He reached into his back pocket and pulled out his wallet. "You can use my account and just pay me the cash. But don't tell anyone."

She beamed. "Oh my goodness, that's a brilliant idea. Thank you!"

Less than twenty minutes later, Leta grinned as she pushed through the front entrance and out into the hot sunshine, a packet of corporate documents tucked safely underneath her arm.

43

"What is all this?" Bart asked, pointing to several documents strewn across the coffee table.

Leta shut the refrigerator door. "Don't move anything!"

Bart held up his hands. "I wasn't. Just asking," he said with an apologetic grin. "Seriously, though, what are you doing?" He examined some of her documents.

She tensed. Perhaps she shouldn't have left everything out for roaming eyes to see.

Trying to buy some time to come up with a plausible answer, she filled her glass of iced tea. "Want some?"

He shook his head. "No thanks."

Trying to sound as nonchalant as possible, she decided on the truth. "Look, this is really confidential."

Katie plopped down next to Bart and snuggled against his arm. "What's confidential, Miss Wearing a Red Wig and Going

Around Looking All Secret-Like?"

Leta sighed and sank into an armchair. "I know you guys might think I'm nuts. Most days you'd likely be right. But I heard something at the debate the other night that got my mental antennas up."

Katie frowned. "Uh-oh. What do you mean?"

"Well, Holiday mentioned he'd formed a 501(c)(3) to fund some philanthropic effort to ease paying for extended nursing care for those who otherwise might not be able to afford a place like Heritage House."

"What's that?" Katie asked.

Bart reached for another document. "May I?"

Leta nodded. "It's a corporation set up under certain provisions of our tax code, mainly a nonprofit-type organization."

Katie leaned back and wedged her feet up on the coffee table. "Where'd you learn that?"

She shrugged, not knowing for sure. It was just something she'd picked up somewhere. Perhaps one of her business classes.

Bart's eyebrows furrowed. "I've seen this name on real estate documents at a recent closing. I swear it's the same."

Leta placed her glass down on the end table. "Are you sure?" She moved and joined him on the sofa. "This name?" She pointed to the articles of incorporation.

"Yup. Same one."

Her heart pounded. This could be the link she'd hoped to find. Then again, it could be nothing.

"Do you have proof? I mean, if you have copies or something, I'd love to see them."

Bart winked back at her. "Get me a glass of that iced tea and I'll see what I can do."

Once again, her gut feelings rang true. As suspected, Holiday's nonprofit was embroiled in transactions that had no connection to any benevolent purpose. Or at least not entirely.

The nonprofit had provided funding for real estate transactions across the state, primarily purchases of long-term care facilities similar to Heritage House.

She pored over the documents Bart provided, all instruments that were recorded and in the public record. His files included numerous transactions. But a dozen or so included elements she wasn't familiar with.

"Oh, those are 1031 exchanges," Bart told her when she asked.

"What? I don't know what that is."

He patiently explained. "Section 1031 of the tax code allows for certain nontaxable exchanges of property. Broadly stated, a like-kind exchange is a swap of one business or investment asset for another. Although most swaps are taxable as sales, if you transfer property within 1031, you'll have either no tax or limited tax due at the time of the exchange. In effect, you can change the form of your investment without cashing out or recognizing a capital gain. That allows your investment to continue to grow tax deferred."

"That's legal?"

"Yup. Everything I've just told you is spelled out in the IRS code." He straightened. "There's no limit on how many times or how frequently you can do a 1031. You can roll over the gain from one piece of investment real estate to another, to another and another. Although you may have a profit on each swap, you avoid tax until you actually sell for cash many years later. People delay paying taxes for years that way."

Leta thought her head would explode. "Okay, slow down. So, what you are saying is that Holiday's nonprofit is exchanging properties? Why? I thought a nonprofit didn't have to pay taxes in the first place."

"Well, not in the same manner you or I might have to — or a business formed to make a profit. But there can still be some advantages, in certain circumstances."

"But what could possibly be advantageous for Holiday's nonprofit, which he says was formed to benefit people who normally couldn't afford long-term care? I mean, he made it sound like he's being so generous, but . . ." She let her words fade. "Bart, what was Holiday exchanging for?"

He lifted a file and flipped it open. "Well, here's an example you'll likely be interested in."

She took the file and pulled it closer. "He used to own Heritage House? Man, I didn't know *that*. Who is this corporation on the other side of the transaction?"

Bart flipped through a couple of the documents fastened in the file. "This company," he said, pointing. "Which is really odd, because that is a for-profit company."

"Are you joking?" Leta flipped several more pages, scanning quickly. Her heart stopped. "Wait. Oh my goodness. You're kidding me! Look at this."

"What?"

She pointed to the signature line on the documents.

Brainchild Enterprises, LLC
Bernard Geisler, Managing Member

44

"So, you're back again?"

Leta stepped up to the counter. "Hi, Arrio! Yup, I'm back." She held up a printed card. "But this time I have my own account. Got my ticket to copy independence in the mail yesterday."

He straightened his bow tie, a shade of blue this time. "That's good." He leaned forward. "Because I can't give you special favors a second time."

She nodded. "Oh, certainly. I understand."

He glanced at the large clock mounted on the wall. "But whatever you need today, you'd better make it quick. It's almost closing time," he warned. "Now, how can I be of assistance?"

"This shouldn't take long." She handed him a piece of paper. "Could you get me the formation articles and all the annual statements for this company, please?"

"Sure thing." He told her it'd take about

twenty minutes. She stepped back and took a seat against the wall to wait.

Leta couldn't wait to report her surprise findings to Nathan and his campaign staff. But first she wanted all her ducks in a row, so to speak. The documents for Brainchild should be the final link she needed to expose what could only be blatant fraud committed against those donating to Holiday's nonprofit, let alone the sleazy way he was using the entire scam to take Nate's bid for governor off course.

She hated to think how close she'd come to being a part of that — working for Jane Ladd and all.

She shuddered.

Thank you, God — for protecting me.

Several minutes later, Arrio stepped up to the counter. "Here you go," he said, sliding a thick manila envelope across the counter in her direction.

She thanked him and paid for her documents using her new account card.

Leta had just slipped the manila packet under her arm when a buzzing sound drifted from her purse. She reached in and pulled her phone out of its pocket and glanced at the screen.

She frowned and brought the phone to her ear. "Erin?"

"Hey, look, I don't have time to talk. I need you to meet me at the Elephant Room in an hour."

Her former co-worker didn't wait for an answer. She simply clicked off.

The Elephant Room was a downtown Austin favorite among tourists and locals alike. The basement location added to the jazz club's appeal, and long lines often formed down the sidewalk before opening time.

Thankfully, Leta didn't have to wait even twenty minutes before she was allowed in. She made her way down the stairs carefully while blinking several times, trying to adjust to the darkened interior.

Tonight the Elephant Room was packed with a noisy crowd, making finding Erin difficult.

A guy with long hair tied back with a lengthy leather strip grinned at her as she stepped up to the bar and ordered a diet cola. "Hey," he said. "Drinking the hard stuff, eh?"

She'd barely nodded in his direction when she felt a hand on her arm and turned to find Erin standing next to her.

"Hey, I have a table over here. Follow me."

Her friend led her to a tiny metal bistro table located under a bright green neon sign in the shape of a martini glass.

Erin had always been an ally. In fact, she'd tipped off Leta on more than one occasion. Even so, her stomach grew a tiny bit nervous, and she was anxious to learn why her former co-worker wanted to talk with her.

A guy on stage delivered a jittery, earthy rhythm on his saxophone, while a guitar player and a drummer hammered out a soulful harmony.

Leta slid a cocktail napkin under her Diet Coke to collect the moisture forming on the glass. "I was a little surprised to hear from you. How've you been?" she said over the music. She hoped for an easy tone as she added, "Still working for the Ladd Agency?"

Her former co-worker nodded. "Yup, money's too good to move along, I suppose."

It dawned on Leta that someone could be watching. She glanced nervously around.

"Hey, I know this must seem odd — me calling you up out of the blue. Especially now that we're . . . well, working a bit cross-sided on everything." Erin looked a bit embarrassed, or maybe even ashamed, as she slid a sealed envelope across the battered tabletop. "Here, this is for you." She stood without saying anything more, leaned down, and gave her a quick hug. "Take care, Leta."

Before Leta had a chance to respond, her former co-worker was quickly lost from sight in the crowd.

Leta suddenly felt a bit nauseous. She bit her lip and slid her finger underneath the seal.

"Hey, you alone?"

Startled, she looked up. The guy from the bar smiled at her. "Not fun to be all alone. Care if I join you?"

She swallowed, trying to find the words to brush him off without him taking offense.

"Hey, wait a minute. You're that girl on the news. The senator's girlfriend. The guy running for governor."

Her eyes darted around the crowded room, and she wondered who might have heard, wishing she could become invisible.

His smile turned to a laugh. "Guess you're not so alone after all." He held up his palms. "Hey, no worries. Sorry for the intrusion." He backed away, then held up his glass as if to salute her. "Can't say I like your guy. But then, all politicians are lying sacks these days."

Shaken by the encounter, she gathered her bag and hurriedly picked her way back through the crowd to the stairwell. She wanted out of there. And she needed to see what was inside that envelope without prying eyes looking over her shoulder.

She quickly made her way to her car, where she locked the doors and used the flashlight feature on her phone to illuminate the single piece of paper. With trembling fingers, she unfolded the page and shined the light at the letters carefully printed in thick black ink.

Back off, or your mother may find herself lost again. This time permanently.

45

Amanda Joy Holiday tossed her Louis Vuitton bag onto Jane Ladd's desk. The python leather puddled like a dead snake while its owner hissed with anger. "The two of you had better have a plan, because if that Breckenridge girl is as smart as you earlier touted, my husband's campaign is teakettled and we might all go to jail. And that is entirely unacceptable!"

Wyndall reached for her hand. "Sweet peaches, calm down. These folks are all on our side."

She pulled back from his grip. "Don't 'sweet peaches' me." She whirled and pointed a bright pink fingernail in Jane's direction. "We want this thing turned around. Now!"

Wyndall shrugged and straightened his tie. "There is merit to what my wife is saying. Clearly you've fumbled twice. Now my opponent is in a position to pick up the ball and is no doubt planning to run with it. As you can well imagine, our team isn't exactly anxious for that to happen."

Jane steeled herself against their incriminations. "We're developing a plan now."

Amanda Joy continued to glare. "Excuse me, but that brings little comfort. Your original plan to hire this girl and use her to get inside information failed to anticipate she might throw your big paycheck back at you in order to run into Emerson's arms," she accused.

Jane leaned back in her desk chair and folded her arms tightly against her chest. "No one could possibly have predicted a romantic attachment would develop. Especially when he was rumored to be marrying Tiffany Shea."

Amanda Joy held up her palm. "Save the excuses. Next, you tried to salvage the day by leaking information to the press and creating a distraction. That tactic was a bit short-lived, don't you think? And now the girl has opened an account with the secretary of state and is getting copies of things we don't want her to have. She's fishing and we're going to get caught!"

Wyndall placed his hand on his wife's shoulder. "What my wife is trying to communicate is that I'm going to spend the next four years in the governor's mansion . . . maybe move into the White House. No one is going to uncover anything that might thwart that effort and place me behind bars. Are we understanding each other?" He turned to Bernard, who was sitting quietly eyeing them from over by the windows. The governor's smile turned both gracious and ominous. "If you're smart, you'll consider this your two-minute warning."

Bernard lifted his chin so slightly it was barely noticeable. "We've already sent the girl a message — one that should get her attention and make her back off."

Wyndall's lumpy fingers squeezed the bottom of his nose in frustration. "Please tell me you weren't stupid enough to threaten her."

Bernard's eyes turned even darker. "Not her exactly."

Amanda Joy buried her head in her hands and groaned. "Oh my stars! And it gets worse."

Jane stood. That was enough. She circled around and leaned back against the front of her desk. "I founded the Ladd Agency, and we didn't get to where we are today by dropping the ball. We're extremely good at what we do, but our backs are against a wall here. Like it or not, we're up against that wall together. If you lose the election, we stand to go down with you. So do your job and get elected. I guarantee we will hold up our end of this bargain."

Despite her earlier tirade, Amanda Joy's expression turned hopeful. "And you are sure of that?"

Jane let her lips draw into a calculated smile. "Wyndall, Amanda Joy. You know me. I always have something up my sleeve."

46

Leta stormed through the front doors of Heritage House and up to the receptionist. "I'm Leta Breckenridge — here to see my mother."

Without waiting for the receptionist to acknowledge her, she bolted for the elevators and punched the button several times. There was a ding and the door opened.

Lester slowly toddled out of the elevator, this time with his pants on and Lucy holding his arm. "Oh, hey, Leta," Lucy greeted her. "If you're going to see your mom, she's not up there."

Leta panicked. "Where is she?" Without waiting for a response, she grabbed her phone and punched out 911.

"Honey, what's the matter?" Lucy frowned. "It's Wednesday. Your mother always has her hair done down in the salon on Wednesdays."

Relief flooded over Leta.

"Hello. What's your emergency?"

Feeling foolish, Leta spoke into her phone. "Cancel. No emergency. I apologize."

Lucy looked concerned. "Honey, is everything all right?"

She assured Lucy all was fine and headed for the salon. Inside were four stations where residents who still had some level of cognitive ability could have their hair washed and styled. Her mother was sitting in the station nearest the window.

Leta headed that way. "Mom?"

A woman pulled the towel from her mother's hair and grabbed a comb. "You her daughter?"

Leta nodded, wiggling her nose at the pungent odor of hair products heavy in the air. "Yes. Do you know how long before she's finished up?"

The lady smiled. "Not long. Say, twenty minutes. Tops."

Leta thanked her and pulled her phone from her bag a second time. "I'll just wait over here, if that's all right."

She tucked herself into a hard plastic chair with wobbly legs and dialed Nate's private number. The phone immediately went to voice mail.

"This is Senator Nathan Emerson. Sorry to have missed your call. Please leave me a message."

Leta nervously rubbed her forehead. She needed him to be there.

"Look, uh, Nate — I can't go into details, but I need you to call me. Please call me."

She was about to end the call when suddenly Nate picked up. "Sorry, babe. I was trying to get off the phone with my mom. What do you need?"

She couldn't help it. All the fear and emotion of the last several hours washed over her with the power of a tsunami. Tears flooded her eyes. "Nate, I'm scared and I need your help."

With hands gripping the steering wheel tightly, Nate drove down the MoPac Expressway and across the Colorado River heading south.

He glanced in the rearview mirror at Leta. "I don't understand. Who wrote that note?"

She clasped her mother's fragile hand a bit tighter, worried the change in environment might frighten her and spur her to more confusion. Instead her mother watched out the window in fascination. "I'm not certain. But I have my suspicions."

She told him about her findings at the secretary of state's office, of what Bart had told her and what his files revealed.

"We're calling the authorities."

"Nate, are you sure? I know these people. They are willing to do anything, stoop to any level, to get Holiday elected. And now it looks as if there is a criminal element at play here. Shouldn't we wait and make sure we have all the facts tied up in a manner that won't let them wiggle free of any charges before breaking this into the open? I mean, I'm sure they have some backup plan. Even with Mom hidden away, I don't trust them. They can find other ways to hurt us."

She thought of Bernard Geisler, of his creepy black eyes and gold-rimmed glasses. "Clearly I failed to recognize how dangerous the situation really was." She bit her lip. "Nate, I'm scared."

"These are scary people," Nate admitted. "Which is why we have to involve the authorities. And quickly."

She could tell by the way he kept glancing in his side mirrors that he was nervous too.

"You did the right thing in calling me. I don't want you to worry. This situation looks bleak, but everything will work itself out."

She wanted to believe him, but even he didn't sound all that convinced.

"You and your mom are safe. That's what

matters most."

"But what about the campaign?" she argued.

"We have time to figure all that out. After we tell the authorities," he assured her.

She looked out at the darkening horizon. The yuccas poking out from the ground looked like spears against the bloodred sunset.

"Okay, you're right. We should get law enforcement involved."

"I am right," he said and gunned the engine.

They remained quiet as he continued driving. The lights of the metro area faded behind them, and soon Nate pulled off the highway and into his mother's circular driveway.

Leta glanced over at her mom. She'd fallen asleep.

"Momma, Mom — wake up." She gently nudged her mom, who slowly opened her eyes.

"Is that the castle?"

Leta couldn't help but smile. "Yes, Momma. We're at the castle."

Nate parked the car and got out. He opened the rear door. "C'mon, Mrs. Breckenridge. Here, let me help you."

Leta gave her mother over into his capable

hands, then slid across the seat and opened her own door and got out of the car.

Porter and Vera stood out on the front portico. Vera waved.

Leta waved back, grateful for their offer of help. Suddenly another woman stepped into view. Her breath pulled from her chest as she saw the familiar woman standing next to them.

Jane Ladd.

47

"Mother, what's going on?" Nate demanded. "What's she doing here?"

Vera held up her hand. "It's all right. Come inside."

Leta reached for his arm. "Nate?"

Porter moved to join them at the car. He gave her a reassuring smile. "Ms. Ladd isn't here to do anyone harm. She came to help."

Despite wanting to believe his declaration, something thrummed just beneath her skin, a feeling of impending disaster. In a protective motion, she tucked her mother behind her for safety. Nothing about Jane Ladd could possibly be good.

Leta saw a flash of something on Jane's face that she'd never seen before, just the ghost of an expression, and in another state of mind she might not even have noticed it. A look of fear. Jane Ladd was one of the strongest women Leta had ever known, and when she saw the look on her face, her heart went cold.

Reluctantly, she allowed Nate's stepfather to help them inside. "Careful, Momma. That's it."

"I've taken the liberty to arrange for a nurse," Vera said. She motioned over a woman who looked to be in her fifties. She wore nursing scrubs and a bright smile.

Nate's mother rubbed the back of her neck. "Please escort Mrs. Breckenridge up to the room we've prepared."

Leta glanced across the expansive room and gave Jane Ladd a wary look. While their nemesis hadn't said a word the entire time, her face said a lot. Dark circles shadowed her eyes, and her typically bright eyes were filled with sallow defeat.

The nurse gently extricated Leta's mom from her tight grasp and led her away.

"I'll be up in a minute, Momma," Leta promised. She watched them retreat up the stairs.

"Okay, time to spill," Nate insisted with a deep scowl. "What's going on here?"

Vera motioned to the sofa. "Please, let's all sit."

Nate moved to the sofa. Leta followed and took the place beside him.

Jane lowered herself into an armchair opposite them. "No doubt, I am the last person you expected to see tonight. And any apprehension you have in what I'm about to tell you is completely understandable."

Nate's eyes grew dark. "You and your bunch lost credibility with me a long time ago."

Leta felt something fierce rising up in her chest, making her strong. "You threatened to hurt my mother."

"Not me. Well, not exactly." Surprisingly, Jane's voice snagged and tears sprang to her eyes. The normally composed woman struggled to get hold of herself even as Porter passed her a box of tissues.

"Thank you," she said, lifting one from the box. She blew her nose. "Look, it's a long story. First, let me tell you that I'm not ashamed of what we do. You may not agree with political opposition tactics, but an operation like ours serves a needed purpose, and we have for a good many years."

Confusion drew Leta's eyebrows together. She glared, trying to unravel the thoughts and emotions tangled inside her head. She'd once looked up to this woman — admired her, even — only to learn an ugly truth. Her association with Jane Ladd had marked her with a deep scar.

Because of her, she'd been paraded across the media, painted as an uneducated and foolish clown, and kicked to the curb with her feelings trampled on, all for the sake of a political joust.

Her mother had gone missing, perhaps at this woman's hand.

Worse, threats were made. Unforgivable threats against a woman with dementia who had no ability whatsoever to defend herself.

That was acceptable politics?

Leta jabbed a shaking finger in Jane's direction. "How do you sleep at night, or even look yourself in the mirror?"

Nate tensed beside her. "I think what Leta is trying to say is to make your point and then get out."

Jane nodded. "I understand your feelings. But I'm here to help you. I have information you're going to need." She looked at Leta miserably. "Bernard Geisler is my brother. While over the years I may not have agreed with his approach one hundred percent of the time, I agree with you that this time he took things too far. He saw an opportunity, became greedy, and crossed the line. By the time I discovered what was going on, it was too late. He'd placed the agency in jeopardy and all of us who worked there in a precarious situation." She lifted her chin. "I built that agency from nothing at a time when this town was ruled by men.

A woman wasn't allowed up to the card table, let alone permitted to deal the cards. I gambled everything. And up until just recently, I was at the top of my game."

"But?" Vera prompted.

She sighed. "But no matter what it means for my brother legally, I am not going down with him. And I have employees to protect." She looked over at Leta. "I want you to know that Erin did not know what was in that envelope."

Over the next minutes, she explained that Bernard had discovered some time back that Holiday had a habit of dipping his hands into pots that weren't entirely his to sample. Small discrepancies in accounting were easy to hide, he'd learned. Especially when those deviations from budget happened in agencies under his purview.

Amanda Joy's tastes ran on the expensive side. In the first year of her husband's initial term as governor, she'd completely redecorated their private quarters in the governor's mansion, using funds from a nearly forgotten appropriation for refurbishing certain art pieces that were no longer even displayed in the mansion but had been stored in the basement, nearly rotting away.

That served to whet her appetite for more. She found her way onto a committee of governors' wives and campaigned for a group of them to travel to Italy under the guise of promoting tourism, financed once again by orphaned funds in earmarked projects never realized.

She and Wyndall bought real property, a ranch outside Amarillo, high-rise condominiums in downtown Fort Worth, shipyards near Galveston.

"Amanda Joy held to the hope there was a chance Wyndall might successfully climb to the White House," Jane reported. "But she was smart enough to realize the odds were slim and a time would come when his political run could come to a halting end. Wyndall was already now much older, and they'd amassed very little fortune over the years. She was desperate to secure their financial future — and that led to what came next."

Like viewing the aftermath of a horrible accident with crushed metal and broken bodies, Leta found herself wanting to turn away from listening to this account of how someone had boldly believed she was somehow entitled and had stolen from people like Leta. Ones who faithfully paid taxes and worked multiple jobs to make ends meet.

The notion infuriated her.

Jane rubbed her forehead, looking pained. "I'm sure neither she nor Wyndall ever anticipated someone like you, Leta."

"I'm not following."

"No matter what you think of me, I am an excellent judge of ability. I knew even before you walked into my office that you were special. And when you showed up that day, I could see in your eyes this thirst for knowledge, this intense drive to never settle for what was apparent on the surface. You made the effort to understand, to keep looking until you knew the entire story. You didn't listen only to what was said, but to the motivations behind every statement, every fragment of data. I was not insincere when I said you have a gift."

Leta looked down at her hands, surprised to see them tremble. She so wanted to believe Jane Ladd's speech was valid, that she truly wasn't just the girl who never finished college. She wanted to be special, to have an identity steeped in regard for her abilities.

Vera leaned forward. "I too am impressed, Leta. Without your knack for sensing when something wasn't right, if you hadn't followed your gut, this situation would have remained status quo. Outside your tenacious investigation, none of Holiday's criminal activity would have come to light."

Nate's hand reached for hers and squeezed. "I'm proud of you."

Leta couldn't help it. Her throat nearly closed with emotion. She could be a little idealistic and a firm believer that anything could be fixed with a bit of grit and some hard work. But the truth was, she hadn't been able to fix a single thing that was wrong in her life since the moment she'd learned of her mother's diagnosis. Everything had spun out of control from that point forward, and she'd somehow lost herself, no longer able to feel her own value.

She looked around the room at Jane, Nate, and his family and saw deep regard reflected in their eyes. For the first time in a long while, she held her head high.

"Thank you," she said, knowing what they claimed was true. It was her efforts that had set everything in motion. She had followed her instincts and uncovered the information necessary to negate a travesty of illegal activity that could be directly linked to the man sitting in the highest office in Texas.

And in so doing, she'd also likely delivered the election to Nathan.

The corners of Nate's mouth tightened. "So, what now? We need to call the authorities."

Vera stood. "That's been done. Even now, I assume arrests are being made."

A deep sadness drifted across Jane's face. "Yes, and of course I will cooperate and provide whatever law enforcement needs to support a prosecution going forward."

Suddenly, Leta was exhausted.

Nate and the others wanted to watch the news, follow the breaking story.

She just wanted to go to bed.

Vera walked over and put her arm around her waist. "Honey, we've prepared a room for you next to your mother's. Please feel free to retire. I hope I don't offend you by saying so, but you look wiped out."

She nodded. "Yes, I am."

Nate followed her up the stairs and to her mother's door. She turned, her heart welling with emotion. "Well, I guess Mom was right after all."

His fingers went to her cheek. "How so, babe?"

"If you do the right thing, everything turns out in the end."

He smiled. "Yes, God has his ways." Nate kissed her gently on the forehead. "And sometimes he uses a very resourceful helper in the process."

48

Election Night

Leta stepped into the ballroom at the Driskill Hotel, feeling buoyed by the high energy and party atmosphere. She'd never attended an election night gala, and certainly never been in the spotlight of all these flashing cameras.

She smiled brightly and followed Porter and Vera to the dais, taking care not to stumble in her heels as she moved up the steps leading to the platform. She took her place under a large arch of red, white, and blue helium balloons and looked out over the enthusiastic crowd.

Katie waved wildly from the floor, as did Bart. Her neighbor Ben Kimey was there too, looking a bit out of place. She greeted him with a little wave. He grinned and smiled back.

Over near the bank of television cameras, she spotted Mike from the store.

On the other side of the room, Edith Styles and Penny Murdock stood chatting. Lucy spotted her and waved.

If able, her mother would've been here as well, beaming with pride. For now, she remained with the Wyatts under the care of their private nurse. She was safe, and happy.

All their friends were gathered, along with a crowd of people she didn't know but who had supported Nathan and were here tonight to celebrate his win.

This was Nate's big night. One well deserved. She couldn't be more proud.

To the right of the stage, a media crew filmed their star reporter — one Leta recognized had been in the group who accosted her at the Pecan Street Festival all those weeks ago, back when she couldn't have imagined this moment.

Three, two, one. The cameraman motioned with his finger, and the reporter instantly pasted on a wide smile.

"Good evening, everyone. Tonight we're broadcasting from the Driskill Hotel where, in just moments, Nathan Emerson will take the stage behind me and give his acceptance speech. As you know, the road to victory took an unusual path when his opponent, Governor Holiday, was arrested, along with his wife, Amanda Joy Holiday, and many of their key campaign personnel and associates, for an elaborate scheme of illegal real estate deals that involved unauthorized use of state funds — proving the old adage, 'In politics, truth can be stranger than fiction.' "

Suddenly, music drowned out the reporter's voice as the band at the back of the ballroom began playing Nate's campaign theme song. The entire crowd swayed to the tune and not only mouthed the words to "Deep in the Heart of Texas" but clap-clap-clapped in unison.

At the side of the dais, a commotion drew Leta's attention. Then she saw him — Nate.

She knew more than most anyone in the room about this man. How he talked and laughed and what he drank in his coffee. She knew what he stood for, and it made her proud.

Her heart fluttered as she watched him shake hands with a small crowd milling around at the base of the steps.

The enthusiasm in the room swelled to towering proportions as the man she loved took the stage, waving.

He stepped to the podium, and applause exploded across the ballroom.

Nate held up his palms to quiet the crowd. "Thank you! Thank you, everyone. And thank you for being here. Tonight the voters of Texas have spoken — and I am honored to serve as your next governor!"

The crowd cheered and applauded.

Nate cleared his throat and continued. "There is no higher calling than service. Across this room tonight, we have nurses, law enforcement officials, teachers, and waitresses who all know that to be true.

"This has been a lengthy race, a long way to the finish line, and I am proud of the contest my campaign has run — a journey made with integrity and heart. We kept our focus — kept the faith that if we did the right thing, this election would turn out in our favor.

"We extend sincere respect and appreciation to my opponent, Kyle Jackson, who stepped up and entered the race during the last lap. He did a fine job, and I wish him and his wife and family all the best."

Leta knew many politicians would take this opportunity to throw mud at Holiday and highlight his downfall. Nate didn't. He was far too classy for that.

"I'd also like to acknowledge a few key people up on the stage with me tonight. My mother, Vera Emerson Wyatt, and my stepfather, Porter Wyatt." He turned to them. "You have my utmost love and respect. Without you, none of this would be possible." Nate looked back over the crowd. "And I'd like to mention a man who went before, a man who first introduced me to the notion of serving in public office. My father, Senator Robert Nathaniel Emerson." Nate gazed upward. "I hope I've made you proud, Dad."

In a rare show of public emotion, Vera wiped her misty eyes.

Leta reached for her hand and squeezed.

Nate expressed to the crowd how hard his campaign team had worked, led by the fabulous efforts of Janesa Morgan. How no team had worked more diligently and with more integrity.

"And last but certainly not least, I want to express my deep respect and love for the woman standing next to me on this stage, Leta Breckenridge. Her tenacious spirit and never-ending quest for truth changed history and secured my ability to stand before you tonight as your new governor."

He motioned her forward and slipped his arm tightly around her waist.

"And now, if you will all indulge me . . ."

He led her out from behind the podium and slid down on one knee.

She looked down with utter amazement. "What are you doing?" she mouthed.

The crowd went crazy wild. Applause and

pandemonium broke out across the room.

Nate simply grinned and held up his hand until they quieted.

Her heart nearly pounded out of her chest as he cleared his throat. "Leta Breckenridge, would you do me the honor of becoming my first lady?"

Her eyes widened and tears flooded, making it hard to see his hopeful expression. She nodded. "Yes — yes!"

He pulled a ring from his pants pocket and slipped it on her finger. "Did you hear that, everyone? She said yes!" He rose to his feet and scooped her into his arms. "I love you," he whispered against her ear.

"I — I love you too!"

He turned back to the podium and leaned into the microphone. "Again, thank you for coming out tonight. I promise I will work every day to serve you!"

He grabbed Leta's hand and his mother's and lifted their arms in a victory pose. Music blared and confetti dropped from the ceiling. Cameras flashed, nearly blinding her.

Leta savored the moment, feeling a little shell-shocked. As if the reality of what had just happened hadn't quite set in.

Still, she couldn't help but recognize something very poignant.

Even though life could sometimes be hard, with unexpected twists and turns, life could also be very good. In the midst of the pain of her mother's decline, of coming face-to-face with others' evil actions, she'd been granted what matters most in life — someone to love.

In what seemed like a flash, a struggling, uneducated nobody who had sacrificed her dreams to do what was right was now poised to become the next first lady of Texas — a princess at the ball on the arm of her prince, a man of immense integrity who delighted in serving others.

While it was unclear what her future would look like exactly, she knew she'd return to school and graduate. Perhaps she could even follow in the footsteps of Lady Bird Johnson and use her role as first lady to influence environmental and landscape management issues for their state.

She and Nate had waited a long time to hear it, but the victory music was finally playing.

The grueling campaign was over.

It was time for them to dance.

ACKNOWLEDGMENTS

Gratitude never seems to be enough for those who influence and support my work. Nevertheless, gratitude is what I have for so many people, because this story (and so many others) would not exist without them.

My publishing team at Revell is incomparable. Jen Leep shared my vision for stories about strong women facing emotional and life-changing circumstances. From the day of our first meeting, I knew I wanted to work with her. Jessica English helped me "kill my darlings" and edited my work with precision. An often seen note: "Kellie, can we reconcile these timing issues?" Thank you so much for all your hard work!

And thank you to the marketing team, publicists, and sales team who worked diligently to get my books in front of readers. You guys all rock!

My agent, Natasha Kern, cares deeply about authors and their careers, and I am fortunate to have her by my side.

This book features a bit of an inside look at political opposition organizations. For many reasons, both of the experts I interviewed wanted to remain anonymous. Without their generous anecdotes and information, I would have been lost trying to assemble this story with any level of authenticity.

While this book paints a story that includes the dark underbelly of politics and those who manipulate the system for their benefit, sometimes crossing the line morally and legally, I know there are elected officials who serve the public with the highest integrity. Former Idaho Secretary of State Pete Cenarrusa is an example. Uncle Pete gave me my first job. My heart is filled with love for him and Aunt Freda, who supported me in ways too numerous to list.

Thank you to the Lady Bird Johnson Wildflower Center and the tour guides who were so helpful and informative. I appreciate the information I gained from the Texas Coalition on Alzheimer's and the numerous unnamed sources who shared their personal insights into what it is like to love someone suffering from dementia.

Early after my first book was published, I was invited to come visit with a local book club. The members of Fiction, Food and Fun are some of my favorite people and have been such cheerleaders for my career as a novelist. This year we lost our founder and good friend, JoAnne Franzenburg, to cancer. Before she lost her fight she was delighted to learn I'd named a lobbyist after her. I'm so sad she was never able to hold the book in her hand and see her name. We love you, Joanne!

I could not have this writing career without the support of my family. Allen, Jordan, Eric and Brandy, and my little Preston and Lydia — you are forever embedded in my heart.

Now I'd like to say something to my readers: Thank you! You buy my books and send me emails and notes of encouragement telling me how much you enjoy my stories. You post such fun notes on Facebook, tweet about my books on Twitter, share pins of my covers on Pinterest, and share reviews on Amazon and Goodreads. Please know this — every minute I sit with my fingertips on the keyboard, you are in my heart and mind.

ABOUT THE AUTHOR

Kellie Coates Gilbert is a former legal investigator and trial paralegal, as well as the author of *A Woman of Fortune, Where Rivers Part,* and *A Reason to Stay.* Gilbert crafts her emotionally charged stories about women in life-changing circumstances in Dallas, Texas, where she lives with her husband. Learn more at www.kelliecoates gilbert.com.